Heartbeat

A Pro-Life Novel

TINA TRUELOVE

WESTBOW
PRESS®
A DIVISION OF THOMAS NELSON
& ZONDERVAN

WestBow Press books may be ordered through booksellers or by contacting:

WestBow Press
A Division of Thomas Nelson & Zondervan
1663 Liberty Drive
Bloomington, IN 47403
www.westbowpress.com
844-714-3454

Scripture quotations are taken from the Holy Bible, New International
Version®, NIV®. Copyright © 1973, 1978, 1984 by Biblica, Inc.™ Used
by permission of Zondervan. All rights reserved worldwide.

ISBN: 978-1-6642-9615-2 (sc)
ISBN: 978-1-6642-9616-9 (e)

Library of Congress Control Number: 2023905746

Print information available on the last page.

WestBow Press rev. date: 10/30/2023

Dedication

I dedicate this book first to God. When I prayed for Him to give me a story to write, He gave me this one. I trust that He has a plan for this book. If you're reading it, then you are part of that plan. You are not here by chance, but by Divine appointment. Thank you for joining me in this journey.

I dedicate this book to my family:

To my son Gabriel Josiah Truelove who never knew life outside my womb. I have never been pro-choice. I have always been 100% pro-life. I have read the pamphlets and I have seen the photos and videos of preborn babies, but when my husband and I held our own son's 15-week lifeless body in our hands, we knew there would never be any person or any circumstance that could ever change our minds. I have seen the evidence with my own eyes. I have held the evidence in my own hands. The sorrow we suffered on March 16, 1997 was felt on every page of this book. It is perfectly fitting that I dedicate this book to our sweet son who waits for us in Heaven.

To my husband, Steve, who read my manuscript with enthusiasm, offering helpful advice along the way. He has always been my biggest cheerleader in life. He's always encouraging me to do things I want to do when I lack the confidence. I love my man so much and I'm thankful God gifted me with him.

To my three children, Drew, Brianne, and Megan and to my Daughter-in-Law, Hillary. Parenting these wonderful people gave me the experiences necessary for developing the characters in this story. They are my inspiration every single day.

To my new little granddaughter, Elainea. She is just the most precious thing ever. When I hold her, everything seems right in the world. Elainea, God knitted you together in your mommy's womb. You are fearfully and wonderfully made. I know this full well, my sweet girl.

I also want to dedicate this book to the women (and some men too) who have volunteered and visited pregnancy care centers across the United States and around the world. It wasn't until I spent time volunteering in our own local pregnancy care center that I realized the magnitude of that ministry in our community. During my time there, I sat with women who wanted abortions. Some of them chose life. Others did not. I sat with women who were young and unprepared for motherhood. They wanted life for their children, but they needed help. In our pregnancy care center, they received it. I helped women complete parenting classes. I witnessed a few first ultrasounds while volunteering there. I watched women's faces light up when they saw their babies on that big screen for the very first time. Most abortion prone women who see their babies on an ultrasound screen will choose life for their unborn children. Our pregnancy care centers help women choose life for their children, but they do so much more. They teach them the value of every life. They give women real choices that do not involve the deaths of their babies. Then, if other pregnancy care centers are like our own, they walk them through the first 18 months to 2 years of parenthood. If you are reading this, I hope you will find your local pregnancy care center and volunteer time there. You will not regret it.

I want to offer a special thank you to my editor, Reba Michelle Dockery. I will always appreciate her professionalism and her work on this book. Her suggestions made the story better. Reba is the author of two Bible studies: Through the Storms and Fresh Oil. She is also the author of Amazing Creation: 7 Week Children's Curriculum.

The characters in this book are completely fictitious. The characters and personalities are a combination of my own personal experiences, but no person is represented as a character in this book.

Some parts of this story are hard because abortion is a hard topic, but beyond the suffering, you will find forgiveness, mercy, grace, love, encouragement, and joy in the full story. If you are in the same situation as any of the characters in this story, it is my prayer that you will find the same forgiveness and peace in the only One who can give it, Jesus Christ.

$\mathcal{B}$

Chapter One

Angela closed her textbook. The library was packed but quiet. The semester was winding down and students at Pleasant Grove University were preparing for final exams. Just a few more weeks and then Angela would graduate and receive her bachelor's degree in psychology. It had been a challenging year to say the least.

Angela's senior year had brought about changes and challenges in her life that she never expected. Her relationship with her boyfriend had become much more complicated over the last few months. Angela had met Brad in the university cafeteria. His dark hair, brown eyes, and playful demeanor had captured her attention from the moment he walked into the room. He had a way of drawing attention to himself. People simply liked him. He was funny, smart, athletic, and handsome. How many guys could check off all four of those boxes? How could she not notice him? Someone from a nearby table had shouted out his name.

"Hey St. James! Nice job sinking that basket last night! Way to go! We almost lost the game. That was a close one."

Angela watched and listened as she finished her salad. The guy who had just captured her attention was tall and slender with dark brown hair and deep brown eyes. *His last name is St. James and he plays on the university basketball team, probably varsity,* she thought. Brad waved back to the other guy and gave him a nod and a thumbs up as he made his way to the buffet counter. The menu that day offered a choice between beef stew or grilled chicken and rice. The lunch segment of the day was almost over. The cafeteria would close soon so the staff could begin preparing the dinner meal. Angela was seated at a table close to the buffet counter. She noticed that Brad took both a bowl of beef stew and a plate of grilled chicken and rice. He added green beans and squash to the chicken and rice plate. *I guess an athlete needs more food ... lots more*, she thought as she noticed Brad moving closer to her table.

That's when Brad became intrigued with this girl sitting alone in a crowded, noisy room. He had turned toward her quick enough to notice her cut her eyes away from him. She obviously didn't want him to notice that she had been watching him, but he noticed. He also noticed her shy smile that she unsuccessfully had tried to hide. She had brown hair and hazel eyes. She was pretty. That was something he noticed and something she couldn't hide.

"Hi, I'm Bradley. My friends call me Brad. Is this seat taken?" He had pointed to the chair across from her.

"I don't see anybody sitting there," she said sheepishly as she glanced up at him. Their eyes met but this time, Angela couldn't cut her eyes away. They were locked there, staring into Brad's eyes as if she were in a trance. Brad cleared his throat.

"Ahem. Do you mind?" He pointed again to the chair across from Angela.

"Help yourself," she told him.

"Come here often?" Brad asked with a grin the size of the Grand Canyon. He knew it was a silly question, but he couldn't help himself. It was a small college town. There were a few other places where students could find food, but freshmen college students didn't have a lot of money to spend at pizza places and fast-food restaurants. Most of the time, the university cafeteria was where they ate their meals.

"Only when I'm hungry," Angela replied. She couldn't help but smile back. "So, you play basketball?" she asked.

"Yep. Varsity." He took a bite of stew.

"Oh, so you're a junior or maybe a senior?"

"I wish. Freshman." He chewed and swallowed a piece of chicken. "I needed a scholarship to come to school here so I trained hard in high school. Finally, I asked a recruiter to come watch me play. He came out during one of my best games and here I am. My scholarship has been a life saver, for sure. I couldn't afford to come to school here without it."

"What are you studying?"

"Marketing. I hope to get a job with an advertising firm after graduation. What about you? Did I catch your name?" Brad continued to eat quickly and had almost finished his plate.

"My name is Angela, Angela Cromwell. I'm also a freshman. I'm studying general psychology. I'm hoping to narrow my studies to child psychology. After graduation, I hope to work with children as an elementary school child psychologist."

The bell sounded. Brad and Angela heard the announcement that the cafeteria will be closing in ten minutes. Students were instructed to take their trays to the bin near the buffet counter and discard their trash. As Brad and Angela made their way to the tray bin and the trash can, Brad decided to take advantage of what little opportunity he had left. "Angela, it was nice to meet you. Without sounding too cheesy, would you mind if I called you sometime?"

Angela smiled and said, "Well Brad, without sounding too cheesy, sure. Here's my number." Angela quickly wrote her number on a napkin and handed it to Brad.

Brad's face lit up and he gave that big Grand Canyon sized smile again. "Ok, great. I'll call you. I'll call you real soon." He turned with a little cocky kind of confidence to head out of the cafeteria. Then, he turned back to her just before he was about to exit through the door. "St. James!" he called back to her. "My last name is St. James."

Angela remembered the other basketball player calling out to him as he entered the cafeteria. She smiled back at him. "I know."

Bradley had called Angela the next evening. There was a basketball game on Thursday night. He asked Angela to come. They would go out for pizza after the game. Then, Bradley would walk Angela back to her dorm. Sometimes they would meet on The Green. The Green was a large grassy area where students would go to have picnics, play Frisbee, walk dogs if they lived in the housing area that allowed pets, or just sit and enjoy the southern summer breezes. Brad and Angela had been nearly inseparable. Where you saw one, you saw the other one. Two years into their relationship, something bothered Angela. Angela began ending their dates with, "Love ya!" She was falling in love with Brad but since he had never told her that he loved her or indicated that he was "in love" with her, she thought the full phrase "I love you" would be too much. A playful "love ya" would have to do for now.

Brad would respond by kissing her good night and then, in the playful demeanor he was famous for, offered her a "Me too. See ya tomorrow."

"Me too?" Angela wasn't sure what to think of that. She wanted Brad to respond with, "I love you." Maybe in time, but they had been dating for two years. They were juniors by then and all she received back from him was "Me too." Something inside Angela told her that Bradley St. James wasn't in love with her, and part of her heart was beginning to break.

How could Brad not love me? Angela couldn't let the question rest. She and Brad had been together day in and day out until recently. A few times, they had let things go too far physically. Angela thought about her grandmother.

Angela's grandmother wouldn't approve of her physical relationship with Brad. She was a fine older woman who never missed a day in church. She was in church on Sunday mornings, Sunday nights, Wednesday nights, and sometimes on visitation nights. Angela's grandparents were always in church. Angela wondered what they did on all those days in church every week. *Wasn't one sermon on Sunday morning enough?*

Angela's parents were not church goers. They talked about God a lot. Sometimes they even mentioned praying for someone or something. Whenever they received news of someone dying, her mom would always console a grieving friend by telling her, "I'll pray for you." Phrases like "Thank God for this" or "Thank God for that" were common but church attendance wasn't important. Sometimes they would go on the big holidays like Easter and Christmas. Whenever they visited Angela's grandparents in North Carolina, that was a different story. Everybody in Grandma's house went to church. There was no arguing about it. You just went. Grandma wouldn't have it any other way. Grandma was always talking about her church groups and how you can have a personal relationship with Jesus.

A personal relationship with Jesus? Angela always thought that was kind of weird. How can you have a personal relationship with Jesus if you can't see Him or talk to Him *in person*. Prayer is one thing, but to have a real relationship with someone, you must *really* talk to them in person. Angela loved her grandmother dearly, but she was glad her parents didn't make her go to church or force her into a weird relationship with a man she couldn't hear or see. Angela didn't understand why all that religious stuff meant so much to her sweet old lovable grandmother. Maybe someday she would make sense of all that but for right now, all she could think about was Brad and why, even after all the time they had spent together, he wouldn't tell her that he loved her, not even after any of the times when they had spent the night together.

By early fall of their senior year, Brad seemed more distant. He didn't call her as much and he didn't always answer when she called him. They rarely met on The Green anymore. Brad always seemed so busy now, like he didn't have as much time for Angela as he once did. They still enjoyed the little time they spent together, but something just seemed different between them. Angela couldn't figure it out, but something wasn't right. Once, she thought she saw him in the distance with another girl, a blonde, but she wasn't sure it was him. It couldn't have been him. That just wasn't possible. Bradley St. James would never cheat on her.

During basketball season, things seemed a little better. Brad invited Angela to the games. They went out for pizza afterward. Things seemed almost back to normal. It was mid-March when something happened that made Angela feel certain that Brad would be hers forever. How could he not love her after what she was about to tell him? It had been earlier that morning when Angela pulled the pink box from the brown paper bag. She took a deep breath and then headed into the bathroom. A couple of minutes later, Angela sat on her bed and waited. She had to remind herself to breathe. She was nervous, yet excited at the same time. A baby was a big deal, but she was coming to the end of time in college and maybe this was the next step of her life. Then, the timer bell sounded. Angela wanted to run but her legs moved slowly to the bathroom counter where the test was laying. As she approached the counter, her eyes made her way past the sink and onto the test where she saw, as clear as day, not one but two lines. The test was positive. Angela was pregnant with Brad's baby. She picked up her cell phone and pushed "Brad" on her speed dial screen. "Brad. It's me. I need to talk to you right away. I have something important to tell you." Angela thought surely Brad would be as excited as she was.

They met at The Pizza Parlor where they spent many evenings together after Brad's basketball games. Angela had secured a private booth for their important conversation. Brad was late but that had become more typical of him lately. He finally strolled in and made his way to the booth where Angela was waiting. She had ordered their drinks and a small pepperoni pizza for them to share. She wanted everything in place by the time Brad got there so the waitress wouldn't accidently disturb them. Angela wanted Brad's full attention.

"So, what's up?" Brad seemed rushed, like he had somewhere else to be, but Angela didn't think much of it. She was about to give him news that would make anything else he had to do seem unimportant.

Angela took a deep breath, "Brad, we've been together for a little more than three years now, right?"

Brad quickly replied as he seemed a little inconvenienced. "Yeah, that's right. What's this all about?"

Why does he seem so rushed? Well, it doesn't matter. "Brad, umm, well." This wasn't going exactly as planned. Angela figured she might as well just say it, "I'm pregnant." Brad just sat there. Motionless. Expressionless.

"Brad, did you hear me? I'm pregnant."

"I . . . I heard you. Umm. Angela. I don't know what to say."

"You don't know what to say? Brad, I just told you that you are going to be a daddy. I'm pregnant with your child and you don't know what to say?" Angela realized she had raised her voice a little too much, so she quieted down to a forced whisper, "You don't know what to say? Aren't you happy about this?"

"Happy? Angela, I need a minute."

Angela was becoming frustrated, "You need a minute? Brad, we are going to have a baby. WE are having a baby!" Angela was just short of shouting but in hard whispers.

"Angela, I . . . I wasn't planning on becoming a father."

"Brad, I wasn't planning on becoming a mother but here we are. I'm pregnant. You're the father."

"OK." The shock was wearing off and Brad was beginning to settle into the idea. "Angela, I want to do the right thing here. Are you sure you want to have the baby? I can take you somewhere and . . . and pay for . . . well, you know."

Angela sat frozen to her seat, her thoughts racing. *What is he saying? He wants me to have an abortion?* This was not at all what she expected. She didn't know what to say.

"Angela. I said I would take care of this, of you. I know it's my responsibility. I'll pay the clinic bill and hospital bill or whatever it takes."

How could this possibly be happening? Angela was completely speechless for what seemed like an eternity. When she found her voice, she was crystal clear. "Bradley St. James, I am having this baby with or without you."

Angela shoved the untouched pizza away from her side of the table, got up, and walked out. She was angry and shocked and a little numb, but an entire ocean couldn't compare to the ebb and flow of tears that Angela Cromwell cried that night as reality began to set in.

Angela had no personal convictions about abortion, but she had heard her grandmother talk about volunteering at a clinic, not an abortion clinic but some other type. It was a clinic for women like herself with an unexpected pregnancy. They offered counseling and helped women make decisions or something like that. Maybe she should call her grandmother. She was a quirky old woman with quirky ways, but Angela loved her, and she knew without a shadow of a doubt that her grandmother loved her. Angela decided not to talk to her parents just yet. Besides, she knew what her mother would say. Her mother would tell her she was out of her mind to even consider having a baby at this stage in her life. Angela knew her grandmother would offer her the best advice.

The next morning, after a full night of crying, Angela pulled herself up off her tear-soaked pillow and called her grandmother.

"Hey Grandma." Angela had not thought about how to approach this conversation, so she stumbled over her words. "I . . . I . . . I need to talk to you about something important. Do you have a few minutes?"

"My sweet Angela Girl, I always have time for you, as much time as you need." Grandma Ruby replied softly and calmly with that reassuring tone to her voice.

Angela's grandmother had always called her Angela girl. When Angela was a baby, Grandma Ruby had called her Angel girl, but Angela's mom put a stop to that.

"Her name is Angela, Mom, not Angel." Angela's mother, Clara, didn't share her mother's love for all things heavenly. She had rebelled as a teenager. She told her mother that she had decided that she wasn't so sure there was a God. She left home, took a bus to Atlanta, Georgia, met and married Angela's father, Robert, all within 3 months time. A year later, they had Angela. That's about all Angela knew about her parents' relationship before she was born. Clara loved her mother but had decided she just couldn't live under her mother's strict religious rules anymore so she left home. Fortunately, Angela's parents made frequent trips back to North Carolina to visit Grandma Ruby, so Angela had many good memories of many sweet times with her grandmother. Angela felt a bond with the woman that she didn't have with her own mother. Maybe that's the reason Angela chose to call her grandmother before telling her mother about her condition.

"Grandma, I'm in a situation and I don't know what to do."

"What is it, Honey?"

With a quiver in her voice, Angela said, "I don't know how to tell you. I don't want you to be disappointed in me."

"Angela Girl, there is nothing you can say or do that will make me love you less. I love you like Jesus loves me. You know I don't like beating around the bush about things so just spit it out. Whatever it is, I promise to hear you out. Everybody deserves a chance to tell her whole story."

"Grandma, I'm pregnant." There it was. Her grandmother had told her to just spit it out so she did.

Grandma Ruby waited a few seconds. She wanted to make sure Angela didn't have more to say. She had promised to hear her out. After a few moments of dead silence, Grandma Ruby offered her response. "Angela Girl, you are definitely in a situation. I know you are a one-man woman so there is no point in asking you if your Bradley is the baby's father." She wasn't exactly asking but still she wanted to confirm that detail.

Angela wasn't bothered by the question. After her own mother's epic rebellion, why wouldn't Grandma Ruby ask this question? "Yes, Grandma. Brad is the baby's father. Here is my problem. I thought

Brad and I would be together forever, but he has been more distant lately. The past several months haven't been the same. Obviously, we still spend time together, but he seems more withdrawn. When I told him about the baby, he had the nerve to suggest I have an abortion." Angela heard her grandmother try hard to withhold a gasp. "I'm not having an abortion, Grandma. I believe other women have the right to do whatever they want, but I could never kill my baby."

"Angela, do me a favor. Repeat that last sentence to me."

"I said I believe that other women have the right to do whatever they want but I could never *kill* my baby." Angela paused and then continued. "Oh, Grandma Ruby, maybe other women should think about this more too." But Angela wasn't interested in talking about what other women do or don't do. She wanted to talk about her and Brad with the only woman she trusted to give her good advice. "Grandma, I told Brad that I am having this baby with or without him. I don't know what Brad will do but I'm pretty sure that after last night, he has no interest in me or this baby. He wants me to have an abortion."

Grandma Ruby paused for a moment to say a little prayer and ask the Lord to give her the right words to respond. "Angela, I'm glad you called me. The first thing you need to do is ask God to guide you through this situation. You said you have made up your mind to keep your baby and I will support your decision. I'm going to send you some information, a packet of information about prenatal development. Be sure to share the information with Brad. Even if he doesn't want to be part of your life or his baby's life, he still needs to be educated about prenatal development. Who knows? The information might at least encourage him to follow through with his responsibility as a father. And Angela, I've told you in the past and I'll tell you again that God's design for intimacy is that it is to be shared only in the context of marriage. He makes this very clear in His Word, but your baby is God's creation, a precious gift. The Bible tells us that He created our inmost being. He knitted us together in our mothers' wombs and we are fearfully and wonderfully made.

Look up Psalm 139:13-14. Read that verse repeatedly. Call me back when you have received the information and you have talked to Brad. Know that I will be praying for you."

A few days later, Angela received a packet of information from her precious Grandma Ruby. Inside the envelope were photos of preborn babies at every stage of development from conception all the way up to birth. There was a list of websites and YouTube channels where Angela and Brad, if he chose to participate, could find more information and watch videos of real babies in the womb. There was also a pamphlet called *Steps to Peace with God* from the Billy Graham Evangelistic Association. Angela had heard her grandmother speak about Billy Graham many times. She glanced through the pamphlet. She had begun to read it when her cell phone rang. The pamphlet would have to wait.

The caller's name was Brad St. James.

Chapter Two

Emily sat in her apartment by the window. It was early spring, and the daffodils were in full bloom. She needed to study but she couldn't get her mind off Luke. The wedding was scheduled for the week after graduation. Emily, the Pleasant Grove University valedictorian, was about to be awarded a degree in pre-law. Luke was about to be awarded a degree in pre-med.

Luke knew that Emily was an ambitious attorney-to-be. She was laser focused on a concentration in Constitutional Law with dreams of a political career in Washington, D.C. He would follow Emily anywhere. Emily and Luke were both devoted Christians. Before they met, they had each prayed about their futures. Emily knew her calling was in Constitutional Law and Luke knew his calling was in medicine.

Luke and Emily met during their junior year at Pleasant Grove University. The Baptist Collegiate Ministries building was packed out at the first meeting of the year. Emily squeezed in and found a seat in the corner of the room where she nearly fell into the lap of the man whose long legs were almost blocking the only chair left available. When Emily landed in the empty seat rather than the lap of the man next to her, she figured the least she could do was introduce herself and apologize for what was almost an embarrassing fiasco. "Hi, I'm Emily. I'm so sorry about that. I'm afraid I'm a bit clumsy sometimes."

"Well Emily, I'm Luke and I'm afraid I didn't give you much of a choice. I'm sorry I didn't see you come in. I was looking around the room and thinking about what a blessing it is that the room is packed out. It looks like God has big plans for the Pleasant Grove University Baptist Collegiate Ministries this year."

"Looks like it! I'm excited about what God has planned. Last year, I chose to stay on campus and settle into college life. I worked with our local mission group here in Pleasant Grove. We volunteered many hours at The Hope House. The Hope House offers food and clothing to not only homeless families but also typical families who have fallen on hard times. Those families need help too. It was an amazing experience. I'm sure I'll volunteer hours there again this year as well, but I hope to go on one of the foreign mission trips this year."

"The Hope House sounds like a great opportunity. I'll have to check that out. Maybe I'll volunteer there as well. I've already signed up for the mission trip to Puerto Rico during Spring Break. They've had several hurricanes to cause catastrophic damage down there. I'll be working alongside a medical team to help children get free checkups, immunizations, and other non-emergency treatments. I'm studying medicine so I'm glad they have a medical missions team already established. This year, they are allowing pre-med students to work with them. Of course, we can't administer medical attention yet, but we can help with supplies, organizing patient loads, transporting children to the clinics . . . things like that. It's a great opportunity."

Emily listened with excitement. "Puerto Rico?" she responded. "That does seem like a great opportunity. I wonder what destination will best suit my field? I'm studying pre-law. Here at PGU, it's a combination of introductory to law classes and a whole lot of political science classes. Later, in graduate school, I want to concentrate on Constitutional Law. Eventually, I'll be moving to Washington, D.C. I don't know if I'll ever run for a political office, but I do know that

I will find a way to fight for religious freedom in this country. It's my calling and I'm passionate about it."

"Well, uh, Senator Emily, I don't know about other trips or their agendas, but I do know that they still need people to sign up for the general cleanup crew for the Puerto Rico trip."

Emily couldn't help but notice his smile. "Well, uh, Dr. Luke, I might have to put my name down for that. We'll see."

The music team started singing "How Great is Our God". Luke and Emily stood up to join in the singing. Luke was tall, Emily noticed. He was tall, blonde, handsome, obviously smart, and he had a heart for helping others in need. Emily began singing the familiar words and she thought about the year ahead. Her thoughts turned to praise, *How great is our God, indeed, and our great God has big things in store at Pleasant Grove University this year. Those plans just might carry me to Puerto Rico in the spring as well.*

Luke towered over Emily. He glanced down at her a few times. Her brown hair had a tint of red to it. He wondered if she might be a little bit temperamental. He had always heard that red headed women were a handful. His cousin has red hair and she is pretty feisty, so he figured it was probably true. Emily certainly seemed focused, driven, passionately devoted to her calling – all qualities of a great lawyer - and she was kind of cute with dimples in her cheeks. He hoped she would sign up for the Puerto Rico clean-up crew in the spring. He decided he wouldn't worry about the red hair issue until he got to know her better and it's only a streak of red anyway. How big of an issue could it be?

The months ahead were filled with hard work for both Luke and Emily. Emily was drowning in case studies, research, and writing assignments. She didn't have much time for sleep. She surely didn't have much time for a social life. She was determined to be the best at what she was meant to do and every assignment she completed proved she had all the qualities of the best attorneys in the country. She was young but wiser than her years. She saw details that others missed and that would prove to be one of her best attributes in the courtrooms of her future. If future law firms were looking for someone who has what it takes to win the hardest cases, then they need look no further than Emily McMaster.

Luke was every bit as busy as Emily. He could barely catch a breath from hours upon hours of clinical research experiences. Relationships in the field are important. Luke needed to prove himself worthy of recommendations for medical school. He also needed to start thinking about the Medical College Admissions Test (MCAT). Pre-med students must pass the MCAT exam before applying to medical school. Luke needed to take the exam in the spring. He still had time to prepare, but he had no intention of failing that exam, not with his eyes on Emily McMaster. That girl didn't miss a beat. There was no way she wasn't moving forward at the pace of a winner. Emily wasn't the type to brag on her own accomplishments, but Luke knew that Emily's college performance was unmatched. Everyone at the college talked about her outstanding grades and commitment. She consistently performed at the top of her class. She was going places and if Luke had his way, he wasn't going to be left behind.

Then there were jobs. Both Luke and Emily had been awarded academic scholarships. Emily had received a full scholarship, but she still needed to provide for some living expenses. She had chosen a private campus apartment so she could focus. That turned out to be a good decision, but she needed to work several hours per week to make all ends meet. She refused to ask her parents for money. They had the means, but their desire to help Emily was no match for their daughter's stubborn independence. Luke had received a partial scholarship, so he had to work more hours than Emily to cover all his expenses even though he lived in the men's dormitory. Working more hours and working harder to keep up with the traditional pre-med timeline proved to be more of a challenge than he had anticipated but Emily McMaster was worth it.

Despite their busy schedules, Luke and Emily had managed to keep up with one another. They rarely missed a Baptist Collegiate

Ministry (BCM) event. As important as their career studies were to them, their relationship with Jesus was first and foremost for both of them. They both saw their careers as an extension of their ministries. Without their service to the Lord, nothing else mattered. They studied hard, worked hard, and saw one another at BCM events. They worked a few fundraising events to raise money for spring mission trips whenever they could. On the rare occasion of a free evening, they managed to get to the local ice-cream shop for a real date. Luke picked up Emily at the door of her campus apartment. He never went inside. He was the perfect gentlemen.

By a force that can only be explained by series after series of Divine appointments and interventions, Luke and Emily were able to keep up the pace and by spring, Luke had met all his personal goals and expectations to warrant a break. He couldn't be more ready for that Spring Break mission trip to Puerto Rico. He had encouraged Emily to go a few times, but he didn't push her. If she went, he wanted her to go because she felt called to go, not just because he wanted her to go. A week before the trip, the campus minister had called a Puerto Rico mission trip meeting to make sure everything was in order with all the students who were going. Luke walked into the meeting room and glanced around. His heart skipped a beat. There by the refreshment table sat Emily. He made his way back to the chair beside her.

Luke's grin was epic. "You never told me you signed up."

Emily returned a playful nod. "Well, uh, Dr. Luke, I kind of wanted to surprise you."

Luke had to respond with her playful nickname. "Oh, I'm surprised, Senator Emily."

"Really?" Emily asked. "To be honest, I thought you knew all along."

With that same smile that kind of hooked Emily when they first met, Luke replied, "I didn't know for sure. I did want you to come but in case you haven't figured it out yet, I kind of like you. I like you a lot, Emily McMaster. I want to share this experience with you, but only if we can keep our focus where it should be, on God's purpose for sending us there. I didn't want you to feel pressured in case our ability to focus on our mission is a problem." He chuckled, "After the year we've had, I think God has trained us well."

"I completely agree, Luke. I'm committed to remaining focused on our mission to serve the people of Puerto Rico. I signed up because I want to share in this experience too, but I looked at the schedules. We won't have much free time and we won't be working in the same areas. We will mainly see one another at our BCM gatherings. Besides, my eyes are hurting from so much reading, writing, and studying. It will be great to get outside and work with shovels and buckets for a change. This will be amazing."

"Of course, you have already checked the schedules . . . in true Emily McMaster fashion. Yes, it will be an amazing week."

Just as the meeting was coming to order, Emily added in a whisper, "By the way, Luke Westmoreland, in case you haven't figured it out yet. I like you a lot too."

The plane trip to Puerto Rico took a little more than 3 hours. The plane departed Atlanta on time and the trip was as smooth as silk. The morning weather in Puerto Rico was warm, sunny, and clear. The hotel where the students would be staying wasn't on the beach, but it was near, only a two-block walk to the sand. The sounds coming from the ocean were relaxing and the breezes were cool and refreshing. The first order of business was a meeting scheduled for 2:00pm.

The mission team had time to claim their bags, get to the hotel, and freshen up before lunch. They enjoyed a homemade Puerto Rican stew prepared by a group of women from the church congregation who would be working with the student teams throughout the week.

After lunch, the students, BCM leadership, and the church leadership moved into a meeting room where schedules were passed to the students. Questions were asked and answered. Any last-minute issues were addressed, and students were broken up into their two groups to meet one another and go over the work details for the week. Luke's group met with local doctors and nurses who would be handling the medical missions part of the trip. The students were briefed on what they were allowed to do and what they could not do. All medical exams and treatments were to be handled strictly by local medical staff. Pre-med students and other students on the medical team were restricted to checking children in, assigning them to a doctor or nurse, and handling supplies. Many children were expected to sign up for treatments, so supplies were expected to run low fast. A few students were assigned to handle transporting supplies from the hospitals and medical offices participating in the mission in a timely manner. Keeping supplies stocked properly was an important responsibility.

Emily's group met with a group of men and women who looked more like a construction team. They were dressed in construction type clothing and wearing hard hats. The cleanup team stressed the importance of following directions. Proper cleanup involved more than simply picking up debris, collecting trash into buckets, and hauling it all away. Contaminants ran rampant after storms. Each student's personal health depended on following directions during the cleanup process. Until this meeting, Emily had no idea how after-storm cleanup worked. This was an area that would challenge her in ways she had never been challenged. Give her a caseload and a few law books and she was a force to be reckoned with. Give her gloves, safety gear, a bucket, and a shovel and she was completely out of her element, but Emily McMaster was not one to back down from a challenge. She bowed her head and said a quiet prayer. "OK Lord. I'm here. Use me as you see fit," and she meant every word.

The week went exactly as expected for Luke. He remained focused on his purpose for the trip. Every morning, he prayed for God to use him in the lives of the children and families he would meet. God did just that. While checking children into the clinic, Luke greeted grateful mothers. Many of the families who came to the makeshift clinic had been displaced for months, their homes still unlivable. Some of them would need to rebuild entirely and still some of them would need to relocate. Most of the children had common childhood symptoms like sore throats, minor ear infections, and an occasional stomach virus. A few times a child would show up with a case of bronchitis or pneumonia. The days were long and busy. The clinic stayed full from the time it opened until early evening. They tried to finish up by 6:00pm so the students could regather back at the hotel for share time and worship time. For Luke, the days seemed to pass by quickly. He couldn't help but notice that Emily looked completely exhausted by the end of each day. He didn't say anything to Emily about his observation, but on Wednesday at dinner, he had to ask. "Hey Senator McMaster! How are you holding up down here in the trenches?"

Deep down inside, Emily wanted to tell him that she was exhausted, but instead, she held up her head, pulled her aching shoulders back and responded, "Making demons shudder."

In that moment, Luke knew. This woman had his heart. She was relentless. She must have been sore from head to toe. Her eyes told him that it was all she could do to keep going, but she kept going. His Emily would not back down from any challenge. Rise or fall, she would never go down without a fight.

Luke and Emily finished their dinner that Wednesday night as they shared stories from the work their groups were doing. Luke told Emily about the children and families he served. Emily told Luke about the families she served out in "the trenches." As Emily spoke, Luke noticed that her voice sounded tired and even a little bit scratchy, but what made her so exhausted was the realization that the families who lived in all the destroyed homes and communities were suffering in ways that Emily had never imagined. "Many of them have lost everything, Luke. Everything. The ones who haven't lost everything are still without so many necessities. The destruction is so widespread. I know the work we are doing here is important but in the scope of all things considered, it seems like so little. I noticed something else. Some of these mothers have lost their homes, their husbands, and their jobs. One of the women from the church down here told us that they have noticed an increase in the number of babies and children dropped off at the orphanage. Even more heartbreaking than that, they've noticed an increase in the number of women going into the abortion clinics too. They can't afford to support their babies. The orphanages are overfilled, and these women are being told that abortion is their only option. My eyes have been opened to situations I didn't know existed. Thank you for encouraging me to come. I'll never forget what I've learned here and it's only our third day."

Luke told Emily that he had heard the same stories from the medical staff working with their mission team. "Some of the doctors and nurses on the medical team have said the same thing. It's heartbreaking."

As the Puerto Rico mission team finished their meals, some of the students began singing worship songs. After a few worship songs, they moved into a Bible study led by the Pleasant Grove University campus minister. The part of the Bible study that stood out most to Emily was the Bible verse from 2 Corinthians 12:9. *But He said to me, "My grace is sufficient for you, for My power is made perfect in weakness." Therefore I will boast all the more gladly about my weaknesses, so that Christ's power may rest on me."* Emily was tired. She felt weak. With two more days to go and much still to accomplish, Emily rested in the truth that God's grace would be sufficient for her and that His power would be made perfect in her weakness.

The next two days were much like the first three but as the workload for the week began to ease, the students were able to spend more time sharing the gospel with more people. By Friday, an entire street of homes was cleaned up and ready for repairs to begin. A community of children and families had received medical care, and many had heard the gospel with 20 adults and 12 children praying to receive Jesus as their Lord and Savior. When this team returns to Pleasant Grove University in Pleasant Grove, Georgia, another team from another college will pick up where this one left off. God's work will continue in this small storm-stricken town.

As Luke, Emily, and the rest of the team made their way to their seats on the plane, they continued to share their experiences with one another. Emily seemed more rested now. Her eyes were bright again, determined. As Luke listened to Emily speak about her week in Puerto Rico and how she would never forget it and how she would find a way to take what she had learned and apply it to her future, he had no doubt that she would do just that. Somewhere in the middle of fighting for religious freedom in a courtroom or fighting for her conservative constituents in Congress in Washington, D.C., Emily McMaster would, no doubt, remember what God had taught her in Puerto Rico and apply it to this life that God has given her.

Luke realized something during that week as well, something he had already wondered about but now he knew. After they get back to their life in Pleasant Grove, somewhere between the clinical research, the writing assignments, the caseloads, the studying, their local BCM responsibilities, their jobs, and somehow managing to make it through the last few weeks of the academic year, Luke was determined to do one more thing. He had prayed about it and he had made up his mind. He would plan a date like Emily McMaster had never known. He would take her to a real restaurant. The local ice-scream shop wouldn't do for this night. He would take her to their favorite spot on The Green, the place on campus where they could go on warm nights and find the perfect spot to watch the sunset over the mountain. They had only had time to experience this a couple of times, but Emily had indicated that it was one of her favorite things to do. There, in that place, at just the right time when the sky behind the mountain top is usually painted with soft pinks, purples, and blues mixed with a million shades of red, he would do it. He would kneel before his Emily and ask her to marry him.

The next several weeks were just as busy as Luke and Emily had expected but they did it. Emily finished the year at the top of her class. Luke had passed the MCAT and finished with his name on the Dean's List. The Saturday after the academic year ended with no clinical research, no case studies, and no written assignments due for either of them, Luke took Emily to the Hungry Hunter for dinner. Luke had worked extra hard at his campus job. He had managed to pull in enough hours to save money for a steak dinner for the two of them and a shiny diamond for Emily's finger. Luke had planned an early dinner so that he could time the sunset scene just right. They made it to The Green in plenty of time, so they spent a few minutes recapping the wild year they had just shared. There were a few benches and a swing nearby. Luke had made the excuse that he had forgotten the picnic blanket that they usually sat on so this time they would have to take a seat on the bench under a big oak tree. Then, when the sun was setting just behind the mountain top and the sky was painted in all the colors of reds, oranges, purples, pinks, and streaks of soft blues, Luke slid from the bench onto one knee, took Emily's hand, and looked into her eyes.

Emily, though taken by surprise, was instantly aware of Luke's intentions. Her eyes filled with tears. Luke wasn't exactly sure if they were happy tears or sad tears, but he was committed now so he was about to find out. "Emily, I have prayed many times that when the time is right, God would gift me with a Godly wife. Emily McMaster, I love you. In you, God has not only gifted me with a Godly woman, but a beautiful, feisty, Holy Spirit filled, Bible studying, obedient woman who faces the devil head on. The devil doesn't stand a chance with you, but I hope I do. Emily, I hope that God has spoken to your heart as He has mine. I want to spend the rest of my life with you if you'll have me. Emily, will you marry me?"

Emily was rarely speechless, but speechless she was although only for a moment. "Luke, I'm . . . I . . ."

"Emily, if you need time to think . . ."

"No, no, it isn't that. It's just that I didn't expect. Oh Luke. Before I answer you, I want to show you something." Emily pulled a man's necktie out of her purse.

Luke was bewildered, but also a little amused. "Emily, why are you carrying a man's necktie in your purse and . . . well, whose is it?"

Emily chuckled, "It's not what you think. A while back, I was going through a dry spell in the area of dating relationships. My mother and I prayed together that God would, when the time was right, send me a Godly man. Then, she went out and bought me this necktie. She told me to hold it when I pray for my future husband and if tears come, to use this tie to dry them. My mother said that someday, when God reveals your future husband to you, maybe he can wear or carry this tie, this tear-soaked tie during your wedding. Now, Luke, will you ask me again?"

Luke was overcome with gratefulness to God for what was about to happen. "Emily, I love you. Will you marry me?"

"Luke, I love you too. I have loved you for a long time. Yes, I will marry you. Will you accept this prayer covered and tear-soaked tie as my gift to you to wear at our wedding as a symbol of God's faithfulness to us?"

Luke placed the ring he had chosen for her on Emily's finger. Then, he kissed her as he pulled the tie from her hands and wrapped it around his neck. "I may never take it off."

Luke and Emily finished watching the sunset and then Luke took Emily home, still never entering her apartment. He was fully resolved to never put them into a position where temptation might take over. He loved Emily too much to take any chances on creating an environment where they might dishonor the God they serve.

Luke and Emily worked their campus jobs all summer, saving as much money as possible as they excitedly planned their wedding and dreamed of their future together, whatever that might look like. When classes started back in the fall, their senior year played out much like their junior year. Their Baptist Collegiate Ministry responsibilities were a top priority. They served hard, worked hard, studied hard, and mostly prayed hard. Emily had been accepted into the College of Law right here at Pleasant Grove University. Luke had been accepted into Medical College of Pleasant Grove closer to Pleasant Grove Medical Center a few miles down the road.

Now, here she is. Emily McMaster who is about to become Emily McMaster Westmorland. Emily turned her eyes off the daffodils outside the window and focused back on her textbook. She decided she didn't need to study after all. She knew the material well. She turned her attention to her computer screen where she had begun to write her valedictorian address. In just a couple of months, her pre-law degree would be in her hands. Luke's pre-med degree would be in his. Luke's and Emily's families would be in town for graduation. Everyone would stay an extra week for the wedding. Emily, being the organized planner that she was, had everything in order. The last few weeks of her senior year would be less stressful for her than last year. The same was true for Luke. All they needed to do now is turn in all their last assignments and take their final exams. Then, they could both enjoy the days leading up to their wedding, celebrate their marriage covenant before God with their families, and move into the next chapter of their lives. The best is yet to be.

Chapter Three

Jessica drove past Pleasant Grove University on her way home from work. The campus was known for its beautiful Magnolia trees scattered in no particular order across The Green. This time of year, in mid-March, students took advantage of warm days by spreading blankets on the grassy areas for picnics or they reserved a larger area for playing Frisbee. On the upper end, shaded by large Magnolia trees and a few Georgia Pines were several benches, all facing west. Students enjoy watching gorgeous sunsets from those benches. One evening, about a year ago, about the time the sunset reached its most beautiful point in its descent, Jessica saw a young male student slide to his knees. She had pulled off to the side of the road as she often did on her way home from work to watch the sunset. If you time it just right, the sunset makes a gorgeous backdrop behind the mountain chain lining the horizon on the west side of the campus. Jessica watched the scene unfold.

The young man looked as if he was presenting an engagement ring to his girl. After a minute or so, the girl pulled something out of her bag. Jessica thought that seemed unusual because it didn't look like she had accepted the man's proposal. She wished she could hear the conversation. The next thing she knew, from what she could tell, the man placed the ring on the girl's finger but then he pulled the item, maybe a scarf, from the girl's hand and wrapped it around his neck as he sealed the moment with a kiss. It was a beautiful scene. Jessica couldn't help but feel jealous.

Jessica wanted to attend PGU after high school, but her family couldn't afford the tuition, not even if she remained at home and commuted during the day. Her grades in high school had been good but not good enough to award her a scholarship. Jessica wanted to study nursing, but she eventually gave up on that dream. Her parents were hard workers, but they didn't make a lot of money. Jessica's father worked at the chicken plant just outside of town. Her mother worked as a seamstress at Alterations for You down near the Pleasant Grove shopping mall. Jessica always thought her mother could make more money if she owned her own seamstress business. She was a talented seamstress. When Jessica was growing up, her mother made many of Jessica's clothes, along with her three younger siblings.

Money had always been tight at the Whitlock house, but they got by OK. Her parents were strict, expecting Jessica and her siblings to obey the house rules. John and Marjorie Whitlock ran a tight household. Jessica never doubted that they loved their children, but they didn't allow her, her brother, or her two sisters much room for error. Often, when growing up, Jessica felt that their punishments were not in proportion to their offenses. Jessica's church pastor spoke about mercy and grace in his sermons. She always wished her parents paid more attention to that part. She and her younger siblings were never offered much of that. The Whitlock house rules were simple. Do as you are told.

Jessica's biggest disappointment is that she didn't have the opportunity to attend college and she probably never will. For now, she would have to be happy working at Carl's Diner. If she performed well enough and tips were good, she made enough money to help her parents pay the bills. Three months ago, she had made enough extra tip money to buy her brother and two sisters Christmas gifts. Her parents were able to get them the things they needed. Jessica's 16-year-old twin brothers, John Jr. and James had received two new shirts and new sneakers. Jessica was always glad her parents never felt the need to dress them exactly alike all the time. Occasionally was enough for her taste. Last summer, the boys had worked extra jobs with a landscaping company so that they could buy a CD player for Christmas, Jessica had bought them each 2 of their favorite CDs. John Jr. and James are huge country music fans. They lit up brighter than the Christmas tree when they opened those CDs. Jennifer, the youngest Whitlock child, is 13 going on 23. She looks up to her big sister way more than she should. In Jennifer's eyes, Jessica can do no wrong. In return, Jessica loves that she has one person always in her corner, someone who thinks she is worthy, and who loves her even when she makes mistakes. Jessica adores her little sister. Last Christmas, John and Marjorie had given Jennifer a pair of jeans and two pair of Jennifer's favorite brand of fuzzy socks. She was excited to receive her jeans and socks. All the Whitlock children appreciated their Christmas gifts. They all knew that their new clothes, shoes, and socks had taken a chunk out of their parents' budget, but they were also pleasantly surprised by their older sister's surprise gifts. Jessica had given Jennifer a set of cool glittery nail polishes. She wanted to add makeup to the gift box, but Jessica's parents wouldn't allow Jennifer to wear makeup yet. Jessica knew that even the nail polish was pushing the boundary lines back a little bit, but the look on her mother's face when Jennifer opened the gift box told her that the nail polish would be allowed. Jennifer was ecstatic.

After a very busy evening at work, Jessica slowed down as she always did when she passed by The Green. The sunset was beautiful, a refreshing sight after a long day at work. Jessica was exhausted, more so than usual. Her feet hurt. Her shoes felt too tight. She didn't pull off to the side of the road this time. Traffic was light so she slowed down to catch the best part of the sunset as the sun prepared to sleep behind the mountain. Jessica gave the car a little gas and headed on home.

It was dark by the time Jessica pulled into the driveway. She felt a chill as she got out of the car. In Georgia, March weather can be unpredictable. March often brings warm spring days, but it sometimes brings the worst snowstorms. One March, a few years ago, Pleasant Grove received 2 inches of snow, much more than usual for north Georgia. The following morning, the sun was shining and the temp was 72 degrees. Jessica remembered wearing her heavy coat one day. The next day, she walked outside in a t-shirt. She walked carefully around remnants of snow still on the ground while wearing sandals. By late that afternoon the snow was gone.

Jessica grabbed her purse, locked her car, and headed inside. John Jr., James, and Jennifer were working on their homework assignments. Her mother was stirring something in a pot on the stove. It smelled like Brunswick stew, one of Jessica's favorite meals.

Marjorie pulled an iron skillet from the oven, cornbread. "How was your day?"

"It was a long day, but the tips were good although most of it was from Jack."

Margorie's lips pursed. "Jessica, you know how we feel about that boy. Your father and I think he is not a good influence on you. Besides, he's too old. You spend too much time with him."

"I'm 19. He's 22, Mom. He's not too old for me and how can I possibly spend too much time with him when I work at least 50 hours a week at the diner. I see him on Friday nights, and we occasionally do something on Saturday. That's all."

"I don't have time to argue with you right now. Would you mind switching the laundry from the washer to the dryer? Then, let your father know that dinner will be ready in about 15 minutes."

Jessica opened the old shutter style doors to the laundry closet on the far side of the kitchen. She switched the clothes from the washer to the dryer. She tossed in a dryer sheet and set the timer for 30 minutes. She made her way through the living room where her father was asleep in his recliner. It was unusual for him to be relaxing before dinner. John Whitlock didn't believe in idol time. "Just because you come home doesn't mean your work is done," he would always say. They all had after work and after school chores. Nobody sat down until all the work was finished. By that time, they barely had time to eat, clean the kitchen, and read at least one chapter of the Bible as was their nightly routine before going to bed. It was all to start over again the next day.

John's boots sat by the chair. Jessica stared at him for a minute or two. He looked tired, older. Years of hard work and hard times were taking their toll on her dad. She decided to freshen up and then wake her dad on her way back to the kitchen for dinner. Jessica went to her room first, hung her purse on the peg behind her bedroom door and plopped down on the side of her bed. She needed to get off her feet for a minute. Her shoes felt tight. She bent over and loosened her shoestrings a bit. That felt better. Jessica stood up and made her way to the bathroom across the hall to wash her hands, and then she made her way back into the living room. "Daddy . . . Daddy." Jessica tapped his shoulder. "Daddy . . . wake up. Dinner is almost ready."

John opened his eyes. "Have mercy. How long was I asleep?"

Jessica wasn't sure. "I don't know. Probably not long. I've only been home for a few minutes. You were asleep when I came in. Mom says dinner will be ready in a few minutes. It smells like Brunswick stew."

"Sounds good. I'll go freshen up. Tell your mother I'll be at the dinner table in a few minutes."

"Yes sir," she stated as she made her way back into the kitchen.

Her mother was setting the table. Her brothers and her sister were placing the silverware and napkins beside each plate. Jessica's mother knew how to make a table look pretty. Her mother's antique china was her favorite. She used it all the time. Jessica was always terrified of breaking something. Her mother told them that her mother's china dishes were one of the few nice things she owned. She said she intended to enjoy them while she was still alive. Jessica agreed. It was beautiful china. The plates were white. The rims of the plates were lined with delicate looking red and pink roses. Jessica's grandmother's house had always smelled like roses. She passed away two years ago. Jessica thought of her grandmother often. She missed her hugs and the way she would cup her hands around Jessica's face softly each time she greeted her.

John walked into the kitchen and took his seat at the head of the table. The rest of the family sat in their seats. They joined hands. John led the family in prayer, thanking God for His blessings on their family and for the food they were about to eat. When John ended the prayer, the family began passing the dishes around. Jessica looked forward to the stew but when John Jr. handed her the serving bowl and ladle, something came over her. Suddenly she wasn't very hungry. She dipped the ladle into the bowl and served herself a small amount of stew. The family passed around the cornbread and salad bowl. Jessica's mother could cook, sew, and keep a household better than anyone she had ever known. She could be a regular Martha Stewart if she didn't have to work such long hours at the alterations shop. By the time dinner was done, Jessica had only eaten a bite or two. The stew had smelled good, but Jessica just hadn't been hungry. They all helped clean the kitchen, taking care of their assigned chores except for John who made his way to the living room, picked up his Bible to prepare for the family evening devotional.

After the kitchen was cleaned up, the family gathered in the living room for John to read from 1 Peter. The verses spoke of being holy, for God is holy. The verses that stood out to Jessica were verses 14-16.

As obedient children, do not be conformed to the evil desires you had when you lived in ignorance. But just as he who called you is holy, so be holy in all you do; for it is written: "Be holy because I am holy."

Jessica's thoughts trailed off. *God wants us to be holy because He is holy. What would He think of me now?* Between her parents' expectations of perfection and God's expectation for holiness, Jessica felt helpless. How could she ever measure up to her parents' standards, let alone God's?

This is the reason she likes Jack so much. He believes in God, but he doesn't expect Jessica to be perfect in any way whatsoever. When she's with Jack, she doesn't have to measure up to anything. The only thing Jack expects of her is occasional messing around. Maybe her parents are right. Maybe Jack is a bad influence on her.

Several months ago, he had come into the diner wearing a black leather jacket and tight jeans. He was carrying his helmet under his arm. His hair thick and wavy, all messed up from the wind and the helmet. Jessica had thought he looked like he had just auditioned for the part of that Fonzie guy in the TV series, Happy Days. Jessica only knew about it because her dad would occasionally watch the reruns. He scanned the room and then took a seat at one of Jessica's tables. She approached his table to take his order. He ordered a ham sandwich, curly fries, and a large sweet tea. He first asked for beer, but they didn't serve alcohol at the diner. Jack finished his meal, left cash on the table for Jessica and then sped off on his Harley-Davidson motorcycle. He thought he was so cool. Jessica thought so too.

Jack came back to the diner two days later and then again a few days after that. He always chose one of Jessica's tables. Her work friends teased her about buying a leather jacket and tight leather pants. Then she could go riding off to start a wild life with the bad boy. Soon enough, Jack was at the diner almost every day, always at one of Jessica's tables and he developed the habit of leaving her unusually large tips. Finally, he asked her out. He didn't waste any time making improper advances. Jessica had refused to violate her convictions at first. She believed in saving intimacy for marriage. The Bible teaches that. Her parents had taught her that, and they might disown her if she were to give in and they found out. Jack was handsome and the bad boy air about him surprisingly attracted Jessica to him. Maybe it was because he had given her the attention she had been craving. Eventually she couldn't turn him down and she gave in to his advances. The immediate guilt was crushing. Jessica had disobeyed God. She had violated scripture and the morals she had been taught. Jessica had rarely missed church since she was barely a month old. She had listened to sermons and Bible study teachers speak on the subject all her life, but what hurt her most was knowing that she had read God's Word herself. She knew God's plan for dating, intimacy, and marriage, yet in a moment, she had disregarded all she knew to be moral and wholesome all because a handsome young man had paid her a little bit of attention. She had sinned, not accidentally, but intentionally. She knew it was wrong, but she had done it anyway. The load of her sin was heavy, and Jessica knew she would carry it for the rest of her life.

John finished the devotion and asked John Jr. to pray. He prayed the deepest heartfelt prayers. He was not only a good boy but a young man of conviction. Jessica was convinced that He would become a pastor someday and a good one. When John Jr. finished the prayer, John turned on the TV as was his custom an hour or so before bed. Sometimes the rest of the family would watch TV with him but tonight, Jessica was expecting a call from Jack so she went to her room where she could talk to him in private.

Jessica picked up on the first ring. "Hey Jack! Are you coming by the diner tomorrow? Tomorrow is my day to work on Saturday. My shift is over at 4:00. Maybe we can do something tomorrow evening."

"Absolutely, Babe. You know exactly what I want to do."

"Jack! I don't mean that. I thought we could have dinner somewhere besides the diner and then maybe catch a movie. Maybe you can pick me up here and say something nice to my parents. I would feel a lot better if they had a chance to warm up to you."

Jack sounded a little frustrated, but Jessica didn't think much of it. "I'll pick you up at the diner at 4:15. No way am I picking you up at your house. Your dad is intense, and your mom hates me."

"Fair enough, I guess. I'll see you tomorrow."

"See ya, Babe." Jack hung up the phone.

Jessica was exhausted so she decided to turn in early. She was asleep by the time her head hit the pillow.

The next morning, Jessica's alarm went off at 6:00am. She wasn't a morning person through the week. She sure wasn't a morning person on Saturdays, but her father never let the family sleep in too long on weekends anyway so she might as well go to work and get paid. And tonight, she would see Jack and go on a tasteful date.

Jessica hoped she could tame Jack so she could resist the temptations he brought and return to her moral ways. Maybe one day, her parents might like him.

Jessica had slept well, but she felt sluggish as she dressed for work. She went into the kitchen, placed a slice of bread into the toaster and grabbed the orange juice, butter, and grape jelly from the refrigerator. She sat them on the table and the toast popped up. Jessica spread a little bit of butter onto the hot bread and opened the jelly jar. Suddenly, Jessica felt nauseous. The smell of the butter and grape jelly blended and made Jessica feel even more nauseous. *So weird*, Jessica thought.

She picked up the piece of toast and brought it as far as her lips. That was as far as it got before Jessica ran into the bathroom and vomited. Jessica thought she might have a stomach virus, but she didn't feel that kind of sick. This was a different kind of sick. Maybe it was just something odd. She decided to skip breakfast. She tossed the toast into the trash can, put the loaf of bread back into the bread box, returned the butter, jelly, and juice back to the refrigerator and went to work.

As Jessica entered the diner, the smell of coffee was overwhelming. She had never noticed that before. She turned to Rhonda, her coworker. "Is there something wrong with the coffee maker? It smells like burned coffee in here?"

"Burned coffee?" Everything smelled perfectly normal to Rhonda. "It smells like a normal Saturday morning to me. You look pale. Are you OK, Jessica? Are you sick?"

"I don't think so. I did vomit at home this morning but then I felt fine. I just couldn't eat. Everything smells funny and my feet hurt and it's only 8:00am."

Rhonda looked down at Jessica's feet. They looked swollen. "Jessica, are your feet swollen?"

"My shoes do feel tight, but I just put them on less than an hour ago. They felt fine then."

Rhonda gave Jessica a knowing look. "Jessica . . . I hate to ask you such a personal question, but would you happen to be . . . um . . . late?"

"Late? Rhonda, I'm never late for work. In fact, I was here early, as usual." Jessica had tried not to sound offended.

Rhonda knew Jessica wasn't following. "No, I don't mean that kind of late. Honey . . . I mean . . . LATE."

Jessica suddenly knew what Rhonda meant. For a moment, Jessica was frozen with fear. "Oh, you don't think . . . no, I couldn't be . . . I can't be . . . oh Rhonda . . . my parents . . . what . . . oh no."

Rhonda could see that Jessica was panicking. "Jessica, take a deep breath and calm down. You might not be pregnant. Maybe you do have a stomach virus. Why don't you take the day off just in case and go by the drug store pick up a pregnancy test. I'm sure it will be negative and then you can put your mind at ease."

"I can't take a pregnancy test at home. I can't take a chance on someone finding it. Oh, Rhonda, what am I going to do?'

"Run down the street to the pharmacy on the corner. Pick up a test and come back here. You can do the test here. If it's negative, then assume you have a stomach bug and go home. If it's positive, we can talk about that when we get a break."

Jessica was shaking all over. She was so nervous. She couldn't possibly be pregnant. The pharmacy on the corner of Maple and Main was only a mile down the road but it might as well have been a hundred miles. Jessica thought she would never get there. Finally, she pulled into a parking spot. She exited her car quickly and ran inside. *Slow down, Jessica*, she thought to herself. *Focus.*

Jessica searched for the aisle where they keep the pregnancy tests. She didn't want to have to ask a clerk. She finally found the section of pregnancy tests. *Do they have to have so many? Which one should I get? Oh, my goodness. Maybe it doesn't really matter.* Jessica couldn't think straight. She picked a random box and headed to the checkout counter.

"Will that be all?" The clerk was a nice older lady. Jessica wondered what she was thinking. No one around Jessica could possibly know her circumstances, but still she felt like everyone was staring at her.

"Yes, ma'am. I think so. I mean, I know so. Um, yes, ma'am. That will be all." Jessica swiped her debit card as quickly as possible and got out of there. She ran to her car and headed back to the diner.

With the test shoved deep inside her purse, Jessica entered the diner through the back door and went straight into the bathroom. She locked the door and opened the box. *How does this work? How do I do this? It can't be that hard,* Jessica thought as she read the instructions.

A few minutes later, Jessica was leaning against the bathroom door waiting for the timer on her watch to go off. The test said to give it two minutes to complete. Then, if there is only one line on the tiny screen, she is not pregnant, but if there are two lines, she is pregnant.

There was a knock on the bathroom door. "Just a minute."

"Jessica, it's me, Rhonda. Are you OK?"

"I don't know yet." Jessica realized she was speaking with loud whispers through the door crack. She opened the door. The hallway was narrow and no one else was there. "Rhonda, I don't know. My whole life is riding on that little piece of plastic and the timer on my watch."

Jessica checked her watch. "Only 30 more seconds. Can you wait with me?"

Jessica had worked with Rhonda for almost a whole year. They both worked long hours, so they spent a lot of time together. They had never kept company outside the diner, but that was only because Jessica had barely enough time for Jack, let alone anyone else. Jessica didn't even make it to many activities for young people at church anymore. She was always working. Her parents didn't mind as long as she was in church on Sundays. The family needed the money.

Right now, Rhonda was the only friend Jessica had in the whole world besides Jack, of course.

"Of course, I can wait with you. Tammy and Bobby have everything covered in the dining room." There was a weird alarm sound that echoed in the drafty hallway. They both looked toward the dining room to make sure everything was OK. Jessica realized the alarm sound was her watch alarm.

B

Chapter Four

Sarah stood back toward the corner of the aisle. Another lady was standing where Sarah needed to be, but she didn't want anyone to see her looking at the pregnancy tests. *I shouldn't even be here. Cole and I have been so careful. How could this be happening to me? Then again, maybe it isn't happening to me, but how can I know without taking a test? Will the lady in my way just pick a test already?* Sarah noticed the lady in front of her was wearing a Carl's Diner t-shirt and jeans, the typical Carl's Diner uniform. *Shouldn't she be at work by now?* Whoever she was seemed just as nervous as Sarah felt. There, finally, the woman grabbed a box and fled to the checkout counter. Now it was Sarah's turn. She had to hurry so she could get out of the store before anyone else from school came in.

Sarah made her way down the aisle to the section housing the pregnancy tests. Now she could see why the woman before her seemed so overwhelmed with the choices. *Must there be so many? How do I know which one to pick?* She grabbed a white box with a purple stripe on one end and like the woman before her, raced to the checkout counter.

Sarah hopped into her Toyota Camry and drove to Lilly's house. Lilly's parents wouldn't be home today so she could take the test there. Lilly wouldn't tell anyone. Sarah and Lilly had been friends since kindergarten. They had been through everything together – elementary school, middle school, high school, acne emergencies, first boyfriends, breakups, first school dances, cheerleading tryouts - most all the trials and triumphs kids face from ages 5 to 17. Sarah had been there for Lilly when she had fallen off the balance beam in gymnastics class and broke her arm. Lilly had dreams of becoming an Olympic gymnast until that day. 8 weeks later when the cast finally came off, Lilly hadn't wanted to try again. She decided she would stick to something that kept both of her feet planted securely on the ground. Lilly decided to pursue a degree in Early Childhood Education when she was ready for college.

Now they were high school seniors and Lilly was here for Sarah on one of the scariest days of her life. Sarah pulled into Lilly's driveway. Lilly was waiting for Sarah at the front door. "Thanks for being here for me, Lilly. I'm so scared. Cole and I have been so careful. I just can't be pregnant. I'm only 17. I'm not ready to be a mother and Cole certainly isn't ready to be a father. Neither of our parents will understand. My parents will be so angry with me."

Lilly listened as Sarah expressed her fears. They were good at listening to each other. They had lots of practice over the years. "Don't borrow worry. Maybe you're just stressed out about final exams, college applications, and you know . . . the stuff of life."

Sarah was impressed with Lilly's patience. Months ago, when Cole began making improper advances toward Sarah, she had gone to Lilly for advice. Lilly warned her about giving in to Cole's advances. "You know, Sarah, we've talked about this before. I've explained to you what the Bible says about keeping yourself pure before marriage."

"Yes, I know. Lilly . . . freshman year, when you went on that youth retreat with your church and came back a Christian, I respected that. We've always respected each other's decisions. Most of the time, we are on the same page. Honestly, there isn't much difference between you and me. We like the same things. We are interested in the same things. Neither of us are troublemakers. You don't drink at all, and I don't drink much. We don't steal. We don't hurt people, at least not on purpose. You're my best friend. I love you, but I don't see why I don't have just as much of a chance of getting into Heaven as you. Does the fact that I slept with Cole really make me less worthy of Heaven than you?"

Lilly prayed for wisdom. "Sarah, neither of us are worthy of Heaven on our own merit. The Bible teaches us that there is only one way to Heaven and that is through a relationship with Jesus. Remember when I told you about what is probably the most well-known and most memorized Bible verse there is? John 3:16?"

For God so loved the world that he gave his one and only Son, that whoever believes in him shall not perish but have eternal life.

Lilly was trying hard to help Sarah understand. "Let me share another Bible verse with you."

Jesus answered, "I am the way and the truth and the life. No one comes to the Father except through me. John 14:6

"Sarah, we don't get into Heaven because of the things we do or don't do. Jesus is the Way, the Truth, and the Life. He is the only way." Lilly prayed for Sarah to understand.

Sarah was listening, but she wasn't convinced or maybe she still didn't understand. She probably should have gone to church with Lilly. Lilly had asked her many times, but Sarah always made up an excuse for not going. Maybe time in church with Lilly would help her understand Lilly's faith. "I'll think about what you've told me, Lilly, but right now, I need to do this test."

"OK, you know where the bathroom is. Let me know when you're ready. I hear they take a few minutes to process. I'll wait with you if you want."

Sarah loved that Lilly never judged her harshly. Lilly was never afraid to let Sarah know when she didn't approve of her and Cole's intimacy or of the few times when Sarah had too much to drink, but she loved her anyway. "Lilly, thank you for remaining my friend. Thank you for knowing everything about me, all my mess-ups, but loving me anyway."

Lilly paused. "Well, that's exactly the kind of love that Jesus shows me."

With that, Sarah nodded toward her friend and headed down the hallway.

Lilly prayed.

A minute or two later, Sarah walked back into Lilly's bedroom. "According to the directions on the box, I should know in a few minutes. I set a timer on my watch."

Lilly saw the fear in Sarah's eyes. "Sarah, do you mind if I pray for you?"

Sarah didn't see any harm in that. If anyone could pray a prayer that reached all the way up to God on her behalf, it was Lilly. "No. I don't mind."

Lilly motioned for Sarah to sit down beside her on the bench at the foot of Lilly's bed. She put her arm around her lifelong friend and prayed.

Dear God,

First, thank You for Who you are. Thank you for loving us no matter what we do or don't do. Thank you for guiding my decisions in life. I want to ask you right now to help guide Sarah. Father, help Sarah to understand how much you love her and how much you want to have a relationship with her. Lord, help Sarah to learn to trust you no matter what situation she is about to face. She is my best friend, Lord. Help me to be the friend to her that you created me to be.

In Jesus' Name, Amen

The alarm on Sarah's watch sounded. "Well, this is it. I guess I'm about to find out if I am pregnant." Sarah stood to walk out of the room.

"Do you want me to go with you?" Lilly wanted Sarah to know that she would support her friend no matter the results of the test.

"I think I would like that, Lilly. Thanks," The two girls exited Lilly's bedroom and started down the hallway. Sarah thought the hallway seemed longer this time than before. They reached the bathroom door and Sarah stopped. She took a deep breath. Her knees felt weak.

Lilly sensed Sarah's nervousness. She took hold of Sarah's arm. "We'll do this together. Come on."

Sarah took another deep breath and nodded. She took one step inside the bathroom door. Then another. Then another. Two steps later she was standing in front of the bathroom counter where the test was waiting. She picked up the test and looked at the screen. She wasn't sure how long she had held her breath until Lilly said something.

"Sarah, are you OK? Say something. What does the test say? You can tell me."

Sarah had to tell herself to breathe in and then out. She forced a word but at first, she couldn't get it out. "It says . . . ". Her voice sounded groggy.

Lilly put the toilet seat down and told Sarah to sit. She was tempted to look at the pregnancy test screen herself, but she didn't. "Sarah, are you pregnant?" She figured a one-word answer, either yes or no, would be easier for Sarah, but as soon as she thought that it occurred to here that Sarah wouldn't have had a problem telling her she wasn't pregnant. She would be excited about that. There was only one explanation for Sarah's lack of the ability to speak. She must be pregnant.

Sarah finally found her voice, weak as it was. "Lilly, I'm pregnant. I'm a 17-year-old high school senior and I'm pregnant." She spoke in a voice a little more than a whisper.

Lilly kept her response calm. For the past 3 years, her priority concerning Sarah was leading her into a relationship with Jesus, but Sarah hadn't been willing to take that step. Lilly didn't know if or how Sarah's baby would affect her journey toward faith, but she knew one thing. She would never give up on Sarah. "Sarah, I know this is not what you wanted, but you'll get through this and I'm going to be with you every step of the way."

"I need a minute to let this sink in." Sarah needed way more than a minute, but she could only think ahead one minute at a time.

Lilly gave Sarah a couple of minutes to think before speaking again. "This is new territory for both of us, but I will be here for you as you figure this out. Talk to Cole. Talk to your parents . . ."

Sarah interrupted. "Talk to Cole? Talk to my parents? What? NO! I can't talk to Cole and I certainly can't talk to my parents!"

Lilly wasn't expecting Sarah's short-tempered reaction. "Sarah, you must eventually talk to Cole. He's your baby's father. As far as your parents are concerned, this isn't something you can hide from them for long. Maybe they'll be more supportive than you think."

Sarah had never had a panic attack, but she was pretty sure she was having one in that moment. She wasn't ready to be a mother. She didn't want to be a mother, not yet. She wanted to finish her senior year, cheer in the final cheer competition, go to prom, go to college, join a sorority – not have a baby – and Cole wouldn't want a baby either, not now. He would want to finish his senior year doing all the things guys do, whatever that was. Sarah couldn't think straight. As far as her parents were concerned, they wouldn't be supportive. How could Lilly not realize that? She had known them her whole life. Her parents expected her to be much smarter than this and her father would want to . . . there's no telling what her father would do to Cole. This was all too much for Sarah. For the first time in her life, she didn't think Lilly could possibly understand and if Lilly couldn't understand her situation, then for the first time since Kindergarten, Lilly couldn't help her.

"Lilly, I have to go." Sarah grabbed the test from the bathroom counter and ran down the hallway, down the stairs, and out to her car. She could hear Lilly chasing after her, calling her name.

"Sarah, wait! Sarah, my parents won't be home for hours. You can stay here and think this through!" Lilly nearly fell down the stairs chasing after her troubled friend. She regained her balance and kept after her. "Sarah, please!"

Lilly couldn't catch up after her stumble. Sarah had pulled out of Lilly's driveway in a hurry. As she backed out, Lilly caught a glimpse of Sarah's red, tear-stained face. Her heart ached for her friend. Sarah had gotten herself in a predicament, an unplanned pregnancy. A boyfriend who, Lilly agreed, wasn't anywhere close to ready to be a father. Sarah wouldn't be able to compete with her cheer team in the final competition. The routine was much too strenuous. It would be dangerous for Sarah and her baby. The situation was bound to be complicated. Lilly wished like never before that Sarah had trusted Jesus with her life. Will she trust Him now? Lilly could only pray.

She walked slowly back to her bedroom and got on her knees. And she prayed hard.

Chapter Five

Angela had all the materials her grandmother had sent her spread out over her bed. When her phone rang, she leaned across the pamphlets to pick it up. She couldn't help but notice the photos of the pre-born babies. She wondered what her baby must look like. "Hello, Brad."

"Hi." Brad wasn't sure how to arrange his words. They were all jumbled up in his head. "I've been thinking. Angela, I still don't know what to think about all of this, the baby and all, but I didn't give us a chance to talk it through. I wasn't expecting this. I needed time to sort through it all. Can we meet to try again?"

Angela held on tight to the ray of hope taking aim at her heart. "Yes, of course we can meet again. When and where?"

"Well, I kind of made a mess of our favorite spot the last time we were there. May I have a second chance?"

Angela was more than willing to give Bradley St. James that second chance. "It might be a little crowded on Saturday, but maybe they can squeeze us in."

"I'll pick you up at 4:00. We can get there before the Saturday evening rush and get a quiet booth near the back."

"Ok, sounds good to me." Angela stacked the pamphlets and the *Steps to Peace with God* booklet into her purse. They could look at them together at The Pizza Parlor.

Two hours later, Angela received a text message from Brad. "I'm waiting downstairs in your dorm lobby. Take your time."

"I'll be right down." Angela was ready half an hour ago. She grabbed her purse from the back of her desk chair and headed down the stairs.

Angela bounced down the stairs and rounded the corner into the common room, the only place men were allowed in the dorm, and there was Brad. He paced the room nervously. Earlier in the school year, he would smile, crack a joke, take her by the hand and they would head out to a game, The Green, The Pizza Parlor, or take a drive down to the lake. Their relationship had been youthful and fun until several months ago when Bradley had become more distant. Angela never knew why. She was so sure the news of the baby would bring things back to normal between them. She hadn't even considered that the baby would push him further away from her. Today, he seemed uncomfortable. His smile was hidden somewhere deep inside him. There were no jokes or playful banter between them. He began to reach for her hand but then withdrew. He no longer knew how to act around her. Angela suddenly became aware that tonight's conversation might not go as she hoped. "Ready to go?"

Brad, not knowing what to do with his hands, stuck them back into his jacket pockets. They walked toward the door of the dormitory. Brad brought his hands out of his pockets long enough to open the door for Angela as they exited the building. This isn't something he had been in the practice of doing but maybe he was supposed to do it now. He had no idea. He had never felt so awkward. He wished things were back the way they used to be. Then there was the Becky situation. He could never tell Angela about her now. "My car is parked just around the corner."

When they reached the car, he decided to go on around to the driver's side. Angela could open her own door like she always did. He had felt awkward enough in the common room. No more of that.

When they reached The Pizza Parlor, they didn't have to wait for a booth. The dinner crowd wouldn't thicken until later. They walked to the back booth so they could talk in private. They ordered their usual: pepperoni pizza, one Coca Cola and one sweet tea. After the pizza was delivered to their table, they could talk. Neither of them knew how to start the conversation. At first, they just sat there. Angela was hungry so she grabbed a slice of pizza from the pan that sat on the table between them and put it on her plate. Brad took a sip of his tea. Angela noticed a stray slice of mushroom on her slice of pizza. She picked it off, took one bite of her pizza and looked at Brad.

Brad noticed Angela's look. She didn't have to say anything else. She had made her decision clear to him, but he had hoped they could start all over and come to a mutual decision about their "problem." He knew Angela's mouthful of pizza and the look she gave him meant that she said all she intended to say the last time they were here. This ball was now on his side of the court so if he had something to say, he should say it. "Angela, first, I'm sorry I acted weird. I didn't know what to say and I still don't really know but I want to start this conversation all over again."

The waitress was seating two women at a table near them and she was taking their order. Angela wasn't worried about keeping their conversation a secret. She was having the baby so everyone would find out soon enough. "So, start, Brad. You wanted to meet, and you want to start the conversation over so what do you need to say to me?"

After a long pause, Brad took a deep breath and began to speak. "Well, how about starting from the beginning. How long have you known?"

"I found out the day I called you. As soon as I saw the test result, I called you. To be honest, Brad, you haven't seemed yourself for the past few months. I wasn't sure you loved me anymore. I thought the news of the baby would bring you closer to me again."

Brand's heart skipped a beat or two at the phrase "loved me anymore." He took another sip of tea to wash down the bulb of pizza stuck in his throat. "Loved you anymore? Anymore? Angela, I care about you a lot. Maybe I do love you. I don't know. That's why I went out with . . . I needed to check my feelings for you, but I never once told you that I loved you. I tried to be careful not to mislead you. Maybe I do love you. Maybe I don't. Now, you're pregnant and well, I'm so confused."

Angela didn't miss it. She heard what Brad almost said. "Went out with who?" she asked.

Brad's mind was spinning. "What?"

Her voice raised a little and she repeated, "Went . . . out . . . with . . . WHO?"

Oh her. He had not intended to ever tell Angela about her, but he might as well spill it all. "It was only a few times over the past few months. Her name is Becky Finch. She's a junior. She's a good friend. That's all. I needed to see if dating someone else would help me sort out my feelings for you, Angela. It didn't help. I'm not romantically interested in her. I should have said something. I shouldn't have kept that from you. I care about you, but I don't know if I'm in love with you. Now the baby. I'm not ready to be a father or a husband."

At least Angela now understood why Brad had been so distant over the past few months. At least he was being open and hopefully honest with her now. He had never lied to her before, so she had no reason to doubt him. Bradly St. James was a player on the basketball court only. "Why did you want me to get an abortion?"

"I don't know. I was trying to figure all of this out. I decided that Becky is only a friend and that maybe I do love you. Maybe I'm just scared. Angela, I was still trying to figure out my feelings for you. I guess my initial reaction was that if we could back up and there was no baby, it would be one less thing for me to figure out. Abortion seemed like a good option."

The waitress delivered the super supreme pizza to the ladies at the other table. She was saying something about their Carl's Diner t-shirts. They said something about being tired of diner food and needing a good old pizza. The smell of the peppers and onions were making Angela feel nauseated. She remembered the pamphlets in her purse. "I want to show you something. My grandmother sent me these materials. I think you should see them. In fact, my grandmother suggested I show them to you."

Angela pulled the pamphlets from her purse and spread them out on the table. There was a stack of them. Grandma Ruby intended for them to be fully educated about the development of unborn babies.

Brad picked up the first one. "Wow, I thought at first, they were just blobs of cells and tissues. How old is this one here?" Brad pointed to one of the images in the first pamphlet.

"Well, let's see. I haven't read these yet. I had hoped we could look at them together." Angela turned the pamphlet so she could read the description. "It says this baby is 7 weeks."

"7 weeks. I had no idea." Brad seemed amazed.

"I'm as amazed as you are. I didn't know either. I've always considered myself pro-choice. I've always believed a woman should be able to decide what to do with her own body." Angela read more. "It says here that a baby's heartbeat can be detected as early as 22 days after conception."

Brad looked at more of the pamphlets. "Look at those tiny little feet. I never knew any of this. This doesn't look like part of a woman's body. It looks like a whole separate body depending on its mother to take care of it." Suddenly Brad realized that the baby Angela is carrying, his baby, might look like one of these photos. "Angela, how far along are you? How old is your . . . our . . . baby?"

"Our baby? What are you saying, Brad? Do you want to be involved in this baby's life?" Angela once again felt a ray of hope tug at her heart. Maybe Brad didn't love her, but they would at least share a baby, a child together and that would have to be enough for now.

Brad still didn't know how to move forward but he felt less confused than he did when they came into The Pizza Parlor. "Angela, I don't know what the future looks like. I don't know what our future looks like, but I realize now that the baby you are carrying is in fact a baby, my baby. Not only will I support you in your decision to have the baby but I, even though I'm not ready, will find a way to be a good father to my baby."

Angela decided that was good enough for the time being. At least she wouldn't be alone, and she would have help because the truth was that she had no idea what she was doing either. "I don't know how far along I am. I've only taken a home test. I called a doctor's office to schedule an appointment, but I can't afford it. I haven't told my parents yet so I can't use our family insurance card. I don't know when I will tell them. I called Grandma Ruby. She told me to find a pregnancy care center here in Pleasant Grove. She said they should help me. I called a center, Your Choice for Unplanned Pregnancies, yesterday. With the word 'Choice' in the title, it sounds like a women's clinic that does abortions. I don't know. When I made the appointment, I hadn't seen these photos and I, myself am . . . or was . . . pro-choice, but they'll do an ultrasound and tell me how far along I am, I guess. I have an appointment for Monday afternoon at 3:00. Would you like to go with me?"

"Will they let me in with you? I mean, I'm a guy."

Angela thought she saw one of the ladies at the other table turn toward her when she mentioned Your Choice for Unplanned Pregnancies. She wondered if that woman was dealing with an unplanned pregnancy too. "You're the baby's father so yes, you can go in with me."

Brad realized he was feeling excited about the possibility of seeing a photo of Angela's baby, his baby in just a couple of days. "I'll pick you up at 2:00." Brad had finished his second slice of pizza and his third refill of sweet tea during their conversation.

The waitress came by to ask them if they needed anything else. Angela asked for a to-go box for the rest of the pizza. She noticed the woman at the other table glancing over at her again. When the waitress returned with the box and the check, Brad took the check and paid the bill. Angela had placed all the pre-born baby pamphlets back in her purse. Brad stood and took Angela's hand to help her stand up.

When Angela stood up, the lady at the nearby table motioned for her attention. Angela knew something was up with that woman.

"Excuse me. I'm sorry to bother you. I didn't mean to eaves drop on your conversation, but I heard you mention a place called Your Choice or something like that. Is that a place here in Pleasant Grove?"

Angela wondered why she wanted to know. "Yes, it's over on Magnolia Tree Drive."

The poor woman looked worried and desperate. She looked a lot like Brad had looked the night Angela told him about the baby. "Would you mind sharing their number with me?"

"Sure." Angela didn't want the panicked looking lady to have her phone number that would be revealed in a text message, so she picked up a napkin from the table she and Brad had just vacated. She wrote down the number to the clinic onto the napkin and handed it to the poor, frazzled looking woman. They must have had a long day at Carl's Diner.

Angela and Brad made their way to the restaurant door. Brad held the door for Angela as they exited their favorite pizza place. When they reached Brad's car, he opened the door for her and held her arm to support her as she climbed in.

"What's this? You're becoming a real gentleman, Bradley St. James."

"Becoming is correct. I've been an inconsiderate child for a while now. In case you didn't know, I'm going to be a father. It's time I grow up and become a gentleman."

Brad drove Angela back to her dorm building and walked her up the pathway to the door. He hugged her gently. "Angela, I promise you that I will do whatever it takes to be a good father to our baby. You won't be doing this alone, but I don't know where our relationship is going. I hope you can give me some time to figure this out."

At this point, all Angela cared about was her baby. "Fair enough. I'll see you Monday afternoon at 2:00." She smiled. "Don't be late."

Back at The Pizza Parlor, Rhonda looked at Jessica. "Jessica, are you sure about this? Abortion? You only found out you were pregnant this morning. You have time to decide what to do. You need to talk to Jack and your parents. Your parents are Christians, aren't they? Aren't they supposed to forgive and all that stuff and if you think they will be angry about the pregnancy, won't they be even angrier about an abortion? Aren't they pro-life? I thought all Christians were pro-life because they have some notion that abortion is a sin or something."

"It's not that simple, Rhonda. My parents are Christians, but you don't understand how strict they are. I know they love me, but they would be so disappointed in me. They will see this pregnancy as an embarrassment to our family. They even told me once that if I ever got pregnant, they would kick me out of the house. Where will I go?"

"Do you really think they will kick you out of the house? If they are pro-life, then why wouldn't they support you if you have the baby? I'm confused." Rhonda was trying to understand but this situation with Jessica's parents didn't make much sense.

Jessica tried to explain. "OK, my parents are Christians, super strict ones. I know they love me, my brothers, and my little sister but, honestly, I feel like their love for us is performance based. If we obey the rules, we are well loved. If we mess up a little, the punishment is harsh, but they mean well. They are doing what they feel is best and maybe it is best but something like this? This is off the charts. I slept with a man I'm not married to. That's my first unpardonable offense in the Whitlock house. I'm pregnant is the second unpardonable offense in the Whitlock house. My parents will say that abortion is a sin, but then they turn right around and tell me that if I ever get pregnant, they will disown me. I'll have to leave and never come back. And truthfully, I'm a Christian too but I don't know how I feel about abortion. At first, isn't it just a bunch of cells clinging together or dividing up or something? My parents never talked to us about sex, except to tell us not to have it, and they certainly never talked to us about pregnancy. Rhonda, I really feel like I don't have much of a choice."

Rhonda felt helpless. "I'm so sorry, Jessica. I wish I knew how to help you. Are you sure you don't want to tell Jack? I know he's a big kid with no concept of responsibility. I don't understand what you see in him, but don't you think he has a right to know? He is the baby's father."

Jessica was exhausted. The morning experience with the pregnancy test and waiting in the hallway with Rhonda until her watch alarm sounded, discovering the results of the test, the busy Saturday at the diner – what a day! When Rhonda had asked her to have dinner with her at The Pizza Parlor, her treat, Jessica had welcomed the break. It would also give her and Rhonda a chance to talk. "If I can't tell my parents, then what's the point in telling Jack? All of this will go away if I have the abortion. The sooner the better while it's not a baby yet and before I get attached to it. Rhonda, I need this to all go away."

Rhonda had at least given Jessica a chance to talk it out. "Ok. It looks like you've made up your mind."

Rhonda was right. Jessica had made up her mind. "I'll call this Your Choice place on Monday morning. Maybe I can just get it over with and all of this will be history by Monday afternoon. I just need to figure out how I'm going to pay for it. I don't really have anything much worth selling. Maybe they'll let me set up a payment plan or something. May I give them your address for billing?"

"Of course, you can. Do you need me to drive you?" Rhonda hesitated and then took a deep breath. "I have a little money tucked away in a jar. I can help you pay for it."

Jessica was thankful for Rhonda. She seemed like she was becoming more than just a work friend. Jessica didn't really have any friends except for Jack. She needed a friend like Rhonda.

The next morning, Jessica attended church with her family. She couldn't concentrate on the sermon. All she could think about was that her family and probably most of the people in the sanctuary would think she was a Jezebel if they knew her secret. Her parents were strict, but she loved them. She enjoyed her church, but she hadn't had time for activities for young people lately. Between working at the diner to help her family put food on the table and making time for Jack, Jessica only had time for Sunday morning worship. She didn't have many relationships at church. She didn't even know her pastor very well. *If they knew what I've done, they wouldn't want to know me anyway. After I have the abortion, they will have two reasons to kick me out of here,* Jessica thought. She breathed deeply as her pastor kept talking about something in the book of Ephesians. *By Monday night, everything will be back to normal, and no one will ever know anything.*

Jessica drove by The Green on her way to work on Monday morning. She thought about her dreams for her future, dreams that would never come to pass. Her life was nothing like she planned. She was working hard and helping her family. Her dream of going to college died a long time ago. She was dating a guy with no ambition or even much of a desire to work for anything. What exactly did Jack do all day anyway? Come to think of it, he didn't come by the diner on Saturday like they had planned, and she hadn't even noticed. She had been too upset about the pregnancy test. He was supposed to pick her up at 4:15. The diner had been busier than usual and, by that time, all Jessica could think about was getting off work and taking Rhonda up on her offer to pay for a pizza dinner. They needed to talk about her choices, and she was glad they did. She would worry about Jack later. In fact, Jessica decided that if Jack called her, she wouldn't answer. *It will be better if I don't talk to him or see him today,* Jessica thought. *I'd rather not take a chance on mentioning the pregnancy to him.*

Jessica pulled into the parking lot of Carl's Diner. She was early on purpose. She couldn't take the chance that her parents might hear her calling the Your Choice place. It would be better to call them from the back room at work. Rhonda was opening up and Tammy and Bobby wouldn't be there for another half hour. Carl, the owner of the diner, wouldn't be there at all today. He and his wife were on a spring vacation down in Florida. Jessica wished she were on a warm beach in Florida right now. She parked her blue Chevy Spark in the side parking lot where Carl preferred employees to park, leaving room for diner guests in the front main parking lot. She went inside and made her way straight back to the break room. She pulled the napkin from her purse – the one on which that nice woman from The Pizza Parlor had written down the name and number of the Your Choice pregnancy place. Jessica noticed that she had only been saying half the name. The full name of the establishment is Your Choice for Unplanned Pregnancies. Jessica thought that was a mouthful and decided to stick to just Your Choice. She straightened out the napkin on the breakroom table and pulled out her cell phone and dialed the number.

After 3 rings, a woman answered the phone. "Good morning. This is Your Choice for Unplanned Pregnancies. This is April. How may I help you?"

Angela thought April sounded nice enough. "Umm, hello, yes. My name is Jessica. I would like to make an appointment for later today."

"OK, I can help you with that. Let's see. It looks like we are booked up for today. What is the reason for your calling?"

Jessica realized she was trembling. Was she doing the right thing? "I'm pregnant and well, I don't want to have a baby. I really need to do this today. Maybe I can call another clinic."

"Let me see what I can do. Do you mind holding for a moment?"

Jessica checked her watch. She wanted to end the call before Tammy and Bobby came in. "I only have a minute or two. I'm at work."

"I understand. Just one moment, please."

After about 45 seconds, April came back on the line. "I can get you in at 3:00. Will that work for you?"

Rhonda was the acting manager of the diner while Carl was on vacation. She had already told Jessica that as soon as she had an appointment time, she would call Greg and Cindy in to cover for them for a few hours. They had both already agreed. All they knew was that Jessica was having a minor procedure done and Rhonda needed to drive her.

"Yes, I can be there at 3:00. Thank you." She hung up the phone relieved. She had an appointment. She was one step closer to putting this all behind her and no one would ever know, no one except for herself, Rhonda, and the one other person Jessica couldn't get out of her head. He had been on her mind since the beginning as if he was telling her to find another way. She kept hearing the words, "Have the baby." But it wasn't Jack's voice. He didn't even know. It was the voice of God. He knows and He would always know.

Chapter Six

It was Monday afternoon. Emily had made an appointment at Your Choice for Unplanned Pregnancies to speak to one of the administrators about volunteering at the center. As organized as she is, she had all her studies and final assignments under control. Her upcoming wedding plans were also under control. Her mother was taking care of most of the final arrangements and loving every minute of it. Her parents were excited about the wedding. They loved Luke like their own son. He was perfect for their precious Emily. They had told Emily to enjoy her last couple of months of college. The next few years were bound to be the busiest years of her life as a new wife with both her and her new husband in graduate school. The School of Law at Pleasant Grove University and the medical school Luke was attending were known for their challenging programs. Luke had the potential to become a great doctor and Emily was surely going to become a great lawyer. Her parents wanted her to savor every moment of the next couple of months.

Luke had told Emily about the women who go to Your Choice, the well-known shortened version of the name. He and other Christian medical students knew about the pregnancy care center. He had explained to Emily that women go there for various reasons. Many women go there because they are seeking an abortion. Other women go for STD testing. Some men go there for testing too. Some women go to get help caring for their babies after they choose to parent them. They also help expectant mothers to make adoption plans for their babies. They work with two different adoption agencies. The center holds adoption training classes for their employees and volunteers every year. They do so much for the community. Many of the female medical students volunteer when they can. Some of the nurses at the hospital volunteer their time as well, doing the testing and ultrasounds.

Emily had decided that with a little extra time on her hands, she would volunteer some time there at least for the next few weeks and maybe through the summer. She was scheduled to be there at 2:00 to meet a lady named Veronica.

Emily pulled into the parking lot at 1:45. As far as Emily was concerned, early is on time, on time is late, and late is unacceptable. The building was an older colonial type that had once been a family home. Emily walked up the wide steps between two large columns. She walked into the waiting room of the center. It was a cozy and welcoming room. There was a wide chair rail around the whole room and a fireplace with a beautifully crafted mantle. Above the mantle was a silhouette drawing of an expectant mother and her unborn baby. The sentiment on the drawing was a Bible verse:

> *For you created my inmost being;*
> *You knit me together in my mother's womb.*
> *I praise you because I am fearfully and wonderfully made;*
> *Your works are wonderful,*
> *I know that full well.*
> *My frame was not hidden from you*
> *When I was made in the secret place,*
> *When I was woven together in the depths of the earth.*
> *Your eyes saw my unformed body;*
> *All the days ordained for me were written in your book*
> *Before one of them came to be.*
> *How precious to me are your thoughts, God!*
> *How vast is the sum of them!*
> *Psalm 139:13-17 (NIV)*

Veronica met Emily in the waiting area. Emily could tell from the moment she walked towards her that this lady was full of personality and a woman who loved her job. "Emily McMaster?"

"I'm Emily. I'm a little early. I have an appointment to speak with a woman named Veronica at 2:00."

"Well Emily! That would be me. I'm Veronica Stephens. I'm one of the administrators here. I'll be showing you around today."

"Nice to meet you, Veronica."

Veronica's smile never faded. She was a jolly woman with dark skin and black hair. Her eyeglasses were black and lined with fake diamonds. She wore bright red lipstick. "Well, let's get started Emily. This room here is our waiting room, of course."

Veronica led Emily down a hallway with counseling rooms on each side. Each counseling room was decorated with comfortable furniture, just like a living room in someone's home. Old buildings like this one had a fireplace in almost every room. Beside each fireplace was a small stack of wood and one of those stands that held a small poker and shovel. Above each mantle was a large drawing of a woman holding a baby in her arms. They all looked different, but they all had the same theme, a loving mother and baby and each drawing also included a scripture verse. At the other end of the hallway was one exam room and one ultrasound room. On one wall of the ultrasound room was a large computer monitor, larger than Emily had ever seen.

"Those large screens are very important," Veronica explained. "When our nurse performs an ultrasound, she wants her patient to see every detail of her baby, no matter how small. Most abortion minded women choose life after viewing their babies by ultrasound."

Emily could only imagine what it must be like for those mothers to see their unborn babies on that big screen. "That's amazing. Don't abortion clinics do ultrasounds?"

This was the only moment during Emily's tour that Veronica frowned. "They do but they don't let the mothers see them. They know that if a mother sees her baby on an ultrasound, there is a high probability that they will lose that sale. They aren't interested in helping women make informed decisions. They are interested in selling abortions."

"That's pure evil." Emily felt as if her heart sank all the way down to her knees.

Veronica led Emily around a corner and up an old staircase with large wooden handrails. At the top of the stairs, they turned into a conference room. In the back of the room was a larger table more suitable for conferences or staff meetings. The rest of the room was filled with tables and chairs. At the far end of the room was a sink and a diaper changing table. On the counter was a newborn baby bathtub and other bath and diapering items. At the front of the room near the door, a large TV was mounted on the wall. Beneath it were shelves filled with DVDs and books. "This is our classroom. We teach parenting classes. We also offer marriage counseling, drug education courses, and basic life skill courses. We teach our clients how to care for their children. We teach them how to prepare for job interviews, how to balance bank accounts and how to manage work and family in all sorts of circumstances. We also offer post abortion counseling for women whether that abortion was yesterday or 40 years ago. The emotional scars left from an abortion will last a lifetime."

The last stop on the tour was the larger room across from the classroom. Veronica continued, "This room is what we call The Stork's Nest. Here we store baby supplies. Our budget allows us to purchase a limited supply of diapers, baby wipes, blankets, bibs, and some clothing items. We stick to items we know new mothers need. People in the community supply the rest. We get all sorts of items donated almost every week including small toys, strollers, portable cribs, bottles, pacifiers, baby food, and formula. Sometimes we get full-size cribs. We only accept new car seats into the store."

"Do women come in off the street to shop for their needs?" Emily was impressed with all the work this small center does in the Pleasant Grove community.

"Not just anyone off the street. When our clients complete classes and class assignments, they receive a certain number of what we call 'nest credits.' The number of credits earned depends on the class or the assignment. Our mothers and fathers can come into The Stork's Nest and spend their nest credits to purchase items for their babies, or they can save their nest credits for a later visit to purchase larger items when a need arises. It's a way to encourage our clients to attend classes and complete assignments so that we can help support them after they choose life for their children."

Emily couldn't be more impressed. "Wow! Your center does so much for this community."

"One of the pro-choice arguments is that pro-lifers will move Heaven and Earth to get a woman to birth an unwanted baby, but then we just drop her to fend for herself after the baby is born. Sadly, there may be women out there in some communities who feel abandoned, but we do everything we can here to support our clients through their pregnancies, during the births of their babies, and through their first years of parenting. We offer them every opportunity to learn how to parent and provide for their children after their time with us has run its course. There are centers much like ours all over the country, but I realize we need more." Veronica motioned to the stairway. She and Emily returned to the main floor where a few clients were waiting.

Veronica led Emily into the office, which was once a small sitting room off to the side of the waiting area. Emily wondered what family once lived in the building. She pictured children sitting in front of the fireplace doing whatever children did back then, maybe reading books or playing with handmade wooden toys while their father poked at the fireplace to keep them warm, and their mother prepared their dinner for the evening. "What do you think, Emily? Would you like to volunteer with us?"

Emily abandoned her thoughts about the make-believe family and came back to reality. "Yes, I would love to volunteer. When do I start?"

Veronica looked at the volunteer schedule. "Would you like mornings or afternoons? Are there certain days of the week that work best for you?"

Emily took her phone from her back pocket and pulled up her digital calendar. "Monday afternoons are best for me. I'll have to work around my classes."

"That works for me." Veronica typed Emily's name into the Monday afternoon schedule. "We'll start you off in The Stork's Nest. You can help us shop for items, receive items from those brought in from the community, and keep the shelves stocked. If you would like, you can also help us out in the classroom. If you are interested in counseling our clients, you'll need to complete a two-day training session first."

"Starting out in The Stork's Nest sounds great. I'll let you know about the training classes for counseling. I'm finishing up my last semester at PGU and I'm planning a wedding for the very next week." Emily was thankful for the opportunity before her.

"Girrrrrl, you are busy!" Emily contained an inside chuckle at Veronica's ethnic personality. Veronica put her whole body into her expressions. Emily couldn't wait to spend more time with this charming woman.

Veronica was finishing Emily's tour session and preparing to check in the next two clients. "I need you to complete some paperwork for us, Emily. I also have a folder for you with lots of information about our center. You can wait in the waiting area while I go get some things from the printer down the hall. The one we have in here isn't working at the moment."

Emily smiled and turned toward the waiting area. "Thank you for seeing me today, Veronica. I look forward to spending time here."

Veronica nodded toward Emily as she headed down the hallway. "You're welcome, Emily. We are happy to have you."

Emily found a seat in the room next to a couple that looked very nervous. Just as Emily sat down, the front door opened, and two women walked in. One of them looked scared. The scared girl looked into the side office. Seeing no one in the office, she turned toward the waiting area. Her eyes widened with recognition as she met eyes with the woman sitting next to Emily.

"Oh, hello." The girl moved to a seat on the other side of the couple. The lady with her sat down too.

Recognizing the scared, frazzled looking girl, Angela officially introduced herself. "Hi. I remember you from The Pizza Parlor. I gave you the number to this place. I'm Angela. This is my . . . this is Brad.

"Hi Angela and Brad. Umm, nice to meet you . . . again. I'm . . . I'm Jessica. This is my friend, Rhonda." The poor girl was so nervous.

Emily sat there not knowing what to say. *I'm definitely going to need training*, she thought to herself. There was another woman in the room. She was sitting several chairs away. Her toddler was playing with a stack of blocks. Emily was happy to have something else to focus on. The kid was doing an impressive job with those blocks.

A nurse came into the room. "Angela Cromwell?"

Angela stood up and moved toward the nurse. Brad stood to follow her. "I'm Angela. This is Brad. He's the father."

Brad's heart skipped a beat. He held his breath for a second, maybe 2. He wasn't sure how long it would take him to get used to hearing others refer to him as a father.

"Follow me. You scheduled an ultrasound appointment to confirm pregnancy so we will go straight to the ultrasound room." The nurse led Angela into the room. She asked Brad to remain in the hallway for a few minutes to give Angela some privacy. She gave Angela instructions for changing into a gown and preparing for her ultrasound. When Angela was ready, the nurse helped her onto the table and made sure she was fully covered. Then she called Brad into the room. She told him to take a seat next to the exam table. "Now, Angela, all you have to do is relax. I want both of you to keep your eyes on the big screen on the wall in front of you. In a few minutes, you'll see your baby."

Brad had to remind himself to breathe. He wasn't sure if he was feeling fear, excitement, or both. *Am I really about to see Angela's baby? My baby?*

A few moments later, the large screen on the wall came to life. The nurse explained to Angela what she was seeing. She moved her computer mouse around. "This right here is your baby."

Angela was mesmerized. The image on the screen looked like a bean but she could make out a larger area that was the baby's head.

The nurse pointed her curser to little nubs. "These are your baby's arms, and these are his or her legs. It looks like you are about 8 weeks pregnant. Your baby is due around mid-October."

Brad sat there staring at the monitor, totally stunned. How could he have suggested that Angela get an abortion? He had no idea until Angela showed him the pamphlets back at The Pizza Parlor that a pregnancy at this stage wasn't just a clump of cells. This was definitely not a clump of cells pregnancy. This was a baby with a head and arms and legs, his baby. "This is amazing. I had no idea."

There's more. "Look at this area right here. What do you see?"

Angela was overcome with emotion. "It looks like a fluttering of something. Is that? It can't be. Not this early, right?"

Brad saw the fluttering but had no idea what he was looking at. "Can't be what?"

The nurse smiled warmly. "It can be, and it is. It's your baby's heartbeat."

Back in the waiting room, Emily was still waiting for Veronica to come back with her forms. The girl who had come in with someone Emily guessed was her friend looked so frightened. Emily decided to at least introduce herself. "Hi Jessica. I'm Emily. I'm going to be volunteering here at the center. I came in today for paperwork and a tour, but I'll be here on Monday afternoons. Perhaps I'll see you again sometime soon."

"Oh, I only plan to be here today. I came in for an abortion. After today, I won't have any reason to come back." Jessica wasn't interested in making friends. She just wanted all this over with and soon. Rhonda placed her arm around her work friend to remind Jessica that she wasn't alone.

Emily's heart sank to the floor. *She's here for an abortion?* It occurred to Emily that Jessica had no idea what kind of center she had come to. Your Choice for Unplanned Pregnancies didn't do abortions. The word "Choice" in the center's name was intended to help mothers understand that they do have choices, choices other than abortion. Jessica must have thought the word indicated that Your Choice was an abortion clinic. Emily wasn't sure what to say. She was rarely speechless, and it bothered her to her core that she had no words.

The other lady with the toddler had been called upstairs to shop in The Stork's Nest. The room was quiet. Emily was silently scolding herself. "Come on Emily! Say something to help this poor scared girl."

The nurse came back out with Angela and Brad. They had smiles on their faces and a clear bag filled with what looked like a video, a book, and pamphlets. As they walked out, Emily thought the couple seemed different, maybe more relaxed. She guessed they were happy with the ultrasound experience. She prayed silently that God would help them on this new journey called parenthood.

Another nurse called her next patient. "Jessica Whitlock?"

Jessica stood and walked toward the nurse. "I'm Jessica. This is my friend, Rhonda."

The nurse addressed Jessica warmly. "Hello Jessica. You indicated in your phone call that you wanted an abortion, but you said that you had not seen a doctor prior to your call. Have you seen a doctor since then?"

Jessica answered quickly. "No, I don't want to see anyone else. I just want this over with today and quickly, please."

The nurse could see that Jessica was desperate. "I see. First, we'll need to get you into the ultrasound room so that we can confirm your pregnancy. Those home tests are sometimes wrong."

Jessica hadn't thought of that. "Oh! So, I might not be pregnant?"

"The home tests are pretty accurate, but they can sometimes deliver a false positive. An ultrasound will help us confirm that you are pregnant."

Jessica just wanted to get this done and get out. "OK. So, if the ultrasound confirms that I am pregnant, I can get the abortion and get out of here?"

"It's not quite that simple dear. An abortion is a very serious procedure. It can even be dangerous. Let's just take things one step at a time. Let's get you checked in and get you ready for your ultrasound." The nurse led Jessica into the room where Brad and Angela had just been and gave her instructions to prepare. "I'll let your friend help you get into a gown while I take your paperwork to the front office for filing. Rhonda, you can step outside the door to let me know when Jessica is ready."

Jessica and Rhonda nodded to the nurse and then Jessica went behind the drape to change. When she was ready, she sat on the table as she was instructed. Rhonda stepped into the hallway to let the nurse know Jessica was ready. The nurse came back into the room and told Jessica to relax and focus on the large screen in front of her. A few moments later, a large screen on the wall came on and Jessica saw a big gray area with a kidney shaped black area in the middle.

The nurse explained to Jessica what she was seeing. Jessica watched the curser. "This area right here is the sack where your baby will grow and develop. This little area right here is your baby. It looks like a small bean right now but he or she will grow very quickly."

Jessica was looking intently at the screen. "That little bean shaped area is my baby?" Jessica needed to refocus on the reason she was there. "I don't need to see anymore."

The nurse moved her curser and magnified the image a little bit more. "I understand but while you're here, let's take a look at one more little detail." Her curser rested on a little spot that looked like it was pulsating. "This is your baby's heartbeat."

Heartbeat? Jessica hadn't expected to see a heartbeat. She hadn't expected to see anything. Her head was spinning. "But I thought it was only a clump of cells, not a baby with a heartbeat."

The nurse was compassionate. She took one of Jessica's hands and spoke in gentle tones. "Jessica, your baby has a head, a body, tiny little arms and legs, and he or she most certainly has a heartbeat. I'd say you are 7 weeks along."

Jessica felt sick to her stomach. She could barely think. *What will I do now?* She turned to Rhonda, but words wouldn't come. Rhonda was still staring at the spot on the screen where Jessica's baby's heart was still beating.

"Jessica, I want you to get dressed and then I would like you to come with me into a counseling room so we can help you decide what is best for you and your baby. Rhonda can come with you if you like."

Jessica took another look at the screen. She watched her baby's beating heart. She needed help, help that neither Jack, Rhonda, nor her family could give her right now. "OK. I would like to talk to someone. Thank you."

Veronica entered back into the waiting room. "Whoooo, mercy! Emily, I am so sorry girl. The printer in the side office has been giving us fits for days and now the one in the back room is joining in the great printer rebellion. I finally got it to work. Here are your forms. Just sign those and bring them back with you next Monday when you come back to volunteer. Again, it was so nice to meet you today. I look forward to seeing you next week."

"It was nice to meet you as well. I look forward to spending time here. I'll see you next week." As Emily turned to the door, she saw a nurse walk Jessica and the woman with her into a counseling room. She thought about her experience. She had learned so much on her tour. In the waiting room, she had watched a couple sit nervously together. She had watched a scared girl come in expecting to get an abortion. Before she left, she had witnessed a couple leave looking relaxed and hopefully ready to parent a child. She had witnessed a nurse take a scared girl into a counseling room. Emily prayed for all of them as she walked out the door. "Lord, please be with these young parents. Use me as your vessel if there is any way I can help them." Emily knew that local mission work is just as important as foreign mission work. Her parents and her experiences with her Baptist Collegiate Ministries group had taught her that. "Here I am, Lord. Send me."

Chapter Seven

Sarah's watch alarm sounded. She sat straight up, frightened by the sound. The last time she had heard it was on Saturday at Lilly's house. It was the sound that told her it was time to check the pregnancy test. It had been positive. The rest of that day was a blur. She had run from Lilly's house in a panic. That must have made Lilly feel helpless. She looked at her watch and noticed the date. It was Monday morning. She had to face the day at school. At least no one knew she was pregnant . . . not yet. She would see Cole at school, but how could she face him? She certainly couldn't tell him until she had time to figure things out. First things first. She got out of bed and dressed for school.

As she headed downstairs, she smelled bacon. Her mother, Rachel, would sometimes get up early and make breakfast. Usually, they all grabbed a bowl of cereal or a strawberry pastry from the pantry, but when her mother couldn't sleep, she would get up and start the day with a good, homecooked breakfast for the family.

Sarah's father had just come inside with a handful of eggs. They were not farmers, but her father enjoyed raising chickens and providing fresh eggs for the family. The only plant he grew outside were tomato plants. When her mother had time, she made homemade bread. Lilly thought about the sandwiches she made with her mother's homemade bread, a fried egg, and a juicy tomato from her father's tomato garden. He called it a garden, but it was only three plants. Sarah always smiled when her father referred to those three plants as a tomato garden. *Well, technically, he's right,* she thought.

Sarah sat down at the table and grabbed the butter, a butter knife, and a slice of toast from the center of the breakfast table. As she prepared her toast and spent a minute or two picking out the crispiest strips of bacon, her mother finished whipping up a batch of scrambled eggs. She placed them in a serving bowl and then onto the table.

As they ate their breakfast, Sarah watched quietly as her parents and her little brother chatted about the day's agenda and expectations. Sarah's father, Charles, a successful accountant, thought it might rain today. "My weather app says rain today. Good. I just planted the tomato plants this past Saturday. The rain will be good for them. I hope I didn't plant them too early. If we have another cold spell like that one two weeks ago, I might as well start all over." Sarah knew her father would worry about planting those plants too early for the rest of the day.

Sarah's mother, also known as Dr. Rachel Scott at the Pleasant Grove University School of Law, was excited for the new classes coming this fall. "A few students, seniors who are about to receive their undergraduate degrees, are coming to the School of Law today to tour our part of the campus. I've heard from several of the undergraduate professors that some of the students in this year's graduating class show an incredible amount of potential for success."

"Rachel, they are receiving their bachelor's degrees in a few weeks. Don't they all show a lot of potential for success?" Sarah's father thought it was as simple as that.

"They do. According to several of their professors, they are a great class. They told me to keep my eyes on one student in particular, Emily McMaster. They said she has the potential to become one of the best lawyers in Georgia. She is dedicated, determined, and highly driven. They say she never backs down from a challenge. I look forward to meeting her." Sarah's mother loved her work as both a lawyer and a teacher. Occasionally, she would take a case. She worked independently out of a home office, but she was well known at the university and at the courthouse. The opposing attorneys grimaced when they had to go up against her. She didn't lose many cases and when she did, it was certainly not an easy win for the other side.

Since her father mentioned rain, Sarah's little brother, Tommy, was worried about whether he and his classmates would get to play kick ball outside during PE class. Tommy was only 7. There were ten years between Sarah and Tommy. "We are supposed to play the final game of the tournament. My team was going to win. I hope it doesn't rain, dad. I think your weather app is wrong."

They finished breakfast. Sarah and Tommy headed to school. Sarah dropped Tommy off at the elementary school, and then she drove the one mile stretch down the street and around the curve to the middle school and high school. She found her assigned parking space. She was happy to be a senior. Only seniors had assigned spaces. Her space was close to the door. She would be especially thankful for that if her father was correct about the rain later that day. She grabbed her bookbag and headed inside to her first class. Cole would be there, probably already in his seat beside hers. It was a math class, Trigonometry. Sarah hated it. She often wondered how her father could sit at a desk and add, subtract, multiply, and divide all day. He never mentioned having to use equations or finding cosine, or tangent, or any other word often mentioned in her class. "Remind me why this class is required?" She would ask Cole that question at least once a week.

Cole enjoyed the class. He was great at math and didn't struggle to memorize equations. Sarah wasn't surprised. Two years ago, in Algebra class, Cole could solve algebraic equations faster than anyone else. He knew the values of x, y, and any other letter in the equation before anyone else could get past the first two steps to solve it. If it hadn't been for Cole, Sarah wouldn't even have the C average she was struggling to hold onto until the end of the year. He spotted Sarah as she walked into the room. He pretended to not notice her.

Sarah sat down in her seat. On her desk was a yellow sticky note with a heart drawn on it with red ink. In the middle of the heart was a note, *Love you forever, C.* Sarah looked over at Cole. She could tell he was pretending he didn't notice her, but she knew better. Cole Quinn might be good at math, but he was a terrible actor. "Thanks, Cole. Love you forever too." Sarah had intended to speak in a normal voice, but she could only manage a whisper as her eyes watered.

Cole knew something was wrong, but their teacher called the class to order before he could ask Sarah why she looked as if she wanted to cry.

It felt like the longest math class in history. Sarah thought the bell would never ring but then she also wondered what she would say to Cole. She had to act perfectly normal. She had to be extra careful to keep her secret. Back in the fall, Cole had been the star quarterback for Pleasant Grove High School. The team had enjoyed an undefeated season and Cole was the player most credited for the team's success. He had gotten the letter last week, his acceptance letter into Pleasant Grove University on a full football scholarship. He wanted to study architecture. His math scores were higher than anyone else in their class and he had explained to Sarah that all the Algebra, Geometry, and Trigonometry would be important for success in his field, although Sarah never understood how. She couldn't imagine those subjects being vital to her success for the rest of her life.

Reading and writing were Sarah's best subjects. She read a lot of books and hoped that someday she might write one. She had been accepted into Pleasant Grove University too, but her parents would be paying her way through college. Now, she was pregnant. There is no way her parents would understand. Even though Sarah wanted to study American literature and professional writing with the intentions of someday teaching at least one of those subjects, her parents had insisted on journalism. "We are paying for your college education, Sarah. Good readers and writers make good journalists.

If you don't want to study law or accounting, journalism is the way to go," her parents told her.

Sarah knew that a baby would mess up her plans, or more accurately, her parents' plans for her life. Even if she could somehow figure out a way to make it all work, she couldn't possibly expect Cole to give up his plans. Sarah wasn't sure how she felt about a career in journalism, but Cole was certain and excited about his future in architecture. No. No, she couldn't tell Cole. As far as Sarah was concerned, she had only one option.

The bell sounded. "Finally," said Cole. "Sarah, is everything OK?"

"Yes, I'm fine. Everything is fine." *Come on Sarah,* she thought. *Keep your answers short and to the point. Cole cannot find out.*

Cole was still concerned. "It's just that you seem like something is bothering you."

Keep calm, Sarah thought. "I'm fine, Cole."

Cole wasn't finished pressing her. "Sarah, were you about to cry back there before class started?"

"Cry?" Sarah tried to fake a chuckle. "Cole, why would you think that?"

They kept walking down the hallway, around crowds of their classmates who were talking and laughing in small group huddles. Sarah thought to herself that all those chuckling classmates were having a normal day, talking about the latest clothing styles, Johnny Anderson's new car, and Amy Smith's green hair. Apparently, something went wrong when she tried to color it herself instead of going to her usual hairdresser. *If only I was having a normal day. Cole and I would be planning a date for Friday night instead of me trying to lie to him and avoid his questions.*

"Because your eyes were watering up before Mr. Jones started class. And because I know you, Sarah. Come on. Spill it. What's wrong?"

"Nothing, Cole, really. Nothing's wrong." The one-minute warning bell sounded. They had one minute to get to their next class. "I'll see you after lunch, in American Literature. I hope you studied. We are having a test today." They parted and headed in different directions to their next classes, Sarah to Basic Biology and Cole to Physics.

Sarah spent the rest of the morning trying to dodge her friends, especially Lilly. Lilly was the only other person who knew Sarah was pregnant. Cole and Lilly were both in her American Literature class. If she could get through that class, she would be OK. She ate her lunch in her car. She didn't want to take any chances with her friends at the cafeteria table. There was always too much chatter and school gossip at the cafeteria table. Sarah didn't want to sit there talking about the shenanigans of her classmates when she was in such a predicament herself. She might be a lot of things, but she wasn't a hypocrite. She had learned that from Lilly. Lilly was always honest. She never tried to be someone she wasn't, and Sarah always admired that about her best friend.

She finished the last of the bacon and egg sandwich she had quickly put together from their breakfast table that morning. Then she headed to her American Literature class. They were studying *The Scarlet Letter* by Nathaniel Hawthorne. *How appropriate*, Sarah thought. She pictured herself with a big red "A" on the front of her cheerleading uniform where the "PGHS" had been.

She hid in a nearby bathroom stall until she heard the one-minute warning bell ring. Then, she waited a little bit longer, timing things just so she entered the classroom at the last minute.

"That's a close one, Miss Scott!" Sarah's American Literature teacher was a nice lady, but she did not tolerate tardiness. It was one of her pet peeves. Sarah had no intention of irritating Mrs. Alexander's pet peeve, but she also had no intention of carrying on a conversation with Cole, Lilly, or anyone else until she took care of her situation. While she was eating lunch in her car, she googled terms like abortion clinics, women's clinics, women's healthcare. Sarah knew she couldn't keep things a secret for long and she certainly couldn't keep avoiding her friends. She needed to take care of this problem and soon. In one of the articles, she read that home pregnancy tests can be wrong. For a second or two, she breathed a sigh of relief. Then, as she took the last bite of her sandwich, she reminded herself that she is still a whole month late. After the first two weeks, she shrugged it off as the result of excessive training for the upcoming cheerleading competition. Then, after 2 more weeks, she had called Lilly who had advised her to take a home pregnancy test.

Sarah couldn't concentrate during class. Mrs. Alexander was going over the main points of the book, allowing the class some time to review the material before the test. Sarah wasn't worried about the test. She didn't need to review the material. She knew *The Scarlet Letter* from cover to cover. Now she could relate to it in ways she never thought about before. She could feel Cole's and Lilly's eyes on her. She might as well be wearing the big letter A now. Surely Lilly hadn't said anything to Cole. Sarah hadn't thought about that possibility. Surely Lilly wouldn't say anything. Sarah was suddenly frozen with fear. Mrs. Alexander passed out the test and told the class they had until the bell wrang to finish.

Sarah read each question, but she couldn't think clearly. She felt as if each question was directed at her. *Come on, Sarah, get through this and then you're out of here.* Sarah only had 4 classes. She had already completed all requirements for graduation except for the four she was currently taking. Cole had taken classes he didn't need. He didn't want to take any chances on having too few credits to graduate. Sarah hadn't considered that when she registered for her senior classes. She wasn't particularly fond of school, except for her cheerleading team. As soon as this class was over, she would head straight over to Your Choice for Unplanned Pregnancies. During her lunchtime research, she read about Your Choice. The article said that women could get free pregnancy tests there and women seeking abortions could get their initial ultrasound needed to confirm their pregnancies. The best part was the clinic was in Pleasant Grove not far from the high school.

As Sarah finished her test, she carefully slipped out her phone so that Mrs. Alexander wouldn't notice. She and Cole had become professional texters during classes. She texted Cole first. "I'm leaving right after class. I have somewhere to go, and I'll be late getting home. I'll see you tomorrow." Sarah knew Cole would think the message was strange. She always told him where she was going, and she was never out late on a school night. Her parents never allowed it, but at least the message would buy her some time. She wouldn't have to talk to him for the rest of the day.

Sarah texted Lilly next. "I'm going to take care of my little problem after school. There is a clinic nearby. I'll call you later."

Lilly almost gave away their secret. Mrs. Alexander heard her gasp. "Is everything OK, Miss Campbell?"

Lilly had to think quickly, "Yes, ma'am. I was trying to stifle a sneeze. I'm sorry I disturbed the class."

"OK, then. Class, you have 10 minutes to finish the test. For those of you who have no more classes after this one, you may leave as soon as you're finished. Place your papers face down on my desk and then you may go. The rest of you will wait for the bell to leave class."

Perfect! Sarah had a way out without having to risk a conversation with Cole or Lilly. She was finished with her test. She grabbed her completed test, quickly picked up her bookbag, and headed out. She quickly placed her test on Mrs. Alexander's desk and fled out the door.

Cole and Lilly glanced at one another. Lilly felt sick. Her best friend was in trouble, and she was heading to an abortion clinic. The father of her baby sat across the aisle from her and he didn't even know about the baby. Lilly had to catch Sarah. She couldn't let her friend make this horrible mistake that would haunt her for the rest of her life.

Cole kept looking over at Lilly. Something was wrong with Sarah and maybe Lilly knew what it was. If she hadn't confided in him, maybe she had confided in Lilly.

"Mr. Quinn!" Mrs. Alexander always addressed her students as Mr. or Mrs. Her husband had been a Marine Corps Drill Instructor or something. "Keep your eyes on your own paper!"

"Yes ma'am." Cole looked back down at his paper. There was no way he could finish the test before the bell wrang. He needed to concentrate. He would have to call Sarah later whether she was busy or not.

Lilly had to get out of class before Cole. She couldn't risk talking to him. She was sick at the thought of what Sarah was about to do but it wasn't her place to tell Cole either, or was it? Should she tell him? What would he think? For all Lilly knew, he would want Sarah to have an abortion too. Lilly decided to leave the last few questions blank. She grabbed her belongings, left her paper on Mrs. Alexander's desk and flew out of the room.

Cole watched as Lilly bolted out of the room. Something was wrong with Sarah and Lilly knew what it was, but he had another class after this one. It would be a while before he would have a chance to call Sarah. Cole decided that girls were dramatic about almost everything. He would never understand them.

Chapter Eight

Lilly had her cell phone in her hand when she ran out of the room. She touched Sarah's name as quickly as she could. Sarah's phone was ringing but she wasn't picking up. *Of course, you aren't picking up. You're driving,* Lilly thought to herself. *Where would she be going? What was it she had said in her message during class?* Lilly frantically tried to pull up her text messaging app. There was Sarah's message. She had said something about a clinic nearby. What clinic? Lilly couldn't think of a clinic. *Think, Lilly, think. Where would Sarah be going?* Lilly kept running toward her car. She needed to get off campus. As far as she could tell, Cole was still in class. She couldn't take a chance on allowing him to catch up with her. As soon as Lilly reached her car, she dialed Sarah's number again. Nothing. She left Sarah a message. "Sarah, I know you're probably driving. Listen. Where are you going? Please call me Sarah. Please, please call me."

Lilly pulled her car off campus and drove for a few miles. She pulled into a grocery store parking lot and hid her car around back so she couldn't be seen from the road. In case Cole had followed her out of class, she couldn't let him find her. Not yet. She dialed Sarah's number again. Still nothing. Lilly left another message. "Sarah, please call me. I know that having a baby is scary for you, but you don't have to do this alone. Please Sarah, where are you going? Sarah, please don't do anything to harm your baby."

Sarah had pulled out of her parking spot as quickly as she could. She wanted to get to the clinic as soon as possible. On the way there, she heard her phone ring, but she didn't answer it. The caller hung up. When it rang again, she heard the notification sound that someone had left her a message. "It's probably Cole. I can't talk to him. I just can't." Sarah realized that she was talking out loud. When it rang again the third time, she decided to find out who was calling. She didn't want to pull over, but if someone was calling her three times in a row, then maybe she should at least check it out. She didn't want anyone getting suspicious. She pulled into a subdivision and drove down into an abandoned cul-de-sac. She knew about it because Cole had taken her there a few times. She pulled her phone from her purse. It was Lilly. Lilly had called three times and she had also left two messages. Sarah listened to Lilly's messages.

Don't do anything to harm your baby? What did Lilly mean by that? How could Lilly even suggest that I could harm a baby? What I'm doing isn't harming a baby. Sarah wanted to pull away and ignore Lilly's message. She sat there for a moment or two longer. She and Lilly had been through everything together. Maybe she should call Lilly back. She hated leaving her friend out of this and Lilly sounded so upset. Sarah looked at her watch. It's 3:30. The clinic wouldn't close until 5:00 but she didn't have an appointment. She needed to get signed in so they could work her into their schedule. She placed her car into drive and pulled forward but something inside her wouldn't let go. She put the car back in the park position and picked up her phone. She took a deep breath and called Lilly back.

Lilly's phone rang. She picked it up and saw Sarah's name on the screen. *Thank the Lord!* Lilly pushed the green button to accept the call. "Sarah! Oh Sarah, I'm so glad you called me back. Listen, Sarah, you know I love you. You've always been like a sister to me. Please don't push me out of your life. I felt so helpless when you ran out of my house the other day. Please, Sarah, tell me where you are going."

"Lilly, you've always been like sister to me too, but you can't help me this time. Besides, I don't need any help. I've made up my mind. I know what I need to do. There is only one option out of this. I'm going to Your Choice for Unplanned Pregnancies. It's a clinic not far from here. Please, just stay out of this. By the way, what was that nonsense about me doing something to hurt my baby? This isn't a baby, Lilly. Not yet and it's better that I do this now before it becomes a baby."

Lilly silently prayed a prayer of thankfulness. She was very aware of what kind of clinic Your Choice was, but she couldn't let Sarah know. She didn't want to scare Sarah out of going, but she did feel the need to address the part about Sarah's baby being a baby. "Sarah, you are carrying a baby. It's not just a clump of cells or a mass of tissue. It's a baby with a head and a heart, arms and legs. They are tiny but they are there. Your baby's heartbeat is beating inside of you right now."

Sarah couldn't listen any longer. "Lilly, that's not true. Do you know Leslie Parsons? She's in my biology class. Well anyway, she goes to a bunch of pro-choice rallies and stuff. I didn't tell her about my pregnancy, but she has said in the past that pro-life places lie to you. She said the stuff you're telling me now is just a bunch of lies that pro-life people make up and they just need to mind their own business. She's always saying things like 'my body, my choice.' I agree with her. Lilly, I love you too, but this is none of your business. It's my body, my choice." Sarah hung up the phone and pulled back onto the roadway.

Lilly pulled back onto the roadway and headed toward Your Choice. She and her mother had volunteered there many times. She had to make sure Sarah went inside. She prayed all the way there.

Sarah pulled into the parking lot of Your Choice. It looked welcoming, not institutional like a regular doctor's office. She sat there in her car for a minute thinking about her conversation with Lilly. Maybe she should let Lilly meet her. She felt terrible about leaving her out of this. If the tide was turned and Lilly was in trouble, she wouldn't want Lilly to push her away. Sarah checked her watch. It was almost 4:00. She knew she needed to get signed in if she was to be seen today. She exited her car and began walking toward the flower-lined walkway to the front door. She stopped when she heard a voice. She didn't like listening to other people's conversations, but she couldn't help but overhear.

"Luke, I'm so glad you told me about this place. I can't believe I didn't know about it." The conversation continued. "Yeah, I know I didn't grow up here but still, you would think that at some point I would have found out about a ministry like this."

A ministry? What does this lady mean by ministry? Sarah kept listening, turning a little as the lady kept walking to her car. Now she wanted to hear the rest of the conversation. *What kind of place is this? A ministry?*

"They do so much more than counsel abortion minded women and ultrasounds, Luke. They help people who test positive for STDs. They don't just talk women out of abortions and then drop them like pro-choice people want others to think. They help women parent their babies. They have parenting classes. They are amazing. I can't believe how much a small-staffed center like this does for this community and they do their best to make sure that every client who comes here hears the gospel message before they leave."

Luke was smiling on the other end of the line. He already knew almost everything Emily was telling him, but he loved listening to Emily's voice, especially when she was excited about something. Emily was passionate about everything, especially about anything that helped draw people closer to Jesus.

Sarah stood frozen in place near the walkway to the front door of Your Choice. She was only steps away from entering a place where they would do all they could to talk her out of an abortion. She would also have to hear a gospel message? She had heard Lilly refer to the gospel message. It suddenly occurred to her that she was not standing in front of an abortion clinic. She was standing in front of a pregnancy care center, one of those places that Leslie Parsons says does nothing but spread lies. But why would a place who does nothing but spread lies be sharing the gospel message? Lilly knows the gospel message and shares it herself. People like Lilly don't lie, especially about things like this. Sarah was confused. She wanted to get this done as quickly as possible but no way was she walking in that door and letting anybody talk her out of anything. The ultrasound would have to wait. Sarah ran back to her car and pulled away as quickly as possible. If she knew Lilly, she would be pulling up to the center any minute now to make sure she went inside. Sarah could only drive away and hope she could figure something out and soon.

Lilly parked on the street and got out of her car as fast as she could. She didn't have time to look for a parking spot and the walk to the door was a short one from where she parked. From there, she could see down into the parking lot which was positioned down a short hill. She took a few seconds to scan the parking lot for Sarah's car but couldn't find it. She ran to the front door of the building, stopped, took a deep breath, and went inside. There was a fun-looking dark-skinned woman at the desk. She was humming a song, Amazing Grace. She looked up at Lilly through her black-rimmed, diamond-lined glasses. "Well, hello there. My name is Veronica. What can I do for you today?"

"I'm looking for my friend, Sarah. She's about my age, 17. She's pretty scared." Lilly was about to give the woman Sarah's last name but then she remembered Sarah's commitment to privacy.

"Well, I'm afraid I can't reveal the name of any of our clients, but I can tell you that we haven't had any 17-year-old girls here today. I'm sorry. I'm afraid I can't tell you more than that."

Lilly thanked the lady and went back outside. Where could Sarah have gone? Maybe she had misunderstood. Lilly thought back at the conversation and she thought hard. No, she had not misunderstood her friend. She said she was coming here. She must have changed her mind. Lilly felt helpless. *Sarah, Sarah, Sarah, where did you go?* She reached for her phone to call Sarah, but it wasn't there. She must have left her phone in her car. When she reached her car, she found her phone resting in the cup holder. When she picked it up, her heart skipped a beat. The screen on her phone indicated a missed call. It was Cole. Lilly couldn't deal with Cole right now. She needed to find Sarah. She called Sarah's number. No answer. *Come on, Sarah. Answer your phone.* She called again, and again.

"Lilly, you don't give up, do you?" Sarah answered even though she was frustrated.

Lilly was relieved. "Sarah, I came down to Your Choice, but I couldn't find you. There's no way you had time to go inside. What happened?"

Sarah spoke through her tears. "I went there. I was almost to the door when a lady come outside. She was talking to somebody. She said that Your Choice does all these wonderful things for our community." Sarah sniffed. "She said they not only counsel abortion-minded women but they help them raise their babies and put them in classes, things like that. Lilly, that place is one of those pregnancy care centers. They're the people that Leslie says will lie to you and make you feel guilty and all that stuff. That's not the kind of place I thought I was going to. You probably know all about it, you being a Christian and all. The lady on the phone said they try to make sure all their clients hear the gospel message before they leave. I have you for that. I left. I'm not going back."

Lilly prayed for the right words. "Sarah, they don't lie to you. If you had gone inside, they would have done an ultrasound. You would have seen your baby. They would have shown you pictures of babies as they grow in their mothers' wombs. They would have given you good advice if you had given them a chance to listen to you share your thoughts, feelings, and fears. They would have offered to walk you through this every step of the way. Your baby is counting on you to take care of him or her. Please don't do anything yet. Let's talk more about this, please?"

Sarah didn't know what she would do but she didn't need Lilly putting any pressure on her. "Well, I can't do anything today."

Lilly wanted to see her friend. "Where are you, Sarah?"

"I stopped for gas. I was almost on empty. I'm going home and try to pretend that all of this is just a dream. I'll figure things out tomorrow. Don't come over, Lilly. I can't talk to you about this anymore today. I can't talk to anyone."

"Sarah, don't hate me for saying this, but Cole has a right to know. It's his baby too. He should have a say-so in this."

"Telling Cole would be the wrong thing to do. Don't you understand, Lilly? This would ruin his life. He is about to go to college on a full football scholarship. He's so smart. He will make a great architect. Telling him would ruin all his plans."

"Why don't you let him decide that?" Lilly spoke calmly.

"Lilly, I'm exhausted. I can't talk about this anymore right now. I need to get home or I'll be late and I sure don't want my parents asking any questions. Mom was supposed to check Tommy out of school for a dental checkup. They are probably already home by now. I have to go." Sarah hung up.

Lilly had been facing the door of the center, admiring the flowery walkway and the way the center looked so welcome and cozy. She had forgotten that she had left her window down until she felt a breeze on the back of her neck. You never know what kind of weather you will get in Georgia in March. It changes by the hour. Earlier, it looked like rain, but the afternoon sun was bright and warm. As Lilly turned back to her steering wheel, someone was standing by her window. When she looked up, she forgot how to breathe.

It was Cole Quinn.

Chapter Nine

Back in the counseling room at Your Choice, Jessica sat waiting for a counselor with Rhonda by her side. The room was warm and comfortable. The decorations were simple but pretty. The colors were calming, like the well-kept living room of someone's home. After a few minutes, a lady came into the room.

"Hi Jessica. I'm Kathy, one of the client advocates here at Your Choice. It's so nice to meet you."

Jessica was visibly nervous and seemed confused. "Hi."

"Jessica, I understand that you came in today seeking an abortion. Is that correct?"

"I did. I was. I don't know anymore." Rhonda touched Jessica's shoulder to help calm her nerves.

Kathy proceeded. "What changed your mind, Jessica?"

Jessica knew Kathy was correct, but she was having trouble admitting it to herself, let alone a strange woman. "Well, I didn't expect to see my . . . my baby on that screen in there. I didn't know that pregnancies, I mean babies, developed this soon. The nurse showed me a heartbeat and well . . . now I don't know what to do."

Kathy needed to find out what kind of support system Jessica had or needed. "I see you have a friend here with you today." Kathy smiled at Rhonda. "I'm glad you have a friend by your side. Tell me a little bit about life at home, Jessica. Do you live near family? Do you have a church home?"

"I don't know about support other than Rhonda. I mean, I still live with my parents. We go to Pleasant Grove Baptist Church. My family is active there, but my parents will not take this well. They don't approve of my boyfriend, and they are super strict. I don't know what they will say or do."

Kathy spoke compassionately. "You said you have a boyfriend. Do I assume correctly that he is the baby's father?"

Jessica hung her head low. "Yes, ma'am."

"Does he know about the baby?"

"No. I haven't told anyone except for my friend, Rhonda." Jessica felt embarrassed by her circumstances.

"Jessica, you said you are active in church. How involved are you in your church. Would you have a support system there?"

"I'm not sure. I go to church every Sunday. Sometimes I help with youth activities, although I haven't had much time for that lately. We have a wonderful pastor." Jessica paused and tilted her head down ashamedly. "Miss Kathy, I know I shouldn't have . . . I know what the Bible says about intimacy. I know His plan for marriage. I am a Christian who messed up and I'm so ashamed." Jessica began to sob. Rhonda grabbed a few tissues from the table beside her and handed them to Jessica. Then she grabbed one for herself. Jessica blotted the tears from her eyes. "I know I sinned. I also know that God offers grace and mercy. I know He will forgive me. It's my family I'm worried about. They will be so disappointed in me. Jack will probably bolt. He enjoys his freedom. He will not want to be a father. What should I do?"

"Jessica, are you sure your parents won't understand? If your family goes to church regularly and you grew up in a Christian home, do you believe they won't understand what you did was a sin but your baby is not?"

Jessica paused for a moment thinking about how her parents would respond. "Ma'am, I really don't know how they will react."

"Let's take this one step at a time. First, let's visit the scriptures for a minute and make sure we know what God says about babies in the womb." Kathy reached for a Bible from the table beside her and turned it to Psalm 139. Then, she moved to sit beside Jessica to read the verses with her.

For you created my inmost being; you knit me together in my mother's womb. I praise you because I am fearfully and wonderfully made; your works are wonderful, I know that full well. Psalm 139:13-14

Jessica wiped more tears from her eyes. "That's beautiful. I was raised in church, but I don't remember ever reading those verses."

Kathy comforted Jessica. "Maybe you did but now you relate to these verses in a way that you couldn't before. God is knitting your baby together in your womb. Your child is fearfully and wonderfully made."

Jessica wiped more tears. "I guess he or she is going to grow pretty fast. I can't hide it forever. I need to tell Jack and my parents."

Kathy placed her hand on Jessica's hand which was resting on the Bible they were sharing. "Yes, you need to tell Jack, but I need to tell you something firmly here. I know you said that you are familiar what the Bible says about saving intimacy for marriage. If you want to live in obedience to God and His Word, you cannot continue an intimate relationship with Jack. Tell him about the baby. It's his baby so he has a right to know but you can't sleep with a man you aren't married to if you want to obey God's plan for intimacy and marriage. Do you understand what I'm telling you, Jessica?"

"Yes. Yes, I do. I won't, not anymore." Jessica meant what she said. Jack will probably take off anyway so that probably will not be an issue.

"OK, then. You are also right that you need to talk to your family. I hope they are supportive of your decision to choose life for your baby. I want you to know, Jessica, that no matter what happens, you have a support system here. We, here at Your Choice, will walk beside you through your pregnancy. We will enroll you in classes, if you like, which will help you prepare for the baby's birth. After the baby is born, you can continue in our parenting education program. You'll earn points when you complete the classes and assignments. You can use those points, we call them nest credits, to shop in our Stork's Nest upstairs. You can purchase items you need for your baby with the nest credits. Would you like to enroll today, Jessica?"

"Yes, I would." Jessica was feeling encouraged.

"OK, I'll send you out to the front desk when we are done here, and April can get you signed up. This is what I would like for you to do, Jessica. First, I would like to pray with you. Then, after you sign up for your classes, I want you to go talk to Jack and your family. No matter what happens at home, I would like for you to come back at least once per week to talk with me so I can support you in this journey every step of the way. And Jessica, you need to know, so that you can discuss this with your family, that you do have one more option. If you decide that you are not ready to be a parent, we can help you make an adoption plan for your baby. OK?"

Jessica hadn't even considered the possibility of adoption. "OK. Thank you so much."

Kathy prayed with Jessica and Rhonda:

Dear Sovereign God,

Jessica and I thank you right now for the truth that you are the Creator of all things. You created the baby who is growing in Jessica's womb right now. You have a plan for her baby. He or she is fearfully and wonderfully made. We know this because Your Word tells us so in Psalm 139. Thank you for bringing Jessica here today. We know this meeting was not by chance, but it was your Divine working in her life. We look forward to walking with her in the journey that is before her, and we thank you for promising to be with us every step of the way. Your Word tells us in Deuteronomy 31:8 that You are the One Who goes ahead of us. You will be with us. You will not desert us or abandon us. You tell us we should not fear or be discouraged. Help Jessica to remember this promise as she leaves here to go to her baby's father and her family. Let her feel Your presence with her no matter what. Thank You God, for the comfort of Your encouraging Word. We love you, Lord.

In Jesus' Name,
Amen

Jessica joined in the "Amen." Then Kathy walked Jessica and Rhonda to the office where April was filing forms. "April, this is Jessica Whitlock. She would like to sign up for our pre-birth and parenting classes. Would you help her with that please?"

April smiled warmly at Jessica. "I would be more than happy to help you with that, Jessica. I assume you are starting at the beginning?"

"Yes. I'm about 7 weeks along."

"Today is Monday. Are Mondays always best for you?"

Jessica thought for a minute. She hadn't planned on this at all. "I think so. I work over at Carl's Diner all week, but I think I can make Mondays work." She looked at Rhonda for confirmation. Rhonda smiled and nodded to tell Jessica she would approve her Monday morning sessions.

"OK. Monday it is. How about starting with our 8:00am class. That's our earliest one. It might be easier for you to go in to work a little later instead of coming over here in the middle of your shift or after work when you're already tired. How does that sound?"

Jessica liked the idea, but she looked at Rhonda again for approval to go in to work a little later on Mondays. After Rhonda nodded with a smile, Jessica answered the question. "I think that will work."

April picked up a business card from her desk and handed it to Jessica. "Here's my number here at the office. Call me if you need to choose a different day or time. Otherwise, I'll see you on Monday morning at 8:00am sharp."

Jessica was at ease. The tears were gone. No matter what Jack or her family thought, she had a place to come to for help. "Thank you so much. I'll see you on Monday morning at 8:00am." Jessica smiled for the first time all day long and then she added, "sharp."

Jessica and Rhonda left Your Choice for Unplanned Pregnancies and headed back to the diner. Rhonda had planned to drive Jessica to Your Choice for her abortion. Then the plan was to take her back to Rhonda's house so she could rest for several hours before going home to her parents who would never know what had happened. They would think Jessica was coming home after working overtime at the diner which was not unusual.

On the way back to the diner, Rhonda and Jessica talked about what they had just experienced. Jessica had been so ashamed on the way to the clinic. Now, she seemed at peace. "Rhonda, why have I never heard about a place like Your Choice before? If I had known about them, maybe I never would have considered an abortion."

Rhonda had remained mostly quiet during the whole experience. She had watched in awe the live feed, the image of Jessica's baby's heartbeat, rhythmically pumping the evidence of life on that big screen. "I've never heard of them either. I sure learned a lot today. I had no idea babies developed so early in the womb. I certainly never would have expected to see a heartbeat this early."

Jessica stared at the little "first photo" the nurse had given her to keep. She couldn't take her eyes off the little bean shaped image she held in her hands. The nurse had marked the baby's heartbeat with a tiny little "X." Jessica rubbed her finger over the photo. "I still can't believe it. If I had only known . . . you know, Rhonda, I wonder how many women who have gotten abortions would have changed their minds if they had been better educated in prenatal human development? If I had gone straight to an abortion clinic instead of Your Choice, you would be driving me to your house right now and this baby would be dead. Instead, I saw my baby on an ultrasound. I saw a heartbeat! That was amazing, don't you think?"

Rhonda pulled up to a stop light. As she waited for the signal to change, she glanced over at the photo in Jessica's hands. "It's incredible."

The signal turned green. Rhonda proceeded through the intersection as Jessica kept talking. "And the scripture verses, the part about babies being fearfully and wonderfully made . . . I guess those verses never stood out to me before."

Rhonda listened quietly as Jessica continued. "I don't know how it will all work out. I don't know what Jack will say or what my parents will do but I know I'm having this baby. I guess I need to keep in mind that adoption is another option. I'm going to take it one step at a time. First, I need to tell Jack. Then, I need to talk to my parents. Actually, I'm going to pray first. Then, I'll do the rest."

Rhonda and Jessica pulled into the diner parking lot. Rhonda turned to Jessica. "Jessica, before we go inside to finish our shift, I want to tell you something."

Jessica thought Rhonda's eyes looked a little misty. "Sure Rhonda. What is it?"

Rhonda paused and then smiled at Jessica. "I'm proud of you for deciding to do something hard even if it is painful for you in the long run. You've got guts."

Jessica felt like Rhonda was holding something back, but she didn't press her. Instead, she turned back to Rhonda with a smile that told her friend she was at peace. "No, Rhonda. I have Jesus."

Chapter Ten

After her shift was over, Jessica sat in the parking lot of the diner. So far, things were working out better than she had planned. She had chosen life for her baby. Now that she had calmed down, she couldn't believe she had ever considered an abortion just because she didn't think Jack would want to father a baby and because she thought her parents would disown her for what she had done. She knew the hardest part was only minutes ahead, but she would have to own up to her choices and take full responsibility for her condition. She prayed hard, asking God to give her the right words, and then dialed Jack's number.

Jacked picked up on the first ring. "Hey babe! Sorry about not coming to the diner on Saturday afternoon. I got caught . . . ."

Jessica interrupted. "Jack. That's not important now, but I need to talk to you about something that is important, really important."

"Ok, babe. Want to meet me down at Mickey's Bar?"

"No, Jack. I don't want to meet you at a bar. Can we meet at the school playground? School is out. The playground should be empty. We need to talk."

"Yeah, we do. I got something to tell you too. Do you want to meet now?"

Jessica really didn't want Jack involved but he had a right to know that he has a baby on the way. "Yes, now."

Ten minutes later, Jack and Jessica both pulled into the empty elementary school playground at the same time. Jessica got out of her car. Jack dismounted his motorcycle. Jessica motioned to the picnic table nearby. "Let's sit over there."

They both walked over to the picnic table, neither of them saying a word. When they reached the table, Jack spoke up. "Listen Jess. I'm sorry about Saturday but I need to . . ."

Jessica interrupted. "Let me go first, Jack."

Jack was surprised. Jessica had interrupted him twice in the last half hour. She seemed more authoritative than usual, so Jack figured he better listen. "OK, shoot."

Jessica decided there was no way to dance around the subject so she might as well, as Jack had put it, shoot. "I'm pregnant. You're the father. I'm having the baby." Then, she waited for Jack's response.

Jack was speechless for the first time in his life. He sat there stunned. They sat in dead silence for what seemed like forever. Jessica gave him some time to process what she had just told him. This was big news for a man who was ready for fatherhood. It had to be near devastating for someone like Jack who could barely take care of himself. Jessica was beginning to understand the reason her parents weren't fond of him. "Well, say something, Jack."

Jack spun around a few times while he let out a stream of expletives and then turned to face Jessica. "What the (another expletive)? Jess, but how?"

Jessica didn't want to drag this out. "You know how, Jack. Look, I've made up my mind and there's nothing you can do about it. I'm having this baby. Honestly, I don't know if I can keep it after it's born. My parents are financially challenged already. It takes their paychecks and mine to keep us all fed, clothed, and sheltered. They can't afford to help me so I might have to choose to make an adoption plan. I'm only telling you because you're the baby's father and whether I like it or not, you have a right to know. Now do you want to be this baby's father or not?"

"Jess, I agreed to meet you here because . . ." Jack paused.

Jessica was getting annoyed at this point. "Because what, Jack?"

Jack still seemed a bit stunned. "Jess, I agreed to meet because I had something to say too."

"Yes, you said so on the phone. So, say it."

"Jess, I was going to tell you that I'm seeing someone else."

Jessica wasn't surprised. "That explains the reason you didn't show up last Saturday afternoon." She really didn't care about that anymore. "I'm not surprised. I don't expect anything from you concerning me or the baby. I had to tell you because you are the father. Do you want to be part of your baby's life?"

"Jess. Look at me. I can't be a father. I don't want to be a father."

"Then you don't have to, Jack. That's all I needed to know." Jessica said goodbye to Jack. This time it was forever. Her tears were back, but she wasn't sure why. She had known since the beginning that Jack wasn't right for her, but he was the only guy who had paid her any attention for years. Still, even though she knew that moving forward without him was for the best, her heart still hurt. She felt alone again, and her next task was bound to be the hardest.

A few minutes later, Jessica pulled into the driveway of her home. She grabbed a tissue from the console of her car, wiped away her tears, and prayed again. She asked God for wisdom, courage, and for whatever else she needed for the moments ahead. Then, she got out of her car and went inside.

Marjorie was already setting the table for dinner. "You're a little late, Jessica." Her mother took a closer look at Jessica's red, tear-stained face. "Jessica, are you OK? Honey if Jack broke up with you, then good riddance. He was never good for you. You'll find another nice young man, maybe at church. Help me finish setting the table, please."

Jessica needed to get this out in the open so she could move on to whatever God had planned for her. "Mom, it's not Jack. I mean, it is but it isn't. I need to talk to you and dad, please."

"Sure, honey, after dinner, OK? I need to get the dishes done early tonight. I have a stack of alterations in the sewing room and half of them need to be finished by tomorrow morning. I'll probably be up all night."

Jessica knew the part about being up all night was probably true but not because of the alterations. "Mom, it really can't wait. I need to talk to you both now. I'll do the dishes for you and anything else you need me to do after we talk."

Marjorie looked at her daughter once again with a look of concern. She knew Jessica was serious. "OK, your father is in the living room. Let's go in there."

They walked into the living room. Marjorie asked John to turn off the TV. "John, it's important. Jessica needs to talk to us. I'm pretty sure it's about that boy, Jack."

John turned off the TV and turned around to face them. "What did that boy do to you? Did he hurt you? I never trusted that boy. I always knew he looked like the abusive type."

"No dad. He didn't hurt me, not in the way you think."

Jessica tried to continue. "Mom, Dad. I have something I need to tell you. You aren't going to be happy with me, but I need you both to hear me out. Please?"

Marjorie's heart was sinking deep into her chest. Whatever her daughter had to say, it didn't sound good. "OK, we're listening."

Jessica took a deep breath. Then, she prayed another short silent prayer. "Well, Jack and I did break up. That part, I know you are happy about, but that's not really what this is about. There is really no way to say this in any way that will make you less disappointed in me so I'm just going to say it."

"Disappointed in you?" Both parents were puzzled in unison.

"Mom, Dad." Jessica took a deep breath and almost whispered it. "I'm pregnant." There, she had said it. Now she waited for a response. The room was silent for another moment of what seemed like an eternity to Jessica.

Jessica continued. "Jack is the father of the baby, but as I told you, we broke up. Jack has no interest in me or the baby."

Jessica's mother reacted first. "Jessica! How could you? How could you do such a thing?"

Her father was next. John stood up and threw the TV remote to the floor for effect. "Where is he? Where is that no good . . .

"Dad, that won't help. He's gone. I don't know where but he's not with me, not now, not ever again. I'm on my own in this. To be honest, I'm glad Jack is out of the picture. You were right. He was not good for me, and he certainly wouldn't be good for the baby."

Marjorie began to sob. "Jessica, we raised you to know better. What will the people at church think?"

John paced the floor murmuring the same things. "Your mother is right. What will the people at church think? Jessica, how could you have done such a thing? How could you disgrace this family like this?"

Jessica sat as calm as she could. This is the reaction she had expected. Of course they were more concerned about what people would think than how she was feeling. The only thing she could do was try to calm her parents down if possible.

"You said you would hear me out so may I continue?" Jessica spoke in the calmest voice she could manage.

"There's more?" Marjorie spoke between sobs. "What more could there be?"

Jessica continued. "I knew you would react this way so this morning, I went to what I thought was an abortion clinic."

Marjorie nearly fainted. John stood motionless. Jessica noticed his fist were all balled up on both hands. "I went there because I was terrified of this, of having a conversation like this with you. I know I messed up. I know the sin I committed. Now, I'm dealing with the consequences of my choices. You both did raise me better. I know that. I fell into a trap. Jack paid me the attention that no other guys would. I was mesmerized by him, and I let him talk me into doing things I shouldn't have. I know I was wrong, but here I am in this situation and I'm taking full responsibility for it. I knew you both would be so upset and disappointed and it scared me.

That's the reason I went to what I thought was the abortion clinic. Thankfully, it wasn't. It was a pregnancy care center, Your Choice for Unplanned Pregnancies. They call it Your Choice for short. They gave me two real choices that do not involve killing my baby. They did an ultrasound. It was free. They showed me a live feed on a giant screen. I saw my baby. I saw his or her heartbeat, a heartbeat already! I'm going to have the baby. I know money is tight and we are all barely surviving. I don't know about keeping the baby after he or she is born. The second choice they gave me was adoption. If I choose adoption, they will help me make a plan."

John and Marjorie sat speechless. John finally spoke again. "You were scared to talk to us?"

Jessica was honest. "Yes. Yes, I was."

"Jessica, you know your mother and I love you. We are hard on you because we love you. As angry as I am about the choices you have made, there is nothing you can do to make us love you less."

Jessica had not expected that. Her tears were back. Her mother spoke next. "Your father is right. We are hard on you kids because we expect a lot from you, but nothing will make us love you less. This is all just such a shock. I never would have expected this of you, Jessica." Marjorie was still crying but she was sincere.

Jessica's tears came harder. She hadn't cried this hard since she was a child. "I'm so sorry. I'm so sorry. I know I made mistakes, but I want to make this right. I have prayed for forgiveness. God has forgiven me and given me a peace that I cannot explain. I hope you can forgive me too."

Marjorie looked at John. "I think we should sleep on this tonight, if we can. Let's call your brothers and your sister in here and have dinner. Then, Jessica, I would appreciate it if you could clean up so I can get those alterations done tonight. I'll call Pastor Mark tomorrow and make an appointment for us to discuss this with him. We need someone to counsel us through this."

Jessica agreed to that. "I understand, but I can't go on Monday morning. I have my first pre-birth class at Your Choice. I'll go every Monday morning and I don't want to miss a single class."

Marjorie had finally stopped crying. "OK, not on Monday mornings. I'll make sure the appointment is after work hours anyway so none of us will have to take any time off."

John called the family together. He allowed Jessica time to tell her siblings about the baby. They spent several minutes talking about God's plan for marriage and family. They talked about grace, mercy, and forgiveness. Then, John was ready for the blessing, but this time his prayer was also for wisdom, understanding, and patience as the family moved forward. He also thanked God for the strength and maturity Jessica had displayed as she told them about the baby and her willingness to accept full responsibility.

Jessica hadn't expected that from her dad. They said "Amen" in unison and began their meal together. Jessica decided not to show them the ultrasound image of their grandbaby just yet. She would wait until she decided whether she needed to make an adoption plan for her baby. She didn't want to make this any harder than it already was. When the meal was finished and the dishes were done, Jessica went into the sewing room to help her mom finish the alterations. She knew her mother needed her rest. They finished around midnight. Jessica crawled into bed exhausted shortly after midnight, but she slept better that night than she had slept in months. One way or another, she knew everything was going to be OK.

Chapter Eleven

Lilly reminded herself to breathe. "Cole! How long have you been standing there? How did you know where to find us?"

"I drive by here all the time on my way to Chad's house. I was on my way there when I saw your car parked here. After the way you and Sarah bolted out of class, I was curious about why you are here, and I heard enough to know that Sarah is pregnant. Why didn't she tell me? Lilly, how long have you known this? Did she leave? Is she inside? Where is she, Lilly?" Cole had heard enough to know Sarah was pregnant, but he had a lot of questions and he wanted answers.

"Cole, she was here but she left," Lilly replied sadly.

"Why did she come here? Why did she come to a pregnancy care center?"

Lilly was surprised at Cole's question. "So, you know this place?"

"Yes, my cousin, April, works here. It's a pro-life pregnancy care center."

"So, you know it's not an abortion clinic?" Lilly was impressed that Cole knew the place.

"Of course it's not an abortion clinic. Why would I . . . why would you . . . Lilly, did Sarah think this was an abortion clinic?"

Lilly was frozen speechless. She had no idea what to say.

Cole pressed. "Lilly! Did Sarah think she was coming to an abortion clinic? Tell me!"

Lilly struggled to find her voice. "Cole, she's scared. She didn't want to tell you. She said she didn't want to ruin your life. I've been trying to talk her into telling you."

You haven't answered my question. "Did Sarah think she was coming to an abortion clinic?"

"Yes, Cole. She did."

"How could she? She was going to abort her baby, MY baby without even telling me she was pregnant? How could she do such a thing?" Cole's eyes began to water.

"Cole, she's scared. When I realized she was coming here, I didn't tell her what this place really is. I had hoped she would go inside, get an ultrasound, see the baby, and then she would tell you and her parents. Then, everything would be OK. She overheard a lady talking on the phone as she was about to go inside. The lady was talking about volunteering here and what they do. When I arrived and she wasn't here, I panicked. I thought that she might have gone somewhere else to . . . to get an abortion, but I finally got her on the phone. She's going home. She isn't going to do anything tonight."

Cole was desperate to talk to Sarah. "I need to see her. I'm going over to her house. I need to talk to her. She can't kill our baby."

"You're pro-life, Cole?" Lilly was encouraged. If Cole is pro-life, then maybe he can talk sense into Sarah.

"Lilly, I've done a lot of things I shouldn't have done in my life, and I've said a lot of things I shouldn't have said. I know I've not been living like a Christian, but I am one. I've never talked about my faith at school. I regret that. To answer your question, yes, I am pro-life. I can't let Sarah do this. I have to talk to her." Cole had never felt more convicted about his walk with the Lord, or lack of it, in his entire life.

"I agree. You must talk to Sarah, but she said she was going home, and she hasn't told her parents. I've never seen her like this. She isn't thinking straight."

"I'll call her now and see if we can meet. Lilly, pray."

Lilly closed her eyes to pray while Cole dialed Sarah's number. "She isn't answering. I don't want to leave a message. I'll call again." Cole dialed Sarah's number four times before she finally picked up.

Sarah answered in a whisper. "Cole, I really can't talk right now."

Cole wanted to be sure Sarah was at home. "Where are you, Sarah?"

"I'm at home. I'm tired. I don't feel well . . ."

Cole interrupted. "Sarah, I want to talk to you. It's important."

Sarah noticed frustration in Cole's voice. *Does he know?* "Cole, now is not a good time."

Cole pressed hard. "Sarah, I know about the baby. Please, talk to me."

"Did Lilly tell you? She had no right!" Sarah remembered to keep her voice down. She hoped no one heard her and in a loud whisper she said, "Lilly had no right to tell you."

"She didn't tell me on purpose. I ran into her at Your Choice pregnancy care center ...."

This time Sarah interrupted him. "Cole, you were there? Why? How . . ."

"Sarah, that's not important right now. What is important is that we talk."

"Cole, I'm at home and I haven't told my parents. We can't have a baby, Cole. You have a scholarship to PGU, and my parents will flip out. They expect me to go there and with a baby . . . well, Cole, that just won't work."

"Sarah, we will figure it out. Look, I need to talk to you about my convictions. I know I haven't been living right but, Sarah, I'm a Christian and I want to take full responsibility for this. If I lose my scholarship, then so be it. My first responsibility from this moment on is you and our baby, our family. Sarah, please don't do anything irresponsible. Protect our baby, please."

"Convictions? Do something irresponsible? Since when did you become all morally mighty? And it's not a baby, not yet."

Cole looked at Lilly and motioned for her to keep praying. "But it is. Sarah, the place you went to and then left is a pregnancy care center. My cousin works there. They do ultrasounds and help women like you. On the ultrasound monitor, you can see the baby and sometimes even arms and legs and Sarah, we can see and hear our baby's heartbeat."

"So Lilly knew what Your Choice was when I told her I was going there and she didn't tell me? She let me go knowing they were going to try to talk me out of ending my pregnancy?"

This wasn't going the way Cole had hoped. "Sarah, it's not just ending a pregnancy. It's ending a baby's life. It is a baby, Sarah, and it's ours. We'll figure this out. Just give me a chance."

"I don't know, Cole. I'm so scared."

"Meet me somewhere before it gets too late. Meet me over at The Pizza Parlor. Let's talk."

Sarah started feeling a strange calmness at the sound of Cole's voice. "OK."

Cole thanked Lilly for trying her best to talk Sarah into doing the right thing. He thanked her for being such a good friend and for praying while he spoke to Sarah. Lilly went home feeling a little relieved and Cole headed to The Pizza Parlor.

Twenty minutes later, Cole and Sarah sat at a table snacking on garlic bread sticks and drinking Coke. Cole could see the fear in Sarah's face. He spoke in compassionate tones. "Sarah, this is all my fault. I never should have pressured you into sleeping with me. I never should have done a lot of things. When I stood at Lilly's car window and overheard her talking to you, realizing you were pregnant with my baby, I guess, well, it changed everything - in a heartbeat. Knowing I'm a dad makes me want to straighten up. I want to apologize to you for putting you in this situation. I want you to know that I will not leave you to deal with this alone. I'm also going to apologize to my parents. They raised me right. I just rebelled, I guess. I put high-school popularity over my convictions. Now that I'm thinking about it, I need to apologize to a lot of people but especially God. Sarah, I want to be the man God created me to be and I'm starting right here and right now."

Sarah wasn't convinced that Cole could make it work. "Cole, how? How can you support me and a baby? How can we both go to college and raise a baby at the same time?"

"I don't know exactly how, but my cousin, April, works at Your Choice. She's always talking about women who go to the clinic scared and have no idea what to do. Some women go there to have abortions but when they see their babies on the ultrasound, they almost always change their minds. Less than 10% of the women at her center follow through with an abortion after seeing their babies on an ultrasound. Sarah, I want you, I want US, to see our baby. Let's make an appointment."

Sarah decided that seeing an ultrasound wouldn't hurt. "I'll call them tomorrow. Maybe we can get in sometime tomorrow afternoon."

Cole felt relieved. "Great! April says Tuesdays are usually slower for some reason."

"Then I'll call first thing in the morning." Sarah and Cole finished their meal. Then they said goodnight and they both headed home.

Before Cole went to bed that night, he called his cousin to tell her to expect a call from Sarah the next morning. "April, please start praying now."

Sarah woke the next morning but decided not to get dressed for school. It was a typical morning at the Scott house with breakfast on the table when Sarah came down the stairs. She would tell her parents she wasn't feeling well. Then, when her parents and Tommy were off to work and school, she would call that place to make an appointment for an ultrasound. She hoped the little money she had in her purse would be enough to cover any expenses. Then, she realized that she hadn't even thought about how she was going to pay for an abortion. She would need to figure that out. She wasn't convinced that Cole or anyone else could change her mind. What did he mean about convictions, anyway? She had forgotten to ask him about that. She would worry about that later. Right now, she needed to convince her parents that she wasn't well. She walked toward the kitchen. *Show time*, she thought.

Sarah's mother was placing a stack of paperwork in a bag and grabbing her keys. She looked like she was in a hurry. "Sarah, why aren't you dressed? You need to leave for school in a few minutes. You never oversleep. Get moving."

"Mom, I'm not feeling well. I have a headache and I feel nauseous. Maybe I should stay home today."

"Do you have a fever?" Rachel grabbed the thermometer from the cabinet, the kind that goes in the ear.

"No, I don't have a fever." Sarah stood still as her mother felt of her head and face.

"You don't feel feverish, but you do look pale. Maybe you should stay home. Do you feel like eating breakfast?"

"No, I think I'll just go on back to bed."

"OK then, go on back to bed. I have a busy morning ahead, but I'll call to check on you in a few hours. I hope you don't have a virus that will keep you out of school. Your final exams are in only a few weeks."

"I don't think it's anything like that. It's probably just a little stomach bug."

Rachel checked her watch. "I hope you're right. Tommy, I'll be taking you to school this morning and I'm already running late so grab your bookbag and let's head out."

Charles checked his watch. "I'm late too but I'll take Tommy to school so you can get to that important meeting you told me about." He kissed his wife goodbye and wished her a good day. He tousled Tommy's hair because Tommy thought he was too old for kisses. "Come on, let's get you to school, little buddy." Then he hugged Sarah. "I hope you get some rest today. Maybe you'll feel better this afternoon."

Everyone else headed out the door. Sarah headed upstairs to her room. She grabbed her phone and dialed the number for Your Choice for Unplanned Pregnancies. A sweet girl answered the phone. "Hi, I'm April. How can I help you?"

Sarah slammed down the phone. *Didn't Cole say his cousin worked there and her name was April?* She decided to text Cole. "April answered the phone. Didn't you say she is your cousin?"

Cole texted back right away. "Yes, but it's OK, Sarah. Please make the appointment. She'll take good care of you and she's legally obligated to keep your confidence."

Sarah dialed the number again and heard the same voice as before. "Hello, I'm April. How can I help you today?"

"My name is Sarah Scott." Sarah immediately regretted giving April her actual name but what was done was done. "I would like to schedule an appointment for an ultrasound, please."

Sarah answered a few questions. "Yes, I'm 17 years old. No, I'm not married. I don't know how far along I am. Yes, I'll be bringing my boyfriend. Yes, he's the baby's father." Sarah wondered if April knew who she was. "Ok, this afternoon at 4:00. Thank you." As Sarah hung up the phone, she heard a sound in the hallway. *Oh Tommy, not again.* Tommy had a habit of leaving toys dangling half off the antique table her mother had chosen to accent a wide area in the upstairs hallway. She turned to go pick it up but there in her bedroom doorway stood her mother.

"Sarah, how long have you known you are pregnant?" Rachel was visibly angry.

"Not long . . . Mom . . . I thought you left."

"I forgot an important document that I needed for a meeting this morning that I am now going to miss. Sarah Scott! How could you?" Charles and Rachel Scott were not religious people, but they had warned Sarah about becoming sexually active at such a young age. They had big plans for Sarah. She was supposed to attend Pleasant Grove University in the fall, study journalism, and become a lead anchor on a big network someday. That was the plan, and her parents had no intention of allowing Sarah to deviate from *their* plans for *her* life.

"Mom, I was going to have an abortion but . . ."

"But what? You WILL have an abortion, Sarah. You can't have a baby now!"

"But Mom, Cole was telling me about this place in town called Your Choice for Unplanned Pregnancies. They help young girls like me."

Rachel's anger had not subsided. "How exactly do they help you, Sarah? Are they going to pay for all the expenses for raising a child? Are they going to pay for childcare while you study? Are they going to pay your salary when you can't work because your too busy raising a baby all by yourself?"

"I won't be by myself, Mom. Cole says he will help. He got all religious and started talking about conviction. He said he would find a way to be a good daddy."

Rachel got even angrier. "Conviction? Conviction? Where was his conviction when he got you pregnant? Tell me, Sarah, where was his conviction then?"

Sarah's head was spinning again. "I don't understand that either. I want to ask him about that . . ."

"Oh no, young lady. You've asked him enough. You're going to cancel that appointment. I'm calling an abortion clinic in Atlanta. They can probably get you in right away."

Sarah suddenly wasn't sure she wanted an abortion after all. Hadn't they been referring to her baby as a BABY? "Mom, wait. Maybe I don't want an abortion. Maybe I . . ."

Rachel was determined to take care of this situation under her terms and right away. "Maybe you don't want an abortion? Sarah, you don't have a choice!"

"But I do. Let Cole and I go to the appointment I made for 4:00 today. Let me see what's on the ultrasound Cole keeps talking about and then we'll decide what to do."

Rachel needed to bring Sarah back to reality. "You and Cole will decide what to do? Sarah, do you really think Cole can play football for Pleasant Grove University, keep up with his studies, and take care of you and a baby? How is he going to do that? If he can't keep his grades up, he could lose his scholarship. Do you want that for him?"

"No. No I don't." Sarah's heart began to sink.

Rachel kept her argument going. "Sarah, honey, let's say you both give it a try. You and Cole decide to get married, and you somehow manage to make it work. Do you want Cole committed to you because of a baby when at some point, you both might have otherwise chosen to go your separate ways? Don't you want a man, whether it be Cole or someone else, to marry you because he loves you and for no other reason? Do you really want to trap Cole into this relationship when it could mean his whole life changes and not for the better?"

Sarah sat for a moment and then dropped her head. "Maybe you're right. I'll cancel the appointment."

Rachel Scott loved winning arguments. "Good. I'll call the abortion clinic to make you another one."

Chapter Twelve

April knew she was treading on thin ice, legally, when she called Cole. "Cole, call Sarah."

Cole was between his first and second classes by now and wondering why Sarah wasn't at school yet. The plan was for her to start feeling better after she made the ultrasound appointment and then come on to school. "Why, is something wrong?"

"Cole, just call her. That's all I can say."

Cole was feeling uneasy. "Didn't she make the appointment?"

"You know I can't tell you that. Just call her, Cole. Call her right now. Skip your next class or whatever it takes. Just call her."

Cole sensed an urgency in April's voice. "OK. I'll call her right now." Cole dialed Sarah's number. No answer. He dialed again. No answer. He thought to himself, *The third time seems to be the charm with you lately.* He dialed a third time.

Sarah answered in a whisper. "Cole, I can't talk right now. My mom caught me calling Your Choice. I had to cancel the appointment. I'll call you later." Sarah thought about all her mother had said. She wasn't taking any chances this time on allowing Cole to change her mind. She knew what was best for him.

"Wait. Sarah, why did you cancel?" Cole heard the click. Sarah ended the call. He called her again. No answer.

He decided to text Lilly. The tardy bell had just sounded so he knew she would already be in class, and it might be too late. *Lilly, please get this message.*

Lilly received Cole's text. She asked to be excused from class due to a headache. She wasn't exactly lying. She met Cole on the outside walkway. "Why did she cancel her ultrasound appointment?"

Cole was frantic. "She didn't say. She just said her mother caught her making the call."

Lilly was visibly concerned about what Sarah might do. Her lifelong friend had not been thinking clearly since the day of her pregnancy test. "Let me try." Lilly dialed Sarah's number. No answer. She tried again.

Sarah was getting frustrated. She needed everyone to leave her alone so she could get past this, but she knew Lilly would keep calling until she answered so she might as well answer now. "Lilly, you can't talk me out of this."

Lily tried to speak calmly. "Talk you out of what, Sarah?"

Sarah told Lilly about the conversation between herself and her mother. "She made perfect sense, Lilly. I can't do this to Cole. He has a great future ahead of him. I can't ruin this for him."

Cole could hear Sarah's voice. He frantically grabbed Lilly's phone. "Sarah, please don't do this!"

Sarah hung up her phone. Her mother was on the phone in the next room with the abortion clinic. Sarah's appointment was made for 3:30. Her mother cancelled all her meetings for the day, promising to stay by Sarah's side. She wanted to support her daughter, but she also wanted to make sure Cole or anyone else with *convictions* stayed away from her.

Cole and Lilly decided to skip school for the rest of the day. Cole jumped into his car to head for Sarah's house. Lilly called April to fill her in. April called a special prayer meeting at the center. Anyone who wasn't with a client needed to get to the prayer room. They had a baby to save.

April and Veronica made it to the prayer room first. Tuesdays were slow so all but three employees and volunteers who were counseling clients filed into the room. April filled them in on the situation between Cole and Sarah. The group bowed to pray. They stormed the gates of Heaven as the prayer warriors that they were, lifting Cole, Sarah, and their unborn child before the Father.

Cole pulled into Sarah's driveway. Her car was there and so was her mother's. He ran to the door and banged on it.

Rachel called to him from inside the house. "Cole, go home. This is not your concern."

Cole's heartbeat was speeding up. "Mrs. Scott, the baby Sarah is carrying is my baby, so it is my concern. I know I haven't given you or Mr. Scott much of a reason to like me but I promise you that I will do right by Sarah."

"First of all, Cole, Sarah isn't far enough along to actually have a baby yet. No matter what your mother or your church or wherever else you get your so-called convictions, that just isn't true. Now, go home. This is Sarah's body, not yours."

"But the baby's body is separate from Sarah's body!

"Cole, go home. If you don't leave right now, I'm calling the police and I'll have you arrested for trespassing! I'm not letting you in this house or anywhere near my daughter!"

Sarah called out to Cole from her upstairs window. "Cole, please, go home. Don't make this any harder than it has to be. The people at the abortion clinic will do an ultrasound too. When I see it, I can back out of the abortion if I want to."

Cole looked up to Sarah. "The abortion clinic won't let you see the ultrasound, Sarah! They know that you will most likely change your mind if you do. They want your money!"

Rachel meant business this time. "Get off my property, Cole Quinn! I'm calling the police right now if you don't leave!"

Sarah called out again, "Please Cole, just go!"

Cole was out of breath, out of energy, and out of ideas for getting Sarah to change her mind. He had another thought. He texted Sarah. "Sarah, which clinic are you going to? Maybe I can meet you there. There's a chance we can still see the ultrasound together." Cole knew they wouldn't even let him inside the building, but he had to find out where Sarah was going.

She texted back immediately. "The one on Peachtree Avenue."

Cole called Lilly. Prayer was their only hope. No matter how far Cole had strayed, he knew the power of prayer. His parents had modeled that very well. Heaven only knew the prayers they had prayed for him.

Lilly prayed a quick but heartfelt prayer for Sarah and her mother. Then, she called April to update her. April and Veronica had been waiting. Cole called his parents. He had a lot to tell them.

Cole's parents had been at work, but both went straight home to Cole. When they arrived at their home, Jacob and Alice Quinn could only embrace their son with all the mercy and grace they had. They had prayed over his rebellious spirit for years. Their son had done things he shouldn't have done, and his girlfriend was about to abort their baby, but their son had called them with a repentant spirit that they knew was sincere. Even though the moment wasn't ideal or anything close to what they had hoped for, it was the moment they had prayed for, and they had prayed for it for years.

Cole couldn't contain his tears any longer. "Mom, Dad, I'm so sorry. I'm so sorry, not just for the trouble I've caused you but for the trouble I have caused others and for my lack of trust in God. Right now, my focus is on getting Sarah and her parents to trust me to do right by her and the baby."

Cole's mother had an idea. "I'll call Rachel. Maybe I can talk some sense into her." She dialed Rachel's number.

Rachel saw Alice's name on her phone screen, but she picked up anyway. She might as well face this head on like the spitfire attorney she was. "Alice, I know why you are calling. There is no point in trying to stop us because you can't. We have made up our minds and that's final."

Alice tried again. "Rachel, please listen to me for a minute. This baby is Cole's baby too and our grandchild. Don't you think we have a right to a say-so in this just as much as you do? What if we pay for all of Sarah's medical expenses and we help Cole raise the baby? We won't expect Sarah or you to be involved any more than you want to be."

Rachel was planted firm in her position. "Alice, Cole has no legal right to have any say-so in this and neither do you. It's Sarah's body and this is what she wants. That's final." Rachel hung up the phone.

Jacob, Alice, and Cole were heartbroken. They were out of arguments. Cole called Lilly to update her. It was almost noon, and they were running out of time.

Lilly had one last weapon to fire at the enemy. "Cole, I've talked to April and Veronica. They are going to call another lady named Emily and head down to the clinic on Peachtree Avenue to pray. I'm going with them. My parents are coming too. It's the most powerful thing we can do."

Cole told his parents what Lilly had said. Cole and his parents rushed to the abortion clinic in Atlanta in one last effort to save Cole's baby and their grandbaby.

When the Quinns arrived at the clinic, they walked up to the sidewalk by the fence. It was a gated clinic. Cole had never felt more helpless. Of all the trophies and attention he had coveted in the entirety of his high school career, there was nothing more important to him than this moment. He knelt on his knees with his parents beside him to pray for the life of his unborn baby to be spared. They heard several people running up behind them. It was Lilly with her parents, April, Veronica, Emily, and another man. They all introduced themselves, including Luke Westmoreland who had come with Emily. So many schedules had been shifted and things put aside for these people to come pray for Baby Scott-Quinn. They prayed deeply, boldly, and fervently. There were no protestors on that Tuesday afternoon, just a few groups who had come to pray, including their own.

At 3:00, Sarah and her parents arrived for Sarah's 3:30 appointment. Cole's heart skipped beat after beat. He stood to face Sarah to plead with her to change her mind before it was too late. She looked different, as if she was slightly sedated. He wondered if they had given her something to relax her. She didn't seem as anxious as she had been the day before or earlier that morning. Sarah didn't say much. She looked Cole straight in the eyes and managed only a tearful, "I'm sorry, Cole."

Sarah's mother took her by one arm. Her father, Charles, took her by the other. They said nothing to the Quinns or anyone with them. They simply turned and guided Sarah into the clinic. That was it. There was nothing more to do but pray, but prayer was the most powerful thing they could do so they all knelt. Lilly and her parents, Cole, Jacob, Alice, April, Veronica, Emily, and Luke all prayed like they've never prayed before.

There was still hope.

Inside the clinic, Sarah Scott was getting checked in. Rachel was handling all the paperwork and answering all the questions. "Yes, we gave her a Xanax to help her relax. Her boyfriend and a group of Christians are outside praying for her. She's been so anxious."

The office manager placed the paperwork in a file and handed the Scotts a $700 bill to be paid upfront. A few minutes later, they called Sarah back to the abortion room. Her parents were told to wait in the waiting room. Absolutely no one was allowed into the abortion room with the patient.

The Xanax was taking its toll on Sarah, but she was able to follow directions. She undressed, got into a gown and was on the table in no time. Sarah felt like she was halfway in a dream and halfway awake, like the few moments just before you fall asleep and reality mixes with dreaming. She heard a doctor come in. He told the nurse to hold the doppler so he could measure the fetus' head.

Sarah wasn't completely coherent, but she could hear the doctor and the nurses talking. Sarah spoke in a hard whisper which was all she could manage. "I want to see the ultrasound."

The nurse patted Sarah's shoulder and told her to relax. The doctor said something about the head being small enough so he wouldn't' have to crush the skull. Sarah felt confused. "Head? Skull? I want to see the ultrasound monitor, please."

Sarah had asked to see the ultrasound, but she hadn't told them to stop or that she had changed her mind, so the nurse patted her shoulder again. "You don't need to see the ultrasound, honey. That will just make it harder for you. Just relax and it will all be over soon."

And it was.

Sarah spent half an hour in a post-abortion room. When they were pretty sure she wouldn't bleed out, a nurse helped Sarah get dressed and walked her back to her parents.

Cole was the first to see Sarah come back outside. He looked for any evidence that told him she had changed her mind but there was none to be found. Her parents looked confident that they had spared their daughter the suffering that raising a baby at such a young age would cause her. Sarah looked pale, weak, and confused. As they walked the walkway to come back through the gate, Cole stared at them both heartbroken and angry. "Sarah." He could barely speak through his tears. His throat was hoarse. "Sarah." Her name was all he could manage.

Sarah, just as she had done when she arrived at the clinic, looked into Cole's eyes and said, "Cole, I'm sorry." But this time, Cold heard agony in her voice and sensed grief in her heart.

As Sarah's parents walked toward their car to take Sarah home, Cole fell hard onto the cement walkway and sobbed tears he never knew he had. Jacob and Alice joined him in grief over the tragic loss of their grandbaby. Lilly and the rest of the group knelt beside them and placed hands on them as they prayed over the Quinn family's deep grief. Their hearts were so deeply broken for this big burly popular high school football player who was now on his knees with his face near the cement sobbing uncontrollably for his baby whose heartbeat was no more.

When he was strong enough to stand again, he looked at his parents. "We've never prayed so hard. I thought God would spare us this grief. Why didn't He?"

Cole's dad was the first to respond. "Son, God gives us free will. The Holy Spirit convicts us, but God doesn't force anyone into compliance. What happened here today is a tragedy none of us will ever forget, but God can use it for good if we let Him. It's like what Joseph said to his brothers in Genesis, chapter 50, verse 20. *You intended to harm me, but God intended it for good to accomplish what is now being done, the saving of many lives.* Son, in the last couple of days, you have found your faith again. Don't let the enemy use this tragedy to turn you back in the wrong direction. We're going to take this one day at time and we're going to get through this together. We love you and we will never leave your side. Stay strong in your faith and let God use this heartbreak for His good."

Chapter Thirteen

On Wednesday morning, Cole woke up and realized his alarm hadn't gone off. He looked at his watch. It was 11:30am. Cole jumped out of bed and ran downstairs. As he was about to enter the living room, he saw his parents. They were sitting on the couch with a Bible spread over their legs and they were praying. Cole stood still and listened.

"And Lord, we thank You for restoring Cole's relationship with You. We thank You for his new determination to live a life that honors You. The days, weeks, and months ahead won't be easy for our son, Lord, but we ask You to carry him through. Let him know You are with him and that You will never leave him. And God, we ask that you give his mama and me the wisdom, knowledge, and understanding we need to be the parents to Cole that You created us to be. Thank you, Lord, for loving Cole even more than we do.

In Jesus' Name,
Amen

Jacob and Alice raised their heads to see their son standing in the doorway to the living room as tears streamed down his face. Cole ran to his parents and fell on his knees with his head in their laps. They all cried for a long time.

Sarah rolled over in her bed. She was in pain physically, but the physical pain was nothing compared to the emotional pain she was experiencing. She hadn't slept all night long. She had tossed and turned. The words wouldn't stop repeating in her head. *Measure the head . . . small enough . . . won't have to crush the skull . . . you don't want to see the ultrasound dear, it will just make things harder for you . . . that will be $700 please, up front . . .* Sarah was haunted by them as they repeated over and over again. She felt groggy. She called for her mother.

"Sarah, honey. Mama's here. Try to rest. You'll be home the rest of the week."

Sarah tried to tell her mom about the words in her head. Maybe it was all a dream. "Mom, did you see it?"

"See what, Sarah?"

"The baby."

"Honey, there is no baby."

Sarah tried harder. "No, the ultrasound. My baby's head. Did you see it? Did you stop them?"

Rachel could only look at her daughter's pale face in confusion. She called to her husband. "Charles! Call the doctor at the clinic. Sarah is talking out of her head. She keeps saying something about an ultrasound. She's asking me if I saw her baby's head. She wants to know if we stopped them. Ask them if we should back off her pain medicine a bit. She also looks awfully pale. Ask them if this is normal."

Charles had come to Sarah's bedroom door to listen to his wife's instructions. He dialed the number to the abortion clinic and asked the questions. He repeated their answers to his wife. "Rachel, they said it's normal for some patients to experience some delirium. It's also normal for patients to have pale skin for a few days. We can back off her pain meds a little if we want. That's about it. They didn't seem concerned. Honestly, they didn't seem to care much at all."

Rachel gave Sarah three quarters of her prescribed dose of pain medicine. She tried to quietly talk her back to sleep. Then, she turned to her husband. "Charles, she doesn't look so good. I'm concerned. Please tell me we did the right thing."

Charles was concerned too. "She does look pale, but the doctor just said all of this is normal. Let's just try to get her to rest this week. They told us at the clinic that she could go back to school in a few days."

The following morning, Sarah opened her eyes to the morning sun. Her head felt a little clearer. She thought about where she had been and where she was. She had been to an abortion clinic in Atlanta. She had gone through with the abortion. She remembered most of it but it still seemed fuzzy. She remembered her mother giving her a Xanax when they left their home. She had told Sarah that it would help relax her before the procedure. She remembered the abortion room and the voices. Sarah stared out her window as she realized that the voices she had been hearing in her head on repeat for two days were not voices in a dream. They were memories.

Cole arose on Thursday morning feeling a little more grounded. The past few days had seemed like a nightmare. He had spent all of Wednesday with his parents at home, reading the Bible and praying together. The only time he had grimaced was when he heard his parents pray for Sarah. He couldn't pray for Sarah. Sarah had killed his baby. He had fathered a child that he would never meet because Sarah had killed it. She hadn't even given him a say-so, not even when his own parents had offered to help. Cole wasn't sure he could ever pray for Sarah. Their relationship was obviously over and that was fine with him. He never wanted to see her again. Not ever. He would spend the day checking on his missed assignments and communicating via email with his teachers. The sooner he could get back to normal, the better. He could smell bacon and eggs. He made his way downstairs to the kitchen to talk to his mother.

"Mom, I want to go back to school tomorrow. The sooner I get back to normal the better."

Cole's mother wasn't sure he was ready. "Are you sure about that, Cole? You don't have to go back yet if you aren't ready. Tomorrow is Friday. Why not wait until Monday morning? Your dad and I have arranged to work from home through tomorrow so we can be with you."

"I'm sure. What else is there for me to do? I can read the Bible and pray with you and dad. That has helped, but I need to get back to normal. I can't stay home and dwell on this day after day. I also need to tell you something else."

"OK, what is it?" Alice wanted to know every detail of her son's heart.

"You and Dad can continue to pray for Sarah if you want, but I can't. She killed our baby. I can't pray for her. I won't."

Alice understood. "OK, Cole. If you can heal faster by going back to school, then go. Your dad and I support you. As far as Sarah goes, your dad and I don't really want to pray for her either if we are being honest about it. She killed our grandbaby. We pray for her because the Bible tells us to pray for our enemies. Right now, it is easy for us to see Sarah as our enemy who has done an unimaginable thing. But she is also a young girl who wasn't given a choice by her parents. Abortion itself will leave scars that will never go away, but when she starts making sense of all of this and realizes that her parents pretty much forced her into it, she will have wounds that only Jesus can heal. That's why we pray for her, son."

Cole's parents always made sense of every situation. They always knew exactly what to say. Why had he rebelled? Why had he decided to give his parents such grief? He realized that if he had listened to them from the beginning and had listened to God, he wouldn't even be in this situation. "You're right mom. I guess I will eventually pray for Sarah, but it will take some time."

"And time you will have. Now sit down and eat a good breakfast." A few seconds later, Alice added, "and Cole, you will also have scars that only Jesus can heal. We are here for you as always."

Cole took a bite of bacon. "Thanks Mom, I love you."

By Friday afternoon, Sarah was feeling more like herself. She decided to ask her parents about the things she heard in the abortion room 3 days ago. "Mom, you and Dad were not allowed to go back with me, right?"

Rachel's mom had returned to work on Thursday. She had just come home and placed a large stack of papers on the table. "No, they made us stay in the waiting room."

"So neither of you heard the nurse or doctor say something about my baby's head?"

"Sarah, we've talked about this, honey. At your stage in pregnancy, it's just a clump of cells. It's not a baby yet."

Sarah argued. "But that's not what they said in the abortion room. I heard them talking. The doctor asked the nurse to hold something, something to do with the ultrasound. The doctor said something about measuring the head and not having to crush its skull."

"Sarah! That' terrible. Honey, you were out of it. I gave you something to relax you earlier that morning. You were just dreaming. That's all. Now, it's time you put this behind you. You'll have the weekend to relax. You can go back to school on Monday."

Sarah decided there was no point in pressing this issue further with her mother. Her mother hadn't been in the room to hear the things Sarah had heard. She decided to do something she should have done before her abortion. She would research abortion methods and fetal development. Sarah headed back to her room. She sat at her desk and turned on her laptop. She brought up YouTube and in the search bar, she typed 'fetal development.' *There must be videos,* she thought.

There were lots of videos, good ones. Sarah watched several over the next few hours. Then she typed into the search bar 'abortion methods.' There were plenty of those too and they were all devastating. Sarah's heart skipped beats. She felt faint. *What have I done?* She yelled out in a panic, "MOM!"

Rachel ran up to her daughter's room. "What is it, Sarah? You scared me to death."

Sarah turned to her mother, eyes red and swollen, tears streaming down her face. "Have you seen these?" Sarah pointed to the screen of video thumbnails showing abortion methods and pre-born babies, babies with heads, bodies, fingernails, toenails, babies who had once had a heartbeat.

Rachel glanced at the screen. "Sarah, you can't believe everything on the internet. People post all kinds of stuff on there. Just because it's on the internet doesn't mean it's true."

"Then why didn't they let me see the ultrasound?"

"Honey, the ultrasound is just so the doctor can make sure he gets it all."

"Gets all of what, Mom? All of the baby? All the arms? All the legs?"

"Sarah! So, he can get all the tissue. I don't know exactly, Sarah. I'm not a doctor. I saw ultrasound images of you and your brother a few weeks before both of you were born but you . . . you were much too early in your pregnancy to see any of that."

"The doctor saw a head. I heard him. He measured it. I . . . heard . . . him!"

Rachel was growing impatient. "Sarah, you need to put this behind you. Now find something else to do but not too much. Get lots of rest through the weekend. I have a lot of work to do."

Sarah wasn't sure how she would handle going back to school and seeing Cole. How could she face him? He couldn't possibly forgive her for what she had done. Sarah was sure of only two things. She would never forgive herself and she would never be the same.

Cole Quinn had made it through the day. He was glad it was Friday. One day back after the week he had endured was enough. He hadn't realized it would be so hard. No one mentioned the situation to him. The only person who knew was Lilly and she would never break his or Sarah's confidence. People were probably figuring it all out though with both he and Sarah out of school for a whole week and no one saying why. He would let people think whatever they wanted to think. The only thing he cared about now was graduating from high school and getting on with his life.

Chapter Fourteen

On the Monday morning of March 27, Emily woke up more excited than she could ever remember, except for the day Luke had asked her to marry him. Today would be a big day for her. She would arrive at Your Choice at 8:00am to volunteer for a few hours. Then, she would meet with another group of pre-law students on campus to tour the School of Law. Emily's graduate studies would begin in the fall. The next few weeks were bound to be some of the most exciting weeks of her life. She would receive her undergraduate degree in pre-law as valedictorian of her class. She would marry Luke just one week later. They would begin their graduate degrees as a married couple. Emily knew it wouldn't be easy, but she knew beyond a shadow of a doubt that God had hand-picked Luke for her. They had worked it all out. After their graduate degrees are complete and they are settled into their careers, they would begin a family. But first things first. Today was dedicated to volunteering at Your Choice for Unplanned Pregnancies and touring the graduate school part of the campus.

Emily jumped up, dressed, grabbed a granola bar and a carton of chocolate milk from the frig, and then ran out the door. *Not exactly the breakfast of champions*, she thought, but she didn't want to be late for her first day of volunteering at the center.

Sarah woke up early on Monday morning, but she wasn't going to school. She would go to that Your Choice place again. She wanted to be there as soon as it opened at 8:00am. She had called them on Friday to see what time they opened and to see if anyone would be available to talk to her, even if it was Cole's cousin, April.

Jessica stretched as she got out of bed. She felt refreshed, free. The conversation with her parents had started out rough but it had ended well. They didn't hate her for what she had done. They didn't approve, but they didn't disown her. They loved her and they would figure out how to move forward. Jessica's first pre-birth class started at 8:00am. She dressed quickly. She had no intention of arriving late.

The sunlight streamed into Angela's room as she opened her eyes. It was a bright, sunny morning. She turned on her radio as she began to dress for the day. The weather report promised sunshine all day long with no chance of rain. She called Brad. "Hey!"

"Hey back!" Brad had found his playful demeanor again.

Angela was a little more serious. "You didn't forget, did you?"

"Forget what? The pre-birth and parenting class? Not a chance. Hey, will I be the only dude there?"

Angela chuckled, picturing tall, basketball athlete Bradley St. James as the only dude in a pre-birth class. "Probably not."

"PROBABLY not?"

"Brad, you'll be fine. It's not a class about the actual birth. It's more about what to expect during each stage of pregnancy leading up to birth. We'll learn about things we can both be doing to prepare for parenthood while keeping our relationship biblical. Now do you feel better about it?"

"Yes. I'm all in. I promised you that you wouldn't have to do this alone. I'll be there with bells on. Want me to pick you up? We can go together."

"Sure, but don't be late!"

By 7:30am, Emily, Angela, Jessica, and Sarah were all headed to Your Choice for Unplanned Pregnancies, each in different situations. Emily to volunteer to support mothers who are dealing with unplanned pregnancies, Angela along with Brad to attend their first pre-birth class together, Jessica to attend her first pre-birth class alone, and Sarah to speak to a counselor because she had chosen to end the life of her unborn baby and she wasn't sure she could live with what she had done.

Emily arrived first. She was so excited about her new ministry. It was a warm sunny March morning, so she decided to wait on the front porch until an employee came to open the center. Brad and Angela arrived next. They decided to wait on the front porch as well. Emily introduced herself. She remembered this couple from the day of her tour, but she wasn't sure they recognized her. "Hi! I'm Emily. I'm here to volunteer today. It's my first day."

Angela responded, realizing that Emily looked familiar. "I'm Angela. This is my boyfriend, Brad. We are here for our first day in the pre-birth class. We know we aren't in the best of circumstances, but we're both excited about the baby."

Emily started counseling before she even realized it. "Babies are a gift from God no matter the circumstances. It's nice to meet you both."

There were footsteps. It was Jessica. "Hello. I guess they aren't open yet."

Emily introduced herself again. "Hi. I'm Emily. They open at 8:00 so we have a few more minutes to enjoy this beautiful sunshine."

Jessica looked at the familiar faces. "I'm Jessica. I'm here for a pre-birth class."

Angela was delighted. "Oh Hi! I'm Angela. Actually, I think I remember both of you ladies from the last time I was here. We were all in the waiting room. Anyway, this is Brad and we are both here for the pre-birth class as well. I guess we are classmates!"

They all heard another set of footsteps. Sarah hadn't been sure she should get out of her car. The people on the front porch looked happy but she was suffering through her worst days. What would they think of her? Then it occurred to her that almost everyone who comes to Your Choice is in the same boat or at least in similar ones. She decided to go on up the steps. The center would be opened within the next few minutes anyway.

Angela, and Jessica welcomed Sarah in unison. "Hi!" The two women giggled at their perfectly synced welcome. Emily had not joined in the welcome. She stood there speechless. She only offered a smile as words would not come. She immediately recognized Sarah as Cole's girlfriend, the girl she and Luke had prayed for outside an abortion clinic just days ago. Emily noticed that Sarah still looked weak and pale. She decided she needed to say something. "Hi. I'm Emily." Sarah had been sedated on the day of the abortion. Emily didn't think Sarah recognized her.

Sarah didn't smile but she introduced herself. "Hi. I'm Sarah, Sarah Scott. I guess we are all early." Sarah noticed the other ladies were older than herself. She wondered what their stories might be. They were all too happy to have had abortions. Sarah felt she would never be happy again.

They all turned back to the sidewalk again as April came up the flower lined walkway with a key. "Good morning! Y'all are early birds today. Give me just a second to get this door opened. This is the original door and lock. It's old and sometimes the lock doesn't want to cooperate with me." April fiddled with the lock for a few seconds and then let everyone inside. "Ok, let's see. First, I don't think I have officially met all of you. I'm April. If you're here for the pre-birth class, it will be upstairs and to the left, in the big room with all the tables and the sink in the back. Veronica will be teaching the class today. She'll be here shortly."

Angela, Brad, Jessica, and Emily made their way up the stairs to the big classroom. A few other women and a couple of men came inside and joined them. Sarah stood there silently. She felt out of place. She didn't know what to say or what to do. She was standing in front of Cole's cousin. Sarah thought April looked familiar, but they had never actually met face-to-face. After a minute, it hit her. The day of her abortion, she had seen April on the sidewalk outside the abortion clinic. She was one of the people there with Cole and his parents. Her memories were still fuzzy due to the medication her mother had given her, but Sarah was sure that April had been there. She almost ran out of the building. Her shame weighed so heavily on her shoulders, but she couldn't run now. April was looking straight at her.

April noticed Sarah standing there looking lost. "Hello. I assume you aren't here for the pre-birth class?"

Sarah answered shyly, unsure if April recognized her. "No ma'am. I'm not." Sarah secretly wished she was heading to the class with the other women. Admitting that she wasn't here for a pre-birth class was almost more than she could handle. She felt her eyes tear up. "I'm here for counseling. I don't have an appointment, but I need to talk to somebody."

April could see this young girl was deeply troubled and she seemed so familiar. "I see. Did I catch your name?"

There was no avoiding the situation now. If April didn't recognize her, she would find out who she was soon enough. "Umm, I'm Sarah. Sarah Scott. I'm Cole's girlfriend . . . well, I was. You probably already knew that."

April tried to hide her shock. She should have recognized Sarah right away. Standing in front of her was the same girl she had prayed for on the sidewalk outside an Atlanta abortion clinic just days ago, the same girl who had left her larger-than-life cousin, Cole, sobbing like a baby himself face down on concrete sidewalk beside that busy Atlanta street. April wasn't a counselor. Even if she was, she wasn't sure how to handle the situation in front of her. She knew the agony Cole was suffering and yet, here she was in her workplace ministry where she warmly greets women like Sarah every day. This time, the situation was too personal. April had no words, but maybe she didn't necessarily need words to help Sarah in that moment. April silently prayed for God to tell her how to show Sarah the compassion she needed and for herself to gain a heart of forgiveness concerning Sarah. April stepped forward with outstretched arms to embrace Sarah as she spoke the only words she could say until God gave her more. "Hi Sarah. Yes, I'm April. I understand why you are here. I can see you are suffering and I'm so sorry for all that you have lost. I'm not a counselor, but one of our counselors will be here shortly. You can sit right here with me until then. You've come to the right place for help."

Sarah took a seat next to April's desk. She hoped a counselor would come in soon. She hadn't thought about how uncomfortable she would be in the same room with Cole's cousin.

The front door opened. April was happy to see Veronica walk in. "Good morning, Veronica! You have a classroom full of people waiting for you today."

"Good! I'm ready for them. I have some good materials for them today." Veronica was excited to start a new class and meet new people.

Veronica seems way to jolly for 8:00am, Sarah thought.

April checked the appointment calendar for the day. "Sarah, it looks like there is a time slot open this morning with Kathy. She'll be here shortly. I have some paperwork for you to fill out first. You can fill them out here and I'll stay with you until she arrives, OK?"

"Yes. Thank you." Sarah began filling out the paperwork. Some of the questions were hard for Sarah to fill out. She had to indicate on the paperwork her reason for coming in. Writing down on paper that she had an abortion was almost too much for her to handle.

She wished Kathy would get there quickly, before she changed her mind and ran outside, and far away to some place where she could pretend the past few weeks were just a bad dream, a nightmare that she could try to forget.

A few minutes later, Kathy walked in. "Good morning, everyone! It's a beautiful day outside. This is the day that the Lord has made. Let us rejoice and be glad in it!"

Are all these people this happy in the mornings? Sarah questioned to herself.

April drew Kathy's attention with a look that told Sarah that maybe Kathy knew who she was too. "Kathy, this is Sarah Scott. She doesn't have an appointment, but she wants to talk to someone."

Kathy smiled at Sarah. "Hello Sarah. As you heard April say, I'm Kathy. It's nice to meet you. Let's walk down the hallway to the second room on the right. We can talk privately in there."

Sarah stood to walk with Kathy. She had no idea how to talk about what she had done but she did know that if she didn't get help, she couldn't live with it. The two women reached the second room on the right and walked inside. The room was painted a soft yellow. There were end tables on each side of the sofa and another one beside a wing-back chair. There were tissue boxes on each table and a Bible on the coffee table. Kathy reached for Sarah's paperwork. "Sarah, make yourself at home. You can sit wherever you like. I'm going to run to my office for a few minutes. I'll be back to talk to you shortly."

Sarah chose the sofa. A few minutes later, Kathy came back in and sat down in the wing-back chair facing Sarah. "Tell me about yourself, Sarah."

Sarah swallowed hard as she searched for the strength to speak. "As you know, my name is Sarah. I'm 17, a senior at Pleasant Grove High School. My boyfriend Cole . . . he and I . . . we did . . . I got pregnant." Sarah reached for a tissue and continued. "I didn't tell him about the baby. He's a football player, a good one. He was accepted into Pleasant Grove University on a full scholarship. He wants to play football there and study architecture. He's so smart. He deserves to follow his dreams." Sarah used her tissue to dab at a tear.

Kathy gave Sarah a compassionate look. "Take your time, Sarah. I'm listening and I have as much time as you need."

"Well, Cole deserves to go to college and get his degree." Sarah paused as if she was lost in her thoughts, swimming in the guilt of what she had done to give Cole the freedom he didn't want.

Kathy encouraged Sarah to keep going. "You said you didn't tell Cole about the baby. Does he know now?"

Sarah spoke between sobs. "He does. He found out when he saw my best friend's car parked outside your place here."

"You came here?" Kathy wondered why she didn't remember Sarah and why there was no paperwork on her until today.

The painful admission cut Sarah to the core. "Yes, but I didn't come in. I was about to come in, but I thought this was a place that offered abortions. When I was almost to the door, I heard a lady come outside. She was talking to someone about volunteering here. As I listened, I realized that this is a pro-life place. At the time, I didn't want anyone talking me out of an abortion, so I left. I didn't know that my friend, a Christian, followed me here. I guess she wanted to make sure I came inside, but she was too late. She was talking to me on the phone with her window down. Cole had walked up to her car and overheard the conversation." Sarah was still sobbing.

Kathy moved to the sofa to sit beside Sarah. She placed her hand on Sarah's shoulder and gave her a clean tissue. "What was his reaction?"

"He begged me to have the baby. He and my friend, Lilly, tried to talk me out of having an abortion, but I wouldn't listen." Sarah could barely speak between her sobs. "I got an abortion at a clinic in Atlanta."

"If Cole wanted the baby, Sarah, why did you go through with the abortion?" Kathy was trying to understand Sarah's full story.

"My parents. My mom said that having the baby would ruin Cole's chances to follow his dreams at PGU. She said that he wouldn't be able to play football, study and keep up with his class assignments, and also take care of a baby and me. She said she expected me to get my degree in journalism. Having a baby would keep us both from getting our degrees and . . . now . . . now those degrees don't seem so important. I mean, they are important, Miss Kathy, but at what expense? I traded my baby's life for a piece of paper, a degree I could still get if I worked hard. And Cole. Cole wanted the baby." Sarah sobbed uncontrollably.

"Sarah, what you have experienced is incredibly painful. Yes, we believe that every life is valuable. We believe that abortion takes a life and from the way you are describing your experience, you believe that too. Am I correct?"

Sarah could barely say the words. "Yes. I mean . . . I think I do now."

"What changed your mind?" Kathy needed to know Sarah's full experience so she could best help her.

"In the abortion room, I heard the doctor say something about the baby's head. I asked to see the ultrasound, but they wouldn't let me. I was really groggy because my mother gave me something to help me relax but I remember asking. A nurse told me that it would only make things worse for me. Now I know why. When I was alert enough a couple of days later, I researched fetal development and abortion methods. I don't know why I didn't do that before. I was so scared and confused. I don't know if I can live with what I've done . . . and Cole. Cole was so broken. He was doubled over on the sidewalk as my parents pulled me away from him and headed back to the car. He will never forgive me. I don't blame him. I will never forgive myself."

It was time for Kathy to tell Sarah about forgiveness that is hers in Jesus. "Sarah, you said your friend, the one who tried to stop you, is a Christian. Has she ever told you about Jesus and the forgiveness He offers?"

"She has tried, but I haven't given her a chance to explain. Cole is a Christian too. I didn't know until after he found out about the baby. He hadn't been living like one. He said that knowing he is a father made him think about the life he is living. He wants . . . he wanted to do right by me and the baby. I took that chance away from him." Sarah's sobs returned at full force.

"Sarah, I'm going to share with you right now about Jesus and how you can have a relationship with Him. In Him, you'll find forgiveness. Once you are His, He will never let you go."

Sarah felt unworthy of this Jesus. "But how could He want me after what I've done? I'm a terrible person. What is it Christians call people like me? A sinner?"

"Oh, Sarah, we are all sinners. We are all bad, but God provided a way for us to know Him, to have a relationship with Him. Then, once we receive this wonderful gift of salvation, we have the Holy Spirit to help us live lives that honor God. We aren't alone. We can't do it on our own. None of us can. That's why we need Jesus. May I share something with you? It's called the Roman Road to Salvation. It will help you understand this better."

Sarah wanted so much to hear what Kathy was about to share with her. "OK, yes."

Kathy shared the Roman Road with Sarah:

"The Bible tells us in John 3:16 *For God so loved the world that he gave his one and only Son, that whoever believes in him shall not perish but have eternal life.*

God so loved the world . . . God so loves YOU. He loves you, Sarah, just as you are. No matter what you've done, He loves you. He loves everyone, not just a few people, but everyone. Everyone includes me too and like you, I'm a sinner. We are all sinners. We have sinned, we sin, and we will continue to sin because we are imperfect.

Kathy continued.

For all have sinned and fall short of the glory of God. —
Romans 3:23

As it is written: There is no one righteous, not even
one. — Romans 3:10

Therefore, just as sin entered the world through one
man, and death through sin, and in this way death
came to all people, because all sinned. Romans 5:12

The Bible tells us that the wages of sin is death. God loves
everyone, but not everyone will spend eternity with Him in Heaven.
The price for sin without salvation through Jesus is eternal death.

For the wages of sin is death, but the gift of God is
eternal life in Christ Jesus our Lord. — Romans 6:23

So there is good news for us! The result of sin is death but the
free gift of God is eternal life. This free gift is Jesus. God loves us
so much that He sent Jesus to die for us even though we are sinful.

But God demonstrates his own love for us in this: While
we were still sinners, Christ died for us. Romans 5:8

So how can you receive this gift? The Bible tells us to confess our
sin and believe in our hearts that God raised Jesus from the dead.

If you declare with your mouth, "Jesus is Lord," and
believe in your heart that God raised him from the
dead, you will be saved. For it is with your heart that
you believe and are justified, and it is with your mouth
that you profess your faith and are saved. Romans
10:9-10

Being a good person is not enough. We cannot be saved just because we are 'good' or because we do a lot of good things. We can only be saved through the grace of God, through Jesus Christ. Once we know Him and He is Lord of our lives, we will still sometimes sin because we remain imperfect, but we will have a desire to live lives that honor Him.

> *For it is by grace you have been saved, through faith*
> *and this is not from yourselves, it is the gift of God not*
> *by works, so that no one can boast. Ephesians 2:8-9*

Sarah, would you like a relationship with Jesus?"

Sarah needed Jesus and she knew it. "Yes, yes I would."

"You can do that by praying right now, right where you are, just as you are, to receive the gift of salvation – confess your sin and believe in your heart that God sent Jesus to die as the ultimate sacrifice for our sin and that God raised Jesus from the dead." Kathy read another Bible verse to Sarah. *For everyone who calls on the name of the Lord will be saved. Romans 10:13"*

Sarah prayed.

"Dear God. I know I am a sinner. I'm so sorry. I can't save myself. I need you in my life. I need a Savior. I believe by faith that Jesus, your Son, died on the cross. I believe He arose from the grave. I turn from my sin. I ask You, Lord Jesus, to forgive my sin and come into my heart. I trust You as my Savior and I receive you as my Lord. Thank You for saving me. Amen

Sarah had just become a new believer in Jesus.

Kathy hugged Sarah and this time, they cried together. Then, Kathy had more information for Sarah. "Sarah, you might be wondering, 'what now?' The next step is to get to know the Lord. The best way to get to know the heart of God is to spend time in His Word. Spend time with the Lord by reading and studying the

Bible. Read it. Study it. Meditate on it. Start trying to memorize scripture verses. Ask the Lord to help you find a Bible teaching church to attend. Surround yourself with other believers. Do you go to church, Sarah?"

"No, ma'am. My family doesn't go to church, but my friend, Lilly, does. Well, I hope she is still my friend."

Kathy encouraged Sarah. "If your friend, Lilly, is a Christian like you say she is, then I'm sure she will be happy with your news."

Sarah believed Kathy was right about Lilly. "I will call her. I'll tell her I want to start going to church with her."

"I think that is a good idea, Sarah. Now, what about your family? Do you think they'll go with you?"

Sarah didn't think so. "I doubt it. They've never talked much about God or Jesus or the Holy Spirit or really anything related to church or the Bible. They are good people. I know they want what is best for me. They love my little brother and me, but they aren't Christians."

"Well, maybe you can share this Roman Road to Salvation with them. I'll give you a bookmark with the Bible verses listed in order so you can always have it handy."

"Yes, ma'am. Thank you so much."

"Sarah, I want to share a few more verses with you." Kathy read the verses from the Bible.

> *Therefore, since we have been justified through faith,*
> *we have peace with God through our Lord Jesus Christ.*
> *Romans 5:1*

> *Therefore, there is now no condemnation for those who*
> *are in Christ Jesus. Romans 8:1*

> *For I am convinced that neither death nor life, neither*
> *angels nor demons, neither the present nor the future,*
> *nor any powers, neither height nor depth, nor anything*

*else in all creation, will be able to separate us from the
love of God that is in Christ Jesus our Lord. Romans
8:38-39*

Sarah, you are a believer in Christ. Nothing can separate you from the love of God. I don't want you to ever forget that."

Sarah would never forget it. "I won't, but the agony over what I did to my baby still crushes me. How do I get over this?"

"I'm glad you asked. We have a post-abortion group that meets here every Monday afternoon. We have several ladies in the group who, like you, have had abortions. They have all found forgiveness in Jesus. Some of them, also like you, are still working on forgiving themselves. I would like you to attend the group. You can come every Monday after school. You will learn how to allow God to use your experience as a testimony to His faithfulness. Would you like that?"

Sarah, despite the guilt still crushing her, felt a sense of relief. Yes, she would learn how to allow God to use her experience for His glory. She couldn't wait to see how He would do it.

Chapter Fifteen

Kathy and Sarah exited the counseling room. They had shared an amazing experience and it showed on their faces. As they made their way into the hallway, Emily, Angela, Brad, and Jessica were coming down the stairs from the pre-birth class at the same time. Emily had been asked to sit in with the pre-birth class to help with the video sessions, handing out class materials, and getting a feel for what the center offers in the class. Sarah suddenly recognized Emily as one of the women who had prayed with Cole outside the abortion clinic. Then, it occurred to Sarah that Emily was the same lady she had overheard talking on her phone the day she came to Your Choice but left without ever coming inside. Shame swept over her again. *Why didn't I recognize her on the porch? She must have recognized me! What does she think of me? She must think I'm a horrible person. Has she kept in touch with Cole? Why am I even here? I wish I could just run away.* Sarah's thoughts were running away with her. She tried to focus and remembered that she was now a daughter of the King. *Get a grip, Sarah. You are no longer alone, and you'll never be alone again.* Emily and Sarah stared at each other for a moment longer, still neither of them knowing exactly what to say.

Kathy broke the ice. "Good morning ladies and I see we have one gentleman as well. Did you enjoy your class?"

Jessica answered first. "Yes. I can't believe there is so much I didn't know about pregnancy and a baby's development inside the womb."

Angela was next. "Tell me about it. I never knew babies in the womb were so well developed. They are certainly not blobs of tissue."

Sarah felt the sting, but she knew she would have to live with the reality of what she had done so she might as well get used to comments, especially those made with good intentions.

Brad chimed in. "I learned a lot too and I'm glad I wasn't the only dude in there."

They all chuckled. Kathy assured Brad that there are plenty of men who come to Your Choice for various reasons. He certainly wouldn't be the only dude around. Sarah was still staring at Emily. If only she had walked past her and came through those doors days ago, she might be in the pre-birth classes with this group of nice people with her baby's heartbeat still pumping beneath her own. Sarah made a mental note to not let the enemy use her guilt against her. She had that testimony to work on and she intended to master it.

As Angela, Brad, and Jessica headed out the door of Your Choice to go about their day, Emily paused to introduce herself to Kathy. She smiled at Sarah to acknowledge their introductions from earlier on the front porch. She moved her eyes from Sarah's to Kathy's. "Hi, I'm Emily McMaster. I'm a new volunteer here. Today, I sat in on the pre-birth class. I don't know what I'll be doing next Monday, but I loved today and I look forward to next time."

Kathy noticed Emily's youthful zest and willingness to serve. "It's nice to meet you, Emily. I'm Kathy. I volunteer here as well, as a counselor." As Kathy spoke, she noticed an awkwardness between the two young women standing there with her. *Do they know each other? Is there something between them? Is it tension?* Kathy knew something felt unsettling. She just didn't know what it was.

Sarah filled in the gap. There was something about Emily that made Sarah want to know more about her in spite of their awkward connection. "It's nice to meet you again, Emily. Actually, I've seen you before . . . before we met on the porch outside. I came here last week, but I left. I never came inside." Sarah wasn't sure how to continue. She was still struggling with her shame. "Anyway, I saw you leaving." Now she felt shameful, nervous, and downright uncomfortable, but she might as well finish what she started. "You might recognize me. You prayed with my boyfriend, well . . . my ex-boyfriend now, I guess . . . on that sidewalk in Atlanta last week. I saw you before I went inside the clinic." Sarah lowered her head. She couldn't look Emily in the eyes as she continued. "I also saw you when I came out of the clinic." Not knowing how to end the conversation, she simply told the truth the best way she knew how in that moment. "I'll be coming back next week too, but I'll be in the post-abortion class." By the time Sarah finished speaking, all three ladies were fighting the tears welling up in their eyes.

Kathy had an idea. "You know, ladies, sometimes we pair a volunteer with a client, you know, to help each other out and build relationships. We call it our Titus 2 Ministry. I can explain that later. Anyway, I'd like the two of you to think about it. You certainly don't have to decide today. Perhaps next week, when you are both here again, each of you can let me know if you are interested in being paired with someone. If you decide to do it, you'll simply encourage one another through the week. Sarah, as the client, you'll decide how you want to communicate with your volunteer, whether it be text messaging, emails, note cards left for you here to protect your privacy, however you are comfortable."

Sarah liked the idea already but decided to take the week to think about it. Between her counseling session with Kathy and recognizing Emily the way she did, Sarah was feeling overwhelmed. "OK, I'll let you know next week. Thank you, ma'am."

Emily liked the idea as well. She already knew that if Sarah decided not to participate, she would be willing to pair with someone else. Emily, true to her character, loved a challenge. She and Sarah walked out together.

April was in the front office and overheard the conversation. After Emily and Sarah exited the building, she looked up at Kathy who had followed them into the waiting area. "Titus 2 Ministry? We don't have a Titus 2 Ministry."

Kathy took a deep breath. "We do now."

Emily and Sarah walked down the flower lined walkway that Emily had come to love. Emily was aware of the awkwardness between them, but she wanted to find a way to bond with Sarah. She wondered how God might use her to help Sarah, especially since she had not completed any official training to become one of the Your Choice counselors. "It was nice to officially meet you today, Sarah. I hope I get a chance to know you better even if you decide against the Titus 2 Ministry." Emily wanted to know more about that. No one had mentioned that to her, not even the day of her initial tour.

Even though Emily was the same lady who had scared her away just days ago and the same lady who had prayed so hard for her that day on the sidewalk outside the abortion clinic, there was something about her that Sarah liked. She would have to get past the awkwardness between them. Emily seemed like a kind person, but also feisty somehow, like someone her mother wouldn't want to cross in a courtroom. "It was nice to meet you too, Emily. If I decide to let Miss Kathy pair me with a volunteer, maybe I could be paired with you. I mean, if you decide you want to do it too."

Emily was curious about Sarah and wanted a front row seat to watch her full story unfold. She wanted to see how God would use Sarah's story for His glory. "I think I would like that. I look forward to seeing you next week either way. Have a wonderful day, Sarah."

"You too, Emily." Sarah felt better. The weight of her decision was still heavy to bear and would be for a while, maybe always, but she felt like she now had a support system. She wanted to know more about Emily. For now, Sarah would go to school, check in late, and get the tardy slip she knew they would give her. She would have to decide how to react when she saw Lilly and Cole. As Sarah climbed into her car, she decided to do something she had never done before today. She had only done it once inside Your Choice with Kathy, but never by herself. She decided to pray.

Emily checked her watch. She needed to get moving. She and a group of other pre-law students were scheduled to tour the School of Law at Pleasant Grove University in a couple of hours. She tossed a folder filled with informational materials about Your Choice and all they offer to the community into the passenger seat along with her purse. Then she drove back to her apartment for lunch. Back at her apartment, she grabbed a loaf of bread, a container of left-over chicken salad, and a jar of mayonnaise. She made a sandwich and grabbed a bottle of water from her frig as she put back what was left in the refrigerator. She swiped an apple from a bowl on the counter. She dialed Luke's number. If he had a few minutes to talk, she would tell him about her morning before heading out for the tour.

Luke answered on the first ring. "Hey! You caught me between classes. I only have a minute or two to spare but I've been praying for you all morning. How did your first day as a volunteer at the center go?"

Emily was excited. "It went very well. First, they placed me in a pre-birth class with a few women and a couple of dads who decided to choose life for their babies. We had a chance to chat a little before the class started. A few people got their early, like me."

"Imagine that. Someone else out there with the same desire for promptness as Emily McMaster," Luke teased.

"Oh stop! Anyway, one of the girls brought her boyfriend. They have decided to parent. We talked about God's design for sex and marriage. They know they can't be together like that anymore until after they are married, if they decide to get married someday. Anyway, it will be interesting to see how they work out. I have a good feeling about them. Another girl in the class who also got there early is having her baby, but it sounds like she might be considering adoption. There were people in that class in all sorts of different situations. I never realized how complex some situations can be. Luke, there's something else! The girl we prayed for outside the abortion clinic was there! She met with one of the counselors. We officially met and I even had a chance to talk to her a little. She still looked weak and pale, but there was something different about her when she came into the hallway after her counseling session. There was almost a glow about her even though I could tell she was still struggling. I can't imagine the physical and emotional pain she must be suffering. She might be OK physically, hopefully, but she'll need a long time to heal from her decision to have an abortion, I'm sure. That reminds me, one of our counselors asked me about participating in their Titus 2 Ministry where they pair volunteers with clients. I need to look through that folder they gave me. Nobody has said anything to me about a Titus 2 Ministry there." Emily was talking a mile a minute while also eating her lunch.

"Hey, slow down there a bit. You're going to choke on your lunch and I'm not there to save your life." Luke loved Emily's zeal for life.

"That was my last bite. How was your morning?"

"Well, let's see, I had to sit through what seemed like the longest advanced biology lecture ever. I'll be glad to get past the pre-med classes and get on to medical school. Hey, I have about a minute and a half to get to class. I'll call you tonight, OK?

"OK. Goodbye until then. I love you."

Luke's heart was melting into mush. "I love you too, Emily. Goodbye until then."

Emily cleaned up her sandwich crumbs and tossed her water bottle into the recycle bin. She grabbed her purse and headed back to her car. The School of Law was on the other end of the campus. She would need to drive her car if she wanted to be on time, which meant early for Emily. Campus traffic was down. More students were walking than driving due to the warm, beautiful spring day. Emily parked her car and checked her watch. She had a few minutes before going inside. She reached for the folder she had brought from Your Choice which was still in the passenger seat of her car. She pulled out all the informational packets and pamphlets and began looking for information on the Titus 2 Ministry. She searched through one pamphlet, then another, then another. *Funny*, she thought. *There is nothing in here about the Titus 2 Ministry*. Emily checked the time again. She had time to look through one more. *Hmmm, nothing there either.* Emily shuffled the papers back in the folder, grabbed her purse and headed inside. She took the folder in case she had an opportunity to look more during the tour. She made a mental note to tell April, Veronica, and Kathy that they needed to include Titus 2 information in their informational packets.

Inside the School of Law building, a group of students were gathering in the lobby. Emily joined the group. They chatted with one another about their classes and the different law degrees they hoped to earn. Within a few minutes, a well-dressed lady came into the lobby. The group of pre-law students quieted their conversations as the well-dressed lady addressed the group.

"Good afternoon. My name is Dr. Rachel Scott. I'm a practicing attorney here in Pleasant Grove. I'm also a professor here in the Pleasant Grove School of Law. I'll be conducting your tour today."

Emily thought the name sounded familiar. She thought hard, retracing her day in her thoughts. *Where have I heard that name?* As Dr. Scott led the group of students out of the lobby and down a hallway, it hit Emily. The young girl she had prayed for on the sidewalk outside the abortion clinic, the same young girl she officially met at Your Choice earlier that morning was a Scott. She had introduced herself as Sarah Scott. Emily wondered if there was a connection, then it hit her hard. She hadn't recognized her at first. On the day of the abortion, Dr. Scott had been wearing dark sunglasses and a hat, but now that she was here on one of her tours, Emily knew without a shadow of a doubt that Dr. Scott was the same woman who had led Sarah by the arm into the abortion clinic that day. Dr. Rachel Scott is Sarah Scott's mother.

Emily followed the tour through hallways where classes would meet. Dr. Scott led them into a cafeteria where they could purchase lunches or dinners for students with night classes. The most exciting part for Emily was the mock trial auditorium. Just walking into the room made her heartbeat spike. She almost trembled at the excitement of participating in a mock trial. Emily scanned the room. It looked exactly like a real courtroom. The auditorium setting allowed space for other students or anyone in the community to view the mock trials. Emily was lost in the moment.

"Miss. Miss. MISS!" Rachel didn't mean to startle the girl, but she needed to get her attention. This was the end of the tour, and she didn't want to leave the girl alone wondering where everyone had gone. She obviously wasn't paying attention.

Emily jumped, dropping her handful of papers onto the floor. "Oh, I'm so sorry, Dr. Scott. I'm just so excited about attending Law School here this fall. I can't wait to stand down there and practice my role as an attorney. I guess I got lost in the thought, the excitement of it all. I do apologize." Emily picked up her scattered papers and stuffed them back in the folder.

So, the girl wasn't lost in thought because she wasn't interested. She was lost in thought because she was incredibly interested in the field of study that Dr. Rachel Scott loved. The girl looked familiar, but Rachel couldn't place her. "I see. Your name is?"

"Oh, I'm Emily McMaster." Emily wondered why she was so nervous. *Come on Emily! It isn't like you to be intimidated by other people. Get a grip*, she thought to herself.

Rachel recognized the name. "Emily, it's nice to meet you. Every student here eventually attends at least one of my classes. I'm also the one who supervises the mock trials." Rachel's eyes scanned the room. Then, she turned her attention back to Emily. "This is my favorite room too. It seems we already have something in common. Sometimes I play the role of the opposing attorney in a mock trial. Perhaps we will spar off at some point. You'll get a chance to show me what you're made of. By the way, this is the end of the tour. We're done here for today." Rachel smiled. There was something about this Emily McMaster, something she doesn't see every year. No, this something is rare, the something that tells Dr. Scott that she's standing before someone with the potential to become a great attorney. And Dr. Scott was rarely wrong.

Showing Dr. Scott what she was made of was a challenge Emily McMaster couldn't wait to take on at full capacity. "I look forward to sparring off, Dr. Scott. It will give *you* a chance to show me what *you're* made of." Emily smiled, shook Dr. Scott's hand, and left the room.

Emily walked away saying a silent prayer. "Lord, help me help this woman to value the life of the unborn. Help me to recognize every opportunity to reach her."

Rachel watched Emily walk away. She had the personality, the drive, the determination, the spunk, the confidence – all the tools she needed to conquer anything that girl wanted to conquer. No wonder the undergraduate professors had mentioned her name. There was something else about her, something else that she couldn't identify, but something she was determined to find out. *Emily McMaster, what is it that drives you?* Rachel whispered to herself as she watched Emily leave the building.

Rachel turned to leave the mock trial room, but something caught her eye. There was something just underneath the seat where Emily had dropped her papers. Rachel bent to pick it up. There were two items. One was a pamphlet, *Steps to Peace with God* by the Billy Graham Association. She had heard that name before. He was a famous evangelist her parents used to watch on TV sometimes. Rachel remembered liking him somewhat, but to her parents' dismay, she had lost interest. The other item was a pamphlet that caught Rachel's breath so abruptly that she nearly choked, *Stages of Development of the Unborn Baby*. Right there on the front of the pamphlet was an image of a 9-week unborn baby. Rachel steadied herself. She had always believed that images such as this were just lies that pro-life groups used to manipulate girls into having babies they can't afford or were not ready to raise, like her Sarah.

Rachel said her name out loud without realizing it, "Like my Sarah." Normally Rachel would toss pamphlets like this in the trash without giving them a second thought but there was something about the girl who had dropped them. Then it hit her. She was one of the women praying with Cole and Lilly on the sidewalk on the day of Sarah's abortion. She flipped through the pamphlet, looking at all the images. On the back page of the pamphlet was a list of resources, websites, and YouTube video links where people can find more information about the development of unborn babies, even witness live ultrasounds. Rachel looked at the list. *I'm an attorney,* she thought, *a good one. I research topics for cases all the time. Why haven't I researched this on my own? Why didn't I research further before making Sarah . . .*

Rachel shivered at the thought that she might have been wrong about unborn babies all along. She tucked the papers into her jacket pocket. She would go home tonight and after everyone else was in bed, she would check out those resources. She would research all night if needed to prove to herself that she had been correct and that people like Emily McMaster are just liars, but there was a sinking sick feeling in Rachel's stomach. What if she only proves to herself that people like Emily McMaster are correct and people like herself are wrong? She couldn't possibly be wrong, but what if she was? She may have to do the hardest thing she has ever had to do.

She may have to go to Sarah, and admit she had been wrong all along.

Chapter Sixteen

Brad and Angela sat on a sofa in the common room of Angela's dorm building. Earlier that morning, in their first pre-birth class at Your Choice, Emily had given them a large envelope filled with information about prenatal vitamins, nutrition, and other helpful pamphlets for maintaining a healthy pregnancy. Also included in the large envelope was a *Steps to Peace with God* booklet. Angela recognized it as one of the items her grandmother had sent her. She and Brad began reading it. The booklet explained God's purpose for life, the problem with sin and separation from God, and how Jesus paid the penalty for our sin and bridged the gap between us and God. The last step explained that we must trust Jesus as our Lord and Savior. "Brad, my grandmother, Grandma Ruby, has talked about these very points my whole life. I guess I just never really listened to her."

Brad listened intently as Angela read aloud each page of the booklet. "I've never heard of this *Steps to Peace with God* before." Brad examined the booklet. "It says it's from the Billy Graham Association. Who is Billy Graham?"

"He's a famous evangelist. My grandmother used to watch his sermons on TV all the time. When I was a little girl, my mom would let me spend weekends with her. That's when I would watch with her. When she started talking to me about salvation, I sort of tuned her out. My mom left home because she thought Grandma Ruby and her religion and rules were overbearing. I guess I didn't want to get mixed up in something my mom thought was absurd. I was too little then to understand the message he was teaching."

Brad was interested in learning more about the message in the booklet. "What do you think now?"

Angela teared up. "I think maybe I've been wrong."

Brad picked up the envelope. "There's another book in here." He pulled out the book.

"What is it?" Angela was curious.

Brad held the book up so Angela could see it more clearly. "It's a Bible."

"Grandma Ruby always talked about the Gospel of John. She sent me a Bible a long time ago. She was always trying to get me to read one of the gospels. She always told me to start in John. She wanted me to learn more about Jesus. I still have that Bible. I hid it in my room to keep my mom from getting angry with Grandma Ruby. I never read any of it, but I couldn't get rid of it either."

Brad wanted to know more. "Why don't we start now? Let's learn more about the Jesus mentioned in that booklet."

Brad and Angela read for hours. Men were allowed to stay in the common area of the girls' dorms until midnight. By 11:30pm, Brad and Angela were in tears. Angela spoke first. "I'm sure there is a lot more for us to learn, Brad, but one thing I know for certain in this moment is that I want Jesus in my heart, and I want to make Him Lord of my life."

Brad spoke through his own tears. "So do I, Angela. So do I."

Bradley St. James and Angela Cromwell bowed their heads there in the common area of the girls' dormitory and they both prayed to receive Jesus' gift of salvation and make Him Lord of their lives. From that moment on, their heartbeats were in sync as a couple dedicated to living a life that honors God and raising their baby to do the same.

Brad checked his watch. "I should go now. I'll call you first thing tomorrow morning."

Angela had another idea. "Let me call you second thing in the morning instead."

Brad looked bewildered. "Second thing?"

Angela smiled through what was now her happy tears. "Yes. The first thing I want to do in the morning is call Grandma Ruby."

Jessica sat in her room studying all the information Emily had given her during her first pre-birth class earlier that morning. She could smell her mother's homecooked meal from the kitchen. It smelled good but made her nauseous at the same time. She wondered if what she was feeling was morning sickness even though it was evening. One of the pamphlets in the large envelope gave suggestions for easing it. After dinner, she planned to discuss her situation more with her parents. Jessica's mother worked hard during the day and all evening trying to take care of the family. Jessica worked hard all day at Carl's diner and picked up all the overtime Rhonda would allow. Her twin brothers did odd jobs to earn money whenever they could. Jennifer, her little sister, would babysit for friends of the family on Friday and Saturday evenings to help raise a few dollars whenever she could. Jessica had noticed that her father looked different. He used to come home from his job and then go right to work around the house fixing anything that needed fixing or working in the yard. He rarely sat down. For the past several weeks, he would come home and go straight to his chair in the living room. Jessica was beginning to think something might be wrong with him. He worked too hard. He always did, but Jessica felt like whatever was making him look pale and feel tired all the time was more than that.

"What am I doing?" Jessica whispered to herself. Her thoughts kept going. *Jack left me. I can't raise a baby all by myself. Mom is stretched too far as it is. We already have so many mouths to feed and Dad sure can't take on any more responsibilities.*

Jessica placed her hand on her abdomen and spoke, for the first time, to her unborn baby. "Hey little guy or little girl, I don't know what I'm doing. I don't even know if I can keep you once you're born, but I can promise you one thing. I promise to take good care of you until then."

After dinner, Jessica's family gathered in the living room as was their nightly custom for Bible reading. Jessica's father asked John Jr. to read tonight. That was a first. Jessica's father always read the Bible to his family. He always felt it was his responsibility as leader of their household. Not tonight. Tonight, John had asked John Jr. to read instead. He read from the book of Acts. After John Jr. read a few chapters, the Whitlock family spent a few minutes discussing the early church and how blessed they were to live in a country where they could worship in church freely, without the fear of persecution. When the early church conversation ended, Jessica asked if she could talk to her parents privately. Her siblings went to their rooms to work on homework assignments and to give their parents and Jessica the privacy they needed. When their doors were closed, Jessica began. "I want to talk to you about what I should do about the baby."

Jessica's mother looked tired. "About the baby? What do you mean?"

Jessica noticed her mother's tired looking eyes. "Well, I went to my first pre-birth class this morning. We learned about prenatal care and how to maintain a healthy pregnancy. On the way out, I grabbed two brochures about adoption."

"Adoption?" Marjorie was surprised. "You want to put the baby up for adoption, Jessica?"

"I don't know. I mean, I don't want to but . . . how can I possibly raise a child? My job pays minimum wage plus tips. The diner is a great local spot. We stay busy but most of our guests are either students or families surviving on low budgets. Tips don't add up to much. Mom, Dad, I'm a single woman with an extremely low paying job who lives at home and my family needs my income to help us all out."

John felt a personal sting. "I'll get a second job."

"No! No, Dad. That's not what I mean. You have always worked hard to provide for us." Jessica felt the tears, but she couldn't stop them. "Dad, I have never admired anyone more than I admire you, and you too, Mom. The two of you have modeled for all of us the value of hard work and the responsibility to family that we all share." Jessica dabbed a tear from her cheek.

Marjorie had not been able to stop her tears either. "But Jessica, the baby you are carrying is our grandbaby. Your father and I want to be grandparents to this baby, honey."

"I know you do. Despite everything that has happened, I know you do. I know you love me, and I know you'll love this baby. That's the reason I wanted to talk to you about it. I didn't want to make the decision without discussing it with you, but I want you both to know that adoption is an option and I'm considering that option."

John had taught his family the value and the power of prayer. "Jessica, your mother and I know this decision is a hard one for you. It's hard for us too since we have a grandchild to consider. We don't have to make any decisions tonight. Let's pray over it and ask God to guide us."

Jessica was satisfied with that. Her parents had been strict on her and her younger siblings, but they had shown her mercy and grace when she expected to be thrown out of the house. They had personally shown her the heart of Jesus. Her situation wasn't ideal or within God's plan for intimacy, marriage, and family. Jessica knew that. She had prayed. She had repented and she was willing to give the whole situation over to God to allow Him to use her and her situation for His good, even if that meant someday saying goodbye to the child she was carrying.

John prayed for guidance, for wisdom, for knowledge, for understanding, and for discernment so that the Whitlock family would make a God-honoring decision over Jessica's future and the future of her unborn baby.

That night, when Jessica slipped into bed, she placed her hand over her abdomen again and prayed one more time before falling asleep.

"Father God, right now this little one's heartbeat pumps beneath my own. As Your child, God, help my heartbeat pump in sync with Yours. Give me a heart after Your own and the strength to make the right decision for this child that You have created. Amen."

Sarah was exhausted. Her day had been one of her hardest ever, but also one of the best days of her life. She had survived her first day back at school since her abortion. She didn't have the courage to look at Cole or Lilly. She avoided eye contact during class and ran out of one class and into another without speaking to either one. She needed time to figure out what to say to them. She had carried the weight of her abortion on her shoulders. That morning, the heaviness of her sorrow had been crushing, but now she didn't need to bear it alone. Now, she has something she didn't have before. Now, she has Jesus. Sarah knew her abortion would always haunt her. She hadn't known all the facts about abortion but that was her fault too. All she had to do was research it, but she hadn't done that. Her mother may have pressured her into it, but Sarah knew she would always bear the responsibility of ending the life of her baby. Sarah knew something else. She knew that what mattered now was what she chose to do with what she had learned. She would pray for God to show her the next step as far as the knowledge she now owned about abortion. As far as her new relationship with Jesus, she knew the next step already. She had to share Jesus with her parents and her little brother, Tommy. As Sarah climbed into bed, she prayed.

"Lord, I know I have so much to learn about You and about prayer, but well, I just want to ask You to help me share You with my family. Umm, that's all. OK. Goodnight. I mean. Umm, Amen."

Sarah's last thought before she fell asleep was that she would have to ask Lilly to help her learn more about how to pray.

Rachel made sure everyone was asleep. Then she crept into her home office. She turned on her computer. *Come on. Boot up already*, she thought. When her computer was ready, Rachel's hands were shaking so much she could hardly type. Over the next hour, Rachel pulled up all the websites suggested on the pamphlet she had pulled from underneath the chair in the mock trial room at the university. She had typed "fetal development" in the search bar multiple times. She typed in "abortion procedures" several times. The information she pulled up had both amazed her and made her sick to her stomach. She sat there staring at her computer screen. After a few seconds, Rachel clicked the play button on the screen. The video resumed. It was an ultrasound video of a 9-week baby. Rachel's eyes were fixated on one spot. Near the middle of her computer screen, there it was. Rachel couldn't take her eyes off the heartbeat of that 9-week baby. She felt her body began to shake. Guilt consumed her. She began to cry so hard she could barely breathe. Through her sobs, she whispered, "How could I? How could I not have known these things? I'm an intelligent woman. How could I not know? Why have I never researched for myself? I've been so wrong."

When Rachel had pulled herself together, she realized the weight of her guilt had brought her down to the floor. She pulled herself up back into her chair. She pulled from her purse the other item she had pulled from underneath the seat in the mock trial room earlier that day. She looked at the little booklet in her hands. "*Steps to Peace with God*," she whispered. "Emily McMaster, what else do you have to tell me?"

Rachel opened the booklet and read every word. She looked back at the paused video of the baby's heartbeat on her computer screen. She clicked the play button to rewatch the video. Then she reread the booklet in her hands again. Suddenly, it made sense to her that most of the Christians she knew were pro-life. Only a God as powerful as the one they claim to know, the one written about in the little booklet, could create another little human being like the one on her computer screen. Rachel wanted to know more about the relationship with God that was written about in the booklet but what right did she have to know God after what she had done? She had basically forced her daughter to kill her baby. *And my grandbaby*, Rachel suddenly realized.

Deep inside her heart, Rachel wanted to know more about this God that she was so unworthy of knowing, but she had another problem and no idea what to do about it. When the sun came up in the morning, how could she possibly face her Sarah?

Luke and Emily had just finished their dinner. During dinner and on the drive back to Emily's apartment, Emily hadn't stopped talking about her day. "I already told you about my morning at the pregnancy care center, but I haven't told you about the tour at the School of Law. Well, I met one of Pleasant Grove's top attorneys. She takes on huge cases, hard ones. She's tough. She rarely loses a case." Emily had researched the name "Dr. Rachel Scott" as soon as she left the School of Law building. "Anyway, she'll be one of my professors and she'll be supervising the mock trials later in the year. She says she might even play the role of the opposing attorney. I had a chance to speak with her for a few minutes after the tour. She said that playing the role of the opposing attorney would give us a chance to show her what we're made of. I hate to admit it, but that made me just a tad nervous."

Luke found a chance to get a word in. "Just a tad nervous? Emily McMaster nervous about something? Wait. Let me savor the day while I still can, the day that Emily McMaster was actually nervous, just a tad, but still, it happened."

Emily loved the teasing. "Oh stop!" Emily chuckled. "Anyway, Luke Westmoreland, I looked her straight in the eyes and told her that I look forward to sparring off with her. That's how she put it.

Anyway, I told her I looked forward to it because it will give her a chance to show me what *she's* made of."

By now, Luke and Emily had arrived at Emily's apartment. "It was an amazing day, Luke."

Luke could never get enough of Emily's spunk. "Will I get to sit in on one of those mock trials so I can witness all this sparring off?"

"Absolutely! There's a whole stadium, a small one, but the mock trial room has stadium seating so people from the university and the community can come in and watch. That reminds me. I dropped some papers while I was in there. I have a few things missing from the materials I brought home from Your Choice. I'll have to replace them."

"Well, maybe the ones you dropped will end up in the hands of someone who needs to read them."

Emily took a deep breath. "Maybe so. Luke, today I realized that Dr. Scott is Sarah Scott's mother. The lady wearing the hat and sunglasses who led Sarah inside that abortion clinic is the same Dr. Rachel Scott I met today at the School of Law. I don't think she recognized me. On the day of Sarah's abortion, she was probably too focused on getting Sarah into that clinic. How could someone so well-educated not know anything at all about human development inside the womb?"

Luke had no answer for that question. "I don't know Emily. Who knows? Maybe she will somehow find the materials you dropped in the mock trial room. Someone is bound to find them. We'll pray for those papers to land in the hands of someone who needs to read them."

Luke and Emily prayed together while standing outside her apartment. They had agreed that Luke would never be in her apartment alone with her. They would honor God by removing any situation where they might be alone and give in. "Well, this is where I say goodnight."

Luke kissed Emily goodnight and stayed outside her door long enough to make sure she made it inside safely and her door was locked. Then, he made his way back to his car. His heart was overflowing. As he pulled out of the university apartment complex, he said a silent prayer of thanks to God who had blessed him with such a wonderful and Godly woman. He couldn't wait to become her husband and start their married life together with all the goodness of God and His plan for them straight ahead.

Chapter Seventeen

On Tuesday morning, Rachel stared at her bedroom ceiling, wondering how she could face Sarah at the breakfast table. She hadn't slept all night. She had tossed and turned, stared at the dark ceiling, and tossed and turned again. The cycle repeated itself all night long. Even though tears threatened to return, her eyes felt dry. Her head hurt, but her heart hurt more. Charles rolled over and mumbled something Rachel didn't understand. She quietly got out of bed and slipped downstairs to make breakfast. If she could get breakfast on the table early, before everyone else got up, she would leave a note on the table to tell the family that she needed to get to the office early. She knew she couldn't avoid Sarah forever and she didn't want to, but she wanted time to process all that she had learned and time to figure out how to talk to Sarah.

———

Jessica's alarm sounded. For the first time in a long time, she felt rested and ready for a normal workday. She dressed for work and made her way to the kitchen. Her mother wasn't making a big breakfast on that morning, but the combined smells of toast and coffee made her nauseous. Her mother noticed the signs. "Are you feeling OK, Jessica? You look a little pale."

"I'm OK. I guess I'm experiencing morning sickness. Maybe I'll be OK by the time I get to work."

"Jessica, honey, they call it morning sickness, but it should be called morning, noon, afternoon, evening, and night sickness."

Jessica grabbed only a piece of loaf bread and a bottle of water. She hugged her mother and was headed out the door just as her brothers and her sister came into the kitchen. "I'm off to work. Have a good day, everyone! Love you guys!"

As Jessica pulled out of the driveway, she realized that she hadn't seen her father come down for breakfast. *Maybe he's just running late,* she thought as she drove down the street looking forward to a normal day.

Angela's first class wasn't until 10:00am but she was up by 6:30am. She couldn't wait to call her grandmother. Grandma Ruby would be so excited about Angela's decision to trust Jesus as Lord of her life. She decided to get dressed for the day and review a few chapters of class material. Final exams were coming up soon so she might as well get a little study time in. At 8:00am, Jessica grabbed her phone and hit Grandma Ruby's name on her phone. "Hello, Grandma! I have something to tell you!"

Grandma Ruby rejoiced with the angels in Heaven over Angela's and Brad's salvation. She had prayed for many years. Before the call ended, she and Angela agreed to pray together regularly over her parents. Perhaps someday, maybe soon, Angela, Brad, and Grandma Ruby would rejoice with the angels in Heaven again over her parents' salvation. One thing Angela knew for sure was that as long as God gave her breath, she would never stop praying for her parents.

Emily woke up on Tuesday morning wondering if she had been too direct with Dr. Scott. Emily knew she could be a handful at times. Her parents had told her so and she was pretty sure Luke thought the same thing even though he never said as much. Emily wondered if she deserved a man as patient as Luke Westmoreland. She breathed a prayer of thankfulness to God for gifting her with such a treasure.

Emily dressed for the day and ate a quick breakfast of oatmeal and a banana. She had an hour to spare before she needed to head out to class. She had just sat down to review her class assignments when she heard a knock at her door. *Who could that be?* she thought. Emily knew it wasn't Luke. He would be in class already and even if he wasn't, he never came to her apartment alone unless it was to pick her up to go out.

Emily called out, "Who is it?"

"Good morning, Miss McMaster. It's Dr. Rachel Scott."

Emily's first thought was that she had been too direct with Dr. Scott the day before. Her second thought was, *Good grief, Emily, open the door.*

Emily opened the door. "Dr. Scott. Good morning to you. Umm, please come in."

"Thank you. I hope you don't mind that I stopped by. I took the liberty of looking up your class schedule and checked your address in your file. I'm sorry to pry but I need to talk to you . . . if you have a minute. I won't take long."

Emily directed Dr. Scott to a comfortable chair. Emily sat on the sofa across from her. "Yes, of course, Dr. Scott. I do have a few minutes. What can I do for you?"

Dr. Scott pulled a pamphlet and a booklet from her purse. "You dropped these in the mock trial room yesterday. I found them after you left." Dr. Scott paused.

Emily sensed that Dr. Scott was at a loss for words. That certainly didn't seem like the reputation Dr. Scott made for herself on campus. "Yes ma'am. Those are mine. I did drop them. Are those materials the reason you came to see me?" Knowing that Dr. Scott was Sarah's mother and that she had led Sarah into the abortion clinic, Emily wondered if she was about to be presented with an opportunity to defend her pro-life stance. If so, she was ready.

"Yes, they are. After you walked away and I picked them up from underneath a seat, I started looking through them. I must tell you that I have always been pro-choice. I have always been taught that babies don't form for a while. I always thought that women who had first trimester abortions were only doing away with a cluster of cells and tissue. My strongest argument for my case is 'my body, my choice' but after looking through your pamphlet on fetal development . . . well, it looks like a whole other body to me and not just after the first trimester. At first, I thought you were just another pro-life manipulator but then I decided to go home and research for myself, something I should have done years ago." Dr. Scott's voice trailed off as if she slipped into deep thought.

"What do you believe now, Dr. Scott?"

"I believe babies develop much sooner." Rachel nearly choked on the words as she spoke them.

Emily noticed Dr. Scott's watery eyes. "You are correct that babies develop much sooner. In fact, and I'll put it simply, life begins at conception."

"But what about at the very first? In the first few weeks?" Dr. Scott now knew the truth, but she was still searching, perhaps without realizing it, for a way out of the crushing guilt of forcing Sarah into an abortion.

Emily wanted to take full advantage of this opportunity even if it meant she would be late for class. "Look at the youngest unborn baby in the pamphlet. Would you say that image is a baby?"

Rachel looked at the image. She looked at the head, the spine, the little nubs that were the beginnings of arms and legs. She focused back on the head where she saw little eyes and a little bump already forming into a nose. "Yes. This is definitely a very tiny little baby."

Emily continued with another question. "OK, if this tiny little human is a baby now, was he or she a tiny human baby yesterday?"

"It would make sense to say yes. This baby was a baby yesterday."

"What about 3 days ago? Was it a baby 3 days ago?" Emily was still making her point.

"Yes, if this is a baby now, it would have been a baby 3 days ago as well."

Emily was making progress. "OK. What about last week? If this baby is a baby now, a baby yesterday, and a baby 3 days ago, was it still a baby last week?"

Dr. Scott saw where Emily was headed. "Oh, I see. If this baby is a baby today, a baby yesterday, a baby 3 days ago, and a baby last week, we could go all the way back to the beginning and see that . . . life begins at conception."

And there it was. Emily smiled at Dr. Scott. "I rest my case, Dr. Scott."

Dr. Scott smiled back at Emily. "You're very good, Miss McMaster, but I'm not done with you yet. I read over this little booklet last night, *Steps to Peace with God*. I think I understand it but I've done something terrible, so terrible." Rachel's strong attorney image melted as the tears came.

"Dr. Scott. We are all terrible. We are all sinners. Salvation isn't based on anything we do. If we had to earn it, none of us would be saved."

"Umm, you don't understand. I'm unworthy of this Jesus."

"We are all unworthy. The Bible tells us in Romans 3:23 that all of us have fallen short of the glory of God. All of us." Emily paused for a minute. Then continued, "Dr. Scott, I know I'm just a pre-law student and certainly not a professionally licensed counselor, but if I can help you with whatever makes you feel unworthy . . . well, as a Christian woman, I'm willing to listen if you're willing to talk to me."

Dr. Scott realized her awkward position. She was a high-profile attorney in Pleasant Grove and one of the most respected professors at the School of Law at Pleasant Grove University and here she was in a pre-law student's campus apartment spilling out her weaknesses. Her only justification was that she wanted to know more about how she could possibly have a relationship with Jesus and how she could ever face her daughter again. "My daughter, Sarah." That's all she could say without choking on her words again.

"I'm listening, Dr. Scott. It's OK. Go on."

"My daughter, Sarah . . . she's just 17, a senior at Pleasant Grove High School. She's coming here in the fall to study journalism. Well, she . . . she got pregnant. She wanted an abortion at first, but she changed her mind. Her friend, Lilly, is a Christian who is pro-life. She must have tried to talk Sarah out of an abortion. I caught Sarah calling a place called Your Choice for Unplanned Pregnancies or something like that. I convinced Sarah that having the baby would ruin her boyfriend's life. He's a smart kid who is coming here this fall to study architecture. The kid has a great shot at a great career. Anyway, I . . . my husband and I, but mostly me, pretty much forced Sarah to have an abortion. After reading your pamphlet and researching fetal development and abortion methods, I just can't face her." Dr. Scott broke into a full-blown cry.

Emily slid over on the sofa closer to the chair Dr. Scott was sitting in. Dr. Rachel Scott was a strong and reputable fire-ball larger-than-life attorney and now she was sitting in Emily's campus apartment. She was a broken woman who needed Jesus and the forgiveness, grace, and mercy He offers to those who call on His name.

Emily read back through *Steps to Peace with God* with Dr. Scott and then she walked her through the Roman Road to Salvation, the same walk through Romans that Kathy had taken Dr. Scott's daughter, Sarah, the day before. Right there on a beautiful Tuesday morning, Dr. Rachel Scott prayed to receive Jesus as her Lord and Savior.

Emily didn't tell Dr. Scott that Sarah was at Your Choice the day before, but she assured Dr. Scott that talking to Sarah was her next step. Emily told Dr. Scott that she would be praying for her and Sarah and their entire family. Dr. Scott thanked Emily and headed to her office where she would spend a large part of her day praying about a hard conversation she must have with her daughter and soon.

Chapter Eighteen

Rachel pulled into the driveway of her home on Tuesday afternoon. She felt free in Jesus, forgiven, loved, and worthy of a relationship with Him, but she was shaking at the thought of talking to Sarah. God had forgiven her, but He is God and His Son, Jesus, had paid the penalty for her sin. Thanks to Emily, Rachel understood that, but how could Sarah forgive her? Sarah had been a mother and her own mother had sedated her with a pill and pulled her into an abortion clinic where they killed the baby that Sarah had decided she wanted to keep. How could her precious daughter ever forgive her for that?

Rachel knew she couldn't put it off. Avoiding Sarah that morning had been hard enough. She loved her daughter. She wanted a relationship with her but her biggest fear in that moment, sitting in her car, was that her daughter would never speak to her again. Rachel prayed and she prayed hard.

Dear God,

I'm new at this but I know You will hear me. First, thank You for forgiving me for a lifetime of spreading lies and leading thousands of other women astray. Lord, thank You for freeing me of that old life. Now, God, help me as I start anew. Please help my daughter forgive me as You have. And Lord, help me to share with my family the Truth that Emily shared with me. Amen.

Rachel exited her car and walked into the house. Charles, Sarah, and Tommy were seated at the kitchen table. Sarah's and Tommy's school books, notebooks, pens, and pencils were scattered all about. Charles was working on a stack of paperwork as well. Rachel was glad Sarah wasn't alone. Seeing her sitting there with the rest of the family made facing her for the first time since last night a lot easier. "Hi Mommy!" Tommy was always excited to see his mama after school.

"Hi Little Slugger! How was your day at school?"

"It was good. I made an A on my math test. My teacher says I can add numbers real good now! I fell on the playground and hurt my knee but the school nurse put a Band-Aid on it so it's OK now, Mommy. You don't even have to kiss it."

"Wow! That must be some Band-Aid if I don't even have to kiss it."

"Well, that and I'm growing up, Mommy."

"That you are, Tommy, and way too fast." Rachel turned her attention to Sarah. "How was your day, Sarah?"

"It was OK." Sarah had prayed about what she might say to Cole and Lilly at school today. She knew she couldn't keep trying to avoid them and she wanted them both to know that she had entered into a relationship with Jesus. When she told them, Cole had said he was happy for her, but then he walked away without so much as a smile. Lilly stayed behind to engage in a conversation with Sarah. They rejoiced over Sarah's salvation and made plans to talk on the phone later in the evening like they used to. Lilly had told Sarah that Cole would come around in time, but Sarah wasn't so sure and she wouldn't blame him for hating her forever. The rest of the school day had been as normal as ever and Sarah was resolved to face each day as the new believer that she was and trust God with her life and her future.

"Just OK?" Rachel wanted more from Sarah than just 'OK' but she wouldn't press too hard, not if she wanted to have a serious conversation with her later.

"Yeah, just OK, but I would like to talk to you about something, Mom."

Charles looked up from his stack of papers. "She's found religion."

Charles' comment took Rachel by surprise. "She's found what?"

"You heard me. She's found religion. She came home this afternoon with a pamphlet and a booklet and tried to get Tommy and me to join in this whatever it is she's gotten herself into."

Tommy chimed in. "She found Jesus, Mommy. This girl at school, her name is Kayla. She found Jesus one time too. She talks about Him all the time. Her mommy and daddy are moving to some country a long way away over the summer. Kayla has to go there too and be a miss-e-airy."

Sarah grinned. "It's missionary, Little Buddy. Her parents are missionaries."

"That's what I said, miss-e-airy. I might be one someday if I find Jesus like you did, Sarah." Tommy told his parents he was done with his homework and asked permission to go play outside.

"Go ahead, honey. Stay in the backyard. I'll call you inside for dinner soon." Now, Rachel really wanted to talk to Sarah.

Rachel sat down at the table with Charles and Sarah. "Sarah, tell me exactly, as your dad put it, what you've gotten yourself into."

Charles got up from the table, taking his stack of paperwork with him. "I've already heard this once. I'll be at the formal dining room table. I have work to do. You two knock yourselves out."

Sarah told her mother that she had been so upset about the things she had heard the doctor say in the abortion room and how she couldn't get over the fact that they wouldn't let her see the ultrasound images. Rachel swallowed hard listening to Sarah's story but she wanted to hear her out.

Sarah continued, "I skipped my first class yesterday because I wanted to go back to Your Choice for Unplanned Pregnancies. Lilly told me all about the place and how it's a pro-life pregnancy care center. I got there before they opened. A few of us gathered on the front porch while we waited for someone to open up and let us in. I met a few other women. Their names are Emily, Jessica, and Angela."

Rachel interrupted. "Did you say you met a woman named Emily?"

"Yes, Emily is one of the volunteers. She was in the pre-birth class with Angela and Jessica while I was in another room with Kathy."

"Who's Kathy?" Rachel wanted to know every detail.

"She's another volunteer or maybe she works there. I'm not sure, but she's a counselor. She listened to me talk about what happened and how I was feeling. She told me about Jesus and how he paid the penalty for our sin and that if I believe in Him and ask Him into my heart, and well . . . I'm not the best at explaining it all, but she gave me this little booklet called *Steps to Peace with God*. She read through it with me and showed me a lot of verses from the book of Romans. She called it The Roman Road to Salvation. Mom, Kathy helped me understand who Jesus is. Dad thinks I'm out of my mind but, Mom, I believe Jesus is real, what He did was real. I believe He is the Son of God. I believe He was sinless. I believe He died on a cross as a sacrifice for our sin. I believe He rose again on the third day and well . . . there is so much more that we can read about in the Bible. They gave me one of those too. Kathy explained the Father, Son, and Holy Spirit. It sounds overwhelming, I know, but I think we would understand it more if we went to church. I called Lilly a little while ago. I'm going to start going to church with her. I would like to go over this booklet with you, Mom. Do you have time? Mom, why are you crying?"

Rachel pulled a tissue from her purse. She also pulled out her copy of *Steps to Peace with God*. "Oh Sarah. I'm so sorry. I'm so sorry, Sarah." Those were the only words Rachel could speak.

"Mom . . ." Sarah touched her mother's shoulder and glanced down at her mother's copy of *Steps to Peace with God*. Sarah realized that someone had already reached her mother and maybe sometime over the last 24 hours, her mother had already found Jesus. "Mom, who gave you your booklet?"

Rachel was still sobbing. "Yesterday, a pre-law student toured the School of Law part of the campus. She dropped this pamphlet and this booklet while touring the mock-trial room. I picked them up. There was something about the woman that dropped them that made me want to read them, so I did." Rachel had been speaking between sobs. She had to pause for a moment to catch her breath. Then, she continued. "Last night, after everyone went to bed, I slipped into my office and researched fetal development and," she could barely say the words, "abortion methods." Now Rachel was in a full wail.

Sarah was speechless. She didn't know what to think or say so she did the only thing she knew to do. She placed her arm around her mother, and she cried with her and she prayed over her. Rachel and Sarah stayed that way for a few minutes. When they both caught their breath again, Sarah asked her mother again, "Mom, who was the women who dropped the pamphlet and booklet?"

"Her name is Emily McMaster. She's the pre-law student my colleagues were telling me about. She has all the makings of a good attorney. I was impressed with her. There was something about her that intrigued me. I left early this morning to go talk to her. I wanted to better understand these materials and I guess I needed someone to tell me that I am still worthy of God's love and forgiveness even after what I did to you." Rachel had been crying so hard that her eyes were swollen and stinging.

Sarah stood looking at her mom in amazement. "Emily, the same girl I met yesterday is the same girl who led you to Jesus today. Wow!"

"Sarah, I'm so sorry for what I did. I know God has forgiven me, but can you?"

Sarah hadn't realized her mother wanted her forgiveness. "Mom, the abortion was just as much my fault as it was yours. I first went to Your Choice thinking it was an abortion clinic. I had no idea how those things worked. I never even thought about how I might pay for it. All I knew was that I was scared. I was terrified. I was the one who first wanted an abortion, and I wanted it before I told anyone. Lilly was the only one who knew because I took the pregnancy test at her house. My plan was to get an abortion and never tell anyone else, not Cole, not you, and not dad. Lilly tried to stop me and so did Cole once he found out. You and dad may have given me medication, drove me to the clinic, and led me in there, but if I had really wanted to, I would have pulled away and joined Cole, Lilly, and the others with them there on that sidewalk. Mom, Emily was one of the women praying with Cole that day."

"I knew there was something else, something more familiar about her. I wonder if she knew who I was all along? I wonder if she recognized me from that day? If she did, she never said so."

Sarah encouraged her mother. "Even if she did, what she cares about now is that you are her new sister in Christ Jesus. What matters now is what we do next."

Rachel and Sarah sat there for a few more minutes discussing their new relationship with Jesus and how they would move forward as mother and daughter. They couldn't change the past, but they could move forward into the future, resting in the comfort of the One who holds it. Rachel and Sarah bowed in prayer together, thanking God for bringing them both to Him and asking Him to use them in whatever way He sees fit for His glory. When they looked up from their prayer, Charles was standing in the doorway between the kitchen and dining room. There were tears running down his cheeks.

Chapter Nineteen

Jessica had just finished serving the lunch crowd when Rhonda called her behind the counter. "What's up, Rhonda? Does Bobby need help with the oven again? That thing has stopped working 3 times in the last two weeks. Carl needs to replace it."

"No, Jessica. It's your mom." Rhonda held up her cell phone. "She said she's been trying to call you."

"Oh, OK. I'm sorry, Rhonda. I must have left my phone in the car. I'll take the call in the break room. I'll be back in a few minutes." Jessica took Rhonda's phone and headed down the hallway.

"Hi, Mom. I'm sorry. I guess I left my phone in the . . ."

"Jessica, "Marjorie interrupted. "It's your father." Her voice sounded stressed.

Jessica was worried. "Dad? What about him? Mom, what's wrong?"

"Well, I don't know exactly. He has seemed so tired lately. When he didn't get up at his usual time this morning, I thought he was planning to go in to work later. After you left for work, I took your brothers and your sister to school and then I went to work, but I was worried about him, so I called him. When he didn't answer, I went home to check on him. I found him on the floor. He was pale and barely conscious. I called an ambulance. We're at the hospital now. They think your father had a heart attack. They are running tests to be sure."

"Mom, I'll be right there!"

"No, no, Jessica. He's OK for now. He is stable. There is no need for you to come to the hospital. I didn't want to call you at work, but I also knew you would be upset if I didn't let you know. I was going to send Pastor Mark to tell you in person, but no one answered the phone."

"I'll check with Rhonda. If she can let me go, I'll come stay with you."

"If you need to work, then don't worry about me." Marjorie knew she wasn't getting paid for today. They needed Jessica's income, but she didn't want to stop her daughter from coming to the hospital if she really wanted to be there. Besides, Marjorie needed Jessica. She really didn't want to wait alone.

Jessica came back into the dining room to find Rhonda who was refilling drinks at table 7. "Rhonda. Here's your phone. My dad is in the hospital. They think he had a heart attack. I know things have been chaotic with me lately."

"Oh no, Jessica. I'm so sorry. Listen, I'll cover for you here. Go be with your dad."

Jessica grabbed her purse from behind the counter and headed out the door. Rhonda called out to her. "Call me later to give me an update on your dad!"

"I will!" Jessica crossed the parking lot, unlocked her car and hopped inside. There on the console was her cell phone. On the screen were several missed calls from her mom and one missed call from Emily McMaster. Emily had left her a message. Jessica decided to listen to the message later. Right now, she needed to get to the hospital.

Twenty minutes later, Jessica pulled into the hospital parking lot. She was relieved to find a parking spot near the entrance. She ran inside. She slowed a little as she approached the front desk. The receptionist could tell Jessica was in a hurry. "How can I help you ma'am?"

Jessica was a little winded from running inside. "My dad, umm, John Whitlock. He was brought in by ambulance. I need to find my mother."

After a few clicks on her keyboard, the receptionist gave Jessica instructions. She pointed Jessica in the direction of the cardiac wing. "Down that hallway to the end and then take a right. The cardiac waiting room is the second room on the left."

"Thank you!" Jessica decided to walk this time but swiftly. She made her way to the end of the hallway and took a right, just like the receptionist had told her. There in the second room on the left sat her mother with her head down. Jessica wasn't sure if she was just upset or praying. She cleared her throat to get her mother's attention.

Marjorie looked up. "Oh Jessica. You're here." Marjorie stood to embrace Jessica. The minute she locked her arms around her daughter, she broke down. "I didn't know what to do. He looked so pale. The doctor should be here shortly to let me know the test results."

"I've noticed that Dad hasn't been as active as usual. I just thought he was tired and . . . well, getting older." After a brief pause, Jessica continued. "And lately, all I've done is add more stress to the family." She hung her head, her shame felt heavy again.

"Jessica. You were a handful there for a while, I'll admit. I need to tell you something that I should have told you a long time ago."

"What's that?" Jessica was puzzled.

"Thank you." Marjorie's eyes were red and swollen.

Jessica couldn't image what she had done that deserved a "thank you" from anyone, especially her mother. "Thank you for what?"

"For being you, for being the daughter that you are. Jessica, your father and I know that you would like to be in college right now. You should have had the opportunity to go. I'm sorry we couldn't afford to send you. Instead of fulfilling a dream of your own, you're working long hours at a diner for pennies above minimum wage plus tips to help us keep the bills paid and food on the table. Thank you, Jessica. Thank you for helping us, Jessica." Marjorie looked defeated.

"Oh Mom. I don't mind. Really, I don't. I have the rest of my life to go to college. Maybe someday I will, but I don't have to go now. You and dad have taught me how to love people. You taught me the value of personal responsibility. You taught me how to discern right from wrong. You taught me to love Jesus. Is there anything more important than that?"

Marjorie managed a smile. "There is nothing more important than loving Jesus."

Jessica spoke softly. "Mom, let's pray."

In that moment, Marjorie couldn't have been more proud of her daughter. "Yes, let's do."

Jessica and Marjorie took turns praying for her father's health, for their family finances, for direction moving forward concerning her father's recovery, and for the doctors and nurses working on John at that moment. After they finished with their prayer, Jessica wondered about her younger siblings. "Mom, have you told John Jr., James, or Jennifer about Dad?".

"No. They are all at school and they would go wild waiting here with us, but I'm glad you came. I'm glad you are here with me. I'll decide what to tell your brothers and your sister when we know more."

Jessica squeezed her mother's hand warmly. "I'm glad I came too, Mom."

A man in scrubs came into the waiting room. "Mrs. Whitlock?"

Marjorie spoke up. "I'm Marjorie Whitlock."

"Mrs. Whitlock, the tests confirm that your husband has had a heart attack. He is stable but he will need surgery to place a stint in two blocked arteries."

Marjorie was still concerned. "But he'll be OK, right?"

"He is stable now. After surgery, he should make a complete recovery."

"May I see him?" Marjorie looked at Jessica and then back at the doctor. "This is our daughter, Jessica. May we both see him?"

"He should be assigned to a room in the Coronary Care Unit soon. The nurse will let you know when you can see him, but we will need to get him scheduled for surgery soon."

"Thank you, doctor." Marjorie and Jessica sat back down to wait for the nurse to come get them. Marjorie began to cry again.

"Mom, the doctor said that Dad will be OK. The surgery will fix him right up."

"Yes, that's wonderful. Thank the Lord for that. It's just that . . ."

"Just what, Mom?"

"Our insurance policy doesn't cover critical care." Marjorie stopped herself. "But we'll figure it out. Jessica, I really shouldn't burden you with these things." Marjorie's voice trembled.

"Burden me? Mom, we are a family. We'll figure this out, like you said." Jessica thought about her family and how much she wanted to be a mother herself. She thought about the baby she was carrying and how much she wanted her baby to be part of this family too. Jessica had no idea how much her father's hospital bill would cost. She had no idea how her mother, how any of them, would find a way to pay it. There were so many things she didn't know, but she knew one thing.

After today, she knew that neither she, nor her family, had the resources they needed to care for another baby.

Jessica remembered that Emily McMaster had left her a message. "Mom, while we are waiting to see Dad, I need to return a phone call. A lady from my pre-birth class at Your Choice left me a message. Is it OK if I tell her about Dad? I know she'll pray."

"Sure, honey. We need all the prayers we can get." Margorie was thankful Jessica had a new friend to talk to, one who would pray for her John.

Jessica slipped into the hallway to listen to Emily's message. It only said for her to call Emily back when she has a chance. Jessica decided to call now.

Emily read her caller ID and picked up on the first ring. "Hi Jessica!"

"Hi Emily. You left a message. I'm returning your call." Jessica wondered why Emily needed her.

Emily was a cheerful as always. "Yes, I was just calling to check on you. How are things going?"

"Well, I'm OK, but I'm actually at the hospital right now."

Emily was concerned about Jessica and her baby. "Oh my! Are you OK?"

"Oh, I'm fine. It's my dad. He had a heart attack today. The doctor just told us that he needs surgery."

"I'm so sorry, Jessica. Is there anything I can do?"

"We are OK, but I would appreciate it if you would add my dad to the Your Choice prayer list. Please pray over his surgery and his recovery." Jessica paused for a second. She wasn't sure she should mention the family finances, but she decided to continue. Jessica whispered just loud enough for Emily to hear. "My dad should be OK after the surgery but . . . well . . . pray for God to provide the finances my family needs. Things are pretty tight."

Emily spoke compassionately. "Jessica, I will most certainly add those requests to the Your Choice prayer list. I believe the prayer team meets on Wednesday mornings, but they have a phone chain for emergencies. I'll get this out to them right away if that's OK with you."

Jessica didn't know there was a phone chain. She was thankful to find out about it. "That will be just fine. Yes, please send that out." Jessica was thankful God had brought Emily and the people at Your Choice for Unplanned Pregnancies into her life. "And Emily?"

"Yes, Jessica. I'm listening. What else do you need?"

Jessica hesitated, but she took a deep breath and found the strength to continue. "I would like more information about the two adoption agencies Your Choice recommends."

"Yes, one of them offers closed adoptions. The other one offers open adoptions. I'll put information about both into a file for you." Emily wasn't sure if she should be happy or sad for Jessica, but she would pray for God to grant the Whitlock family healing, knowledge, understanding, and wisdom through the weeks ahead.

Chapter Twenty

On Monday morning, April 17th, Brad, Angela, Jessica, Sarah, Emily, April, Veronica, Kathy, and several others sat in the pre-birth classroom at Your Choice. Weeks earlier, with Jessica's permission, Emily had sent information about Jessica's dad out to the Your Choice prayer list phone tree. Word had gotten out. In a small college town like Pleasant Grove, it didn't take long for word to spread through a community. So many people had been praying for Jessica's family. Every Monday, Brad, Angela, and Jessica attended their pre-birth classes. Sarah had been attending the Your Choice post-abortion support group. Emily continued to work in the pre-birth class and occasionally would sit in on the post abortion support sessions. Today, as they had all done for the past several weeks, they met in the pre-birth class first to get an update from Jessica before dispersing into their respective groups. "Dad was in the hospital longer than expected but he is home now and doing well. They don't want him going back to work for a few more weeks. He's getting a little impatient. I think he's driving Mom out of her mind."

There were chuckles. Then, Jessica continued. "Thank you all for sending food and helping with my younger brothers and my little sister. It's amazing how much the homecooked meals and help with transportation challenges have helped us. I think Jennifer has gotten a little too used to Kathy's trips to the ice cream shop after school. Thank you, Kathy, for helping us out."

"You are more than welcome, Jessica. I'll keep picking her up and taking her home for as long as you need. Besides, I've gotten a little too used to after school visits to the ice cream shop too. There's nothing like a hot fudge sundae after school!"

There were a few more chuckles and then Jessica finished her update. "Thank you all so much. My family, all of us, appreciates everything you have done. Between your help with donations plus the donations Pastor Mark collected at church, all our immediate needs have been met. We can't thank you enough."

Veronica stood to address the group. "Thank you for the update, Jessica. We will continue to pray for your family, and you be sure to tell us if more needs arise, OK?"

"Yes, ma'am. I will." Jessica was thankful for the people God had brought into her life through this group. They had prayed for her and her family faithfully. They had helped get her siblings to school and helped get them home. They had provided meals and money. Jessica silently prayed a prayer of thanks for the immediate needs that were met, but she knew her family remained under great financial stress. Jessica worked all the overtime she could. Her mother worked overtime at Alterations for You and Jessica had heard her mother's home sewing machine running late into the night. Sometimes the humming of her mother's machine would wake her up at 2:00am. John Jr. and James had worked so hard at odd jobs that they had missed homework assignments. Even Jennifer had baked cookies and sold them wherever she could. Still, with her father not returning to work for a few more weeks and both Jessica's and her mother's jobs not bringing in much money, even with all the overtime, Jessica couldn't see an end to the financial strain her family was suffering. Jessica patted her growing tummy. "Hey, little one. You know I have to do what's best for you, right? I'll love you always."

"Jessica," Veronica called.

"Oh, Veronica. I'm sorry. I guess I was deep in thought." Jessica smiled through her pain. She knew the next hour would be one of her hardest ever.

"It's time for our meeting about making an adoption plan for your baby. Are you ready, honey?" Veronica adjusted her big black glasses with the fake diamond trim.

"Yes, I'm ready." Jessica didn't mean to lie but she did. She wasn't ready but she had to do this, and she knew it.

Veronica led Jessica into one of the counseling rooms. "Jessica, is it OK if we ask Emily to sit in? She wants to get acquainted with every service Your Choice offers. It's up to you. You can say 'no' if you'd rather it be just the two of us."

"Emily can certainly join us. I don't mind."

Veronica stepped outside and motioned to Emily to come in. Emily came into the room and sat in one of the wing-back chairs near the fireplace. "Thank you for allowing me to sit in with you, Jessica."

Jessica smiled and nodded to Emily. She couldn't manage words. She didn't want to cry. She had to be strong.

Veronica began with prayer. She prayed for God's blessing on Jessica and for wisdom and peace over her decision. After the prayer, Veronica began to explain more about the two different adoption options. "Jessica, Emily sent you information about the two adoption agencies affiliated with us here at Your Choice. One of them offers only open adoptions and one offers only closed adoptions."

"What is the difference between the two?" Jessica was determined to make the right choice.

"An open adoption allows the birth mother to stay in touch with the adoption family. You will still be giving up all rights to your baby. The adoptive parents are the baby's legal parents in every way. You'll have no authority over your baby whatsoever, but you'll be allowed to send and receive letters and photos over the years. If the adoptive parents are OK with it, you might even be able to see your child. Not all families are OK with that. It depends on what the adoptive family is comfortable with. A closed adoption is just that, completely closed. In a closed adoption, the birth mother has no contact or information about the adoptive family. You'll have no right to contact the adoptive parents or your baby as he or she grows up. Do you understand both options, Jessica?"

"Yes, I do." Jessica tried to swallow the knot in her throat.

"Do you know which option you prefer, Jessica?" Veronica asked the question as compassionately as she could. She could see the sadness in Jessica's expressions.

"I don't know yet. I haven't even told my family about this meeting. I need to talk to my parents. The baby is their grandbaby, so I don't want to make the decision or sign anything until after I tell them my intentions. I'll talk to them this week, Veronica. Will that be OK?"

"That will be OK. When you decide which agency you want to work with, I'll arrange a meeting between you and one of their agents."

"Ok. Thank you, Veronica."

"You're welcome, Jessica." As Jessica left the room, Veronica looked at Emily. "There are many great things about working or volunteering here, Emily. There are also really hard things. One of the hardest things is seeing a young woman like Jessica make an adoption plan for a baby she really wants to keep. Jessica made one life altering decision for her baby, and now she is about to make another one. She chose to let her baby live, and now she's about to choose to give her baby a life that she believes she can't give it. Birth mothers like Jessica are stronger than they think."

Chapter Twenty-One

It was Saturday, May 27th. Emily and Luke stood outside the Pleasant Grove University auditorium with their degrees in their hands. Their parents stood nearby. Their mothers had been snapping photos of Luke and Emily, Emily and her parents, Luke and his parents, Luke and Emily with each set of parents, and Luke and Emily with several friends who had passed by them while weaving through the crowds of students and proud parents. Emily's father had asked a stranger to take his camera to take a photo of Luke and Emily with both sets of parents. Emily turned to Luke, "Get used to this. It's good practice for next week."

"Exactly how many wedding photos do we need? Can't we just take one?"

"Luke! One?" Emily knew Luke was teasing. "Exactly which one photo would that be?"

"That's easy. The photo of me stuffing a big slice of wedding cake into that little mouth of yours." The whole group broke into laughter.

"Your mother and I will hang a big copy of that one in the living room for everyone to see!" Emily's father was proud of his little girl. She had just graduated from Pleasant Grove University. In her hand, she held her well-earned pre-law degree and she had just delivered what was sure to be known as PGU's best valedictorian addresses of all time, at least in his eyes. He stood there watching his little Emily as she enjoyed one of the best days of her life. Next week, she would be living what would be *the* best day of her life. In one week, she would marry Luke Westmoreland. Emily's father loved Luke. In his hand, he held his well-earned pre-med degree. Luke and Emily would be just fine. He had no doubt about it.

"We should head on over to the restaurant." Luke's mother had made reservations at the Hungry Hunter, one of Pleasant Grove's best steakhouses. "If we leave now, we should get there right on time."

"OK folks, you heard the lady. Let's get moving." Luke's dad watched his son. He watched how Luke treated Emily. He had raised Luke to be a gentleman and that he was. He treated Emily like a queen. Luke's parents loved Emily. Luke was about to marry one of the godliest women they had ever met. Like Luke, they loved her determination, her zest, her zeal. Emily had a way of lighting up even the dreariest room just by walking in. She certainly had a way of lighting up their son's eyes every time he looked at her. They liked Emily's parents too. They had raised Emily well. Luke's parents looked forward to many opportunities in the future to get the two families together. God had blessed them all with good relationships and maybe someday they would share a set of grandchildren.

As the Westmorelands and the McMasters walked down the sidewalk that led to the parking lot, Emily spotted Brad and Angela. They were standing with a crowd that Emily thought must be their families. "Brad! Angela! Congratulations!"

Angela turned to Emily. "Congratulations to you too, and to you, Luke!"

"Thanks Angela." Luke turned to Brad. "Hey Brad, nice to see you. Emily and I won't be out of town for long after the wedding. Let's plan to get together when we get back. Emily and I would like to have you and Angela over for dinner. What do you say?"

Bradley St. James had finally made a friend who wasn't on the basketball team. "I think that sounds great. Angela and I would love to spend time with you and Emily. We are still new Christians. I know we can learn a lot from y'all."

Emily and Angela had heard their conversation. Emily had a suggestion. "Yes. Luke and I would love to have you and Angela over and by the way, I'm sure we could learn a lot from you. We can all learn from each other. Let's have Jessica and Sarah over too. I want us all to stay in touch."

Angela loved the idea. "That would be awesome. Brad and I would love to stay in touch with everyone. Jessica and Sarah grew up here. I know Jessica is staying in Pleasant Grove. She has so much responsibility on her shoulders with her family and Sarah is coming here to PGU this fall."

Emily and Angela continued to discuss how happy they were for Sarah to become such an active part of the Your Choice family and how wonderful it was that her mother had attended the last two post-abortion support group sessions with her daughter. Then they heard Luke's mom call from the edge of the parking lot. "Luke! Emily! I hate to interrupt your conversation, but we really need to get going. I don't want us to lose our table at the restaurant."

"OK, on our way, Mom." Luke shook hands with Brad and Emily hugged Angela. They congratulated each other on their graduations. Brad and Angela congratulated Emily for her valedictorian address and reminded her that they would see her at the wedding next week. Then, Luke and Emily joined their families and headed to the restaurant.

At the restaurant, they all arrived just in time. They were led to a table in the back of the dining room. "Whew! That was close!"

"You're such a worrier, sweetheart. I told you it would all work out." Luke's father was much more relaxed than his mother.

"Yes, you did, but I didn't believe you." Luke's mother kissed his father on the cheek.

Throughout the entire graduation dinner to honor Luke and Emily, the two families were engaged in conversation about topics ranging from Luke's and Emily's childhood to hunting to politics to the future of digital currency. "I think they all like each other," Luke whispered to Emily."

Emily agreed as Luke kissed her cheek. "I think you're right,"

"Hey! None of that until after the wedding, young man!"

"Oh, Yes Sir!" Luke teased back to Emily's father. Everyone chuckled as they finished their dinner and prepared for dessert, a graduation cake that Emily's mother had made and brought to the restaurant. She had written Congratulations Luke and Emily on the top of the cake with icing.

During dessert, Luke sat back in his chair and listened. He listened to the conversations and watched the expressions on the faces of all the people he loved most in the world. The two families were created to be one. They blended together as if they had all grown up together. Luke prayed a silent prayer of thanks to God for all the people sitting around the table that night and all the blessings still yet to come.

Chapter Twenty-Two

Emily stepped back a few steps. Her mother stood behind her and wrapped her arms around her daughter. "It's absolutely stunning." They gazed at Emily's wedding dress hanging in front of her bedroom window. The sun was up. Its rays took aim at the pearl lined neck and elegant lacy designs running down the length of the dress.

"Oh Mom. I can't believe the day is finally here. I'm getting married today!"

"Yes, you are. I'm so proud of you, Emily. You have grown into a beautiful woman inside and out. You are smart, kind, compassionate, loyal and you possess all the fruits of the Spirit – love, joy, peace, patience, goodness, kindness, faithfulness, gentleness, and self-control. Of all your accomplishments, I'm most proud of your character."

Emily's eyes watered. "Mom, you and dad taught me everything I know. You modeled Godliness for me. I learned more from you and dad than I could ever learn in a textbook."

Emily's mother smiled. "Thank you for saying so, Emily. That means a lot."

Emily's dad tapped on the bedroom door that was standing open. "Hey you two. We need to leave for the church in ten minutes. From the looks of that dress and all the jewelry, make-up, and whatever other pretty stuff that needs to go with us, we had better start loading up right now."

Emily's mother looked at her daughter. "Well, are you ready to become Mrs. Westmoreland?"

"So ready!" Emily and her parents loaded the car with Emily's dress and all the pretty stuff and headed to Pleasant Grove Baptist Church.

Luke stood in front of the mirror in his parent's hotel room adjusting his tie, the one Emily had given him on the night Luke proposed to her. His parents, Emily, and her parents had helped Luke move out of his dorm room and into Emily's apartment during the week between graduation and today's wedding. Luke had stayed with his parents in their hotel room. His mother walked up to Luke and helped him adjust his tie from behind. "It really didn't need adjusting again, Luke. You've adjusted it 7 times now."

"Well, 7 is the Biblical number that represents perfection, right?"

"You look handsome. Your tie is perfect. Your whole suit is perfect. Your shoes are even shined. You look great." Luke's mother tried to calm her son's nerves.

"I don't know why I'm nervous. I wasn't this nervous when I took my final exams."

Luke's father encouraged his son. "It's perfectly normal for you to be nervous, my boy. Just try not to think about how many people will be looking at you. What did Emily's father tell me? I believe he said the guest list included about 300 people, that's all. Don't worry about the photographer either. He'll be snapping that camera at every move you make but just try to ignore him."

"Oh, don't listen to your dad. He's just teasing you. He's right that it's normal for you to be nervous though. Luke, you're a fine young man. You're a Godly man. You possess all the characteristics of a man after God's own heart. You work hard. We have no doubt that you are ready for this. You'll make a great husband for Emily. Your father and I are so proud of you."

"Thanks Mom. I had two of the best examples that have ever walked this earth. Thank you both for all you have done for me over the years. I love you both."

"Before you and your mother get all sappy, let's head to the church. No bride wants to start her wedding day off waiting on the groom to show up. Now get moving." As Luke and his mother headed out of their hotel room ahead of Mr. Westmoreland, Luke thought he saw something in his peripheral vison. He turned back in time to see his misty-eyed father place his handkerchief back into his pocket.

Emily's wedding party were all Baptist Collegiate Ministry friends. The BCM ministry and their dedication to it had given them all a common life purpose while they worked on their undergraduate degrees and worked in both foreign and home mission projects. They had all become like sisters. Today was a bittersweet day for them because Emily's wedding would be the last thing they would all do together. Emily was the only one remaining in Pleasant Grove after today. The other girls were going to various locations around the world. Two of them would travel to their home states of Indiana and Montana. The rest were headed to Africa, Europe, and Asia for various foreign mission assignments.

After the maid-of-honor and the bride's maids had added the final touches to Emily's wedding look, she pulled a few small boxes from behind a table. "I have something for each of you. Now, don't make a fuss because if I cry all my makeup off, we have to start all over again."

The girls giggled and they each took a box from Emily. Inside each box was one large heart with smaller hearts dangling from the larger one. On the larger heart was an engraving that read "Friends are friends forever if the Lord is the Lord of them." It was a verse from an old Michael W. Smith song that they all loved. At one of the meetings during their freshman year, they decided it would be "their song" and it was for the next few years, maybe for a lifetime. On each of the smaller hearts was an engraving of each of their names.

"Oh Emily," the maid-of-honor was especially touched. "This is beautiful." She teared up and the other girls did the same.

"Now I told you all not to make a fuss. We don't have time to redo my makeup." Emily dabbed at a stray tear with her "something blue" handkerchief that her mother had given her. "I have one too. I know we promised that we will all get together regularly, but I also know how challenging that promise will be to keep – but friends are friends forever if the Lord is the Lord of them. That's us. I love you ladies so much. Thank you for sharing this special day with me."

They heard the organ begin to play. Emily's father knocked on the door. "May I come in?"

Emily sucked in a breath. "Yes, come in, Dad."

Mr. McMaster walked in. One look at his baby girl took his breath away. "You are beautiful, Emily, just like your mother."

"Thanks, Dad." Emily took a deep breath. "The music is playing."

Mr. McMaster could have stood there all day just staring at his beautiful grownup daughter, but Emily was right. The music was playing, and Luke was waiting. "Well, are you ladies ready to get this party started?"

"Yes, they all cheered in unison." The wedding party headed out of the bride's dressing room and down the hall to the place they were instructed to meet the wedding coordinator who would tell each couple when to march down the aisle. She was standing just outside the worship center doors with Emily's little cousin who was the 4-year-old flower girl.

Emily took her father's arm and the two of them headed down the hallway to the same spot.

"Emmy! Emmy! Look! I have a basket full of rose petals."

"Yes, you do, my sweet girl. Now, do you remember what to do with them, just like we practiced last night at rehearsal?"

"Yes. Those ladies will go first. Then I will go down, but I have to remember to walk really slow. I'm supposed to sprinkle the petals on the floor but not too much at one time. Do you remember what you are supposed to do, Emmy?"

"I think so," Emily winked.

"Well, just in case you forgot, you're supposed to walk real slow too but try not to step on my petals, OK?"

Emily and her father grinned. "I'll try to be really careful."

"OK." With that, she bounced off with her basket of rose petals.

The wedding coordinator gave instructions for the first couple to go down the aisle, then the next, and then the next. A minute later, the flower girl began her walk, sprinkling rose petals on the floor. Then, Emily and her father stood at the door as the organist begin to play the wedding march. Emily's eyes met Luke's and she forgot how to breathe. Her father reminded her. "Just breathe, baby girl. I can't have you passing out on me. Don't embarrass me. They are all looking at me, you know."

"Oh Dad," Emily almost laughed out loud, but she was breathing again.

Emily's march down the aisle was timed perfectly although she was pretty sure she had stepped on a few rose petals. Emily's pastor from her hometown had watched Emily grow up. He had come into town to marry Emily and Luke. "Who gives this woman to be wed?"

Emily's father almost lost his composure, but he found it again. "Her mother and I." Mr. McMaster took Emily's hand and placed it in Luke's. He looked at Luke with eyes that told him, *I love you like a son. I know you'll take good care of my daughter.*

Luke's eyes had locked onto his soon-to-be father-in-law's eyes that told Mr. McMaster that he understood and that he loved Mr. McMaster and that, yes, he would not only take care of Emily, but he would love her until the day he died.

The wedding was traditional with traditional vows, just like Luke and Emily wanted. It had gone perfectly except for the part toward the end when their little flower girl had been standing still long enough. She decided to start picking up all her rose petals. She started at the front of the worship center where the bridal party stood and picked up petals all the way back to the back door where she had started. Then, she found her mother and sat with her. Everyone thought she was adorable and quiet laughter filled the worship center.

The pastor pronounced Luke and Emily man and wife and told Luke that he can now kiss his bride. And Luke did. Then, the pastor introduced them to their guests for the first time as Mr. and Mrs. Luke and Emily Westmoreland. The happy couple marched out of the worship center and into the fellowship hall. They had chosen to take their wedding photographs before the ceremony so they would have more time to visit with their guests. They served their guests grilled chicken, mashed potatoes, green beans, and rolls.

Luke and Emily Westmoreland enjoyed every second of their special day. They tried to visit with everyone in attendance. They had all the people who meant the most to them all in one place. Angela, Brad, Jessica, Sarah, April, Veronica, and Kathy were all there. When it was time to leave for their short honeymoon, Luke and Emily took the opportunity to thank their guests for coming and made sure they knew how special each person in attendance was to them. Then Luke flung the garter that Emily had worn during the ceremony to a crowd of single men. Brad caught it. Emily tossed her bouquet to a crowd of single women. Angela caught it.

When Luke and Emily pulled away from the church, leaving the best day of their lives behind them, their hearts couldn't have been more full. "It was absolutely perfect, Luke. It was a perfect day, even better than I have ever dreamed."

"I couldn't agree more, Mrs. Westmoreland." Luke had one arm around Emily's shoulders and one hand on the steering wheel. As they drove away as husband and wife, their hearts no longer beat separately, but together as one heartbeat until death do them part.

Chapter Twenty-Three

Angela had become close to the women at Your Choice. She wanted to remain in Pleasant Grove so that she could continue her pre-birth classes. She obtained her bachelor's degree in psychology back in the spring, so April offered her a paid position as a full-time on-site counselor. She would start that position as soon as her maternity leave was over which should be in late October. Brad was hoping he could stay in Pleasant Grove so that he could stay close to Angela and the baby. He had applied for several positions in June. In the first week of July, Brad had been offered a job with a Pleasant Grove advertising firm where he would draw enough money to rent a small apartment and if he could convince Angela to say "yes" to his upcoming proposal, he would have enough room for her and the baby. Brad looked around his apartment. He had rented a two-bedroom apartment only a few miles from Your Choice and only a few miles from Kathy's house where Angela had moved in after she had to vacate her dorm. His mother had come back into town to help him decorate the apartment. He had told her to help him make it cozy. He wanted it to look like a home Angela would love.

"There. Now it looks like home." Mrs. St. James had placed the last cushion on the sofa. "She will love it, but she is a woman and she'll be a mother by the time she moves in as your wife so don't be hurt if she decides to change a few things around."

"I won't mind. I want her to make this her home." Brad smiled at the thought of Angela as his wife. "Now I just have to get her to say 'yes.'"

"She'll say yes, Brad. I know she loves you. I know you love her. You two had a rough start but I have to say that I'm impressed with you and how you are handling this now. By the time you and Angela are married, you'll both have good jobs. This apartment is nice, and the rent is manageable, but the best part of it all is that my grandbaby is alive and he or she will have a good home and the best mommy and daddy on the planet."

"Thanks, Mom. Your support means a lot to me. I could never repay you for all you and Dad have done for me over the past couple of months. I couldn't have made it through the stress of all those interviews without you and I certainly couldn't have made this apartment a home without you."

"There is one thing you could do to repay me." Mrs. St. James grinned at her son.

"Mom, I'm not telling you the sex of the baby." Brad's expression lit up. "We want it to be a surprise. Angela will kill me if I let that cat out of the bag." They both laughed.

"Well, I guess I'll have to wait then." She smiled at her son. "Well, I need to pack up. I want to leave early in the morning if I'm going to make it back home before dark. It's a long drive and your dad doesn't like me traveling this far alone."

Brad watched his mother leave the room to go pack up her belongings. The next time she comes to Pleasant Grove, he would be handing her his baby, her grandbaby. Brad's heart was overflowing with gratitude. The best was yet to be.

Jessica sat on her front porch rocking chair sipping a glass of cold lemonade. She could feel her baby kicking and squirming inside her womb. "I know it's hot out here, little one. We'll go inside soon."

Jessica's father continued to improve after his surgery. He had gone back to work last week and had told his wife that he wanted to get a little yard work done. Jessica's mother had begged him to stay inside out of the heat, but her father had gotten a taste of freedom again and wouldn't have it any other way. Giving in, as if she ever had a chance to convince him otherwise, Margorie had asked Jessica to keep an eye on her father. "Don't' take your eyes off him," her mother had told her.

Jessica decided her father had been out long enough. "Hey Dad, let's go inside now. It's awfully hot and you know mom won't let me go back inside unless you go with me."

Knowing his daughter was right and knowing she needed to be inside as much as he did, he nodded in her direction, set the weed-eater aside, and joined his daughter on the front porch. "OK, we'll go in for now, but I'm coming back outside after it cools down."

"Fair enough." Jessica and her father headed inside. "Besides, I think Mom has dinner almost ready. It smells amazing."

A few minutes later, Jessica and her family were seated at the dinner table. Her father asked the blessing. Then, they began their meal accompanied by the music of chatter. Jessica loved family dinner conversations. No matter how tired she was from sewing day and night, Marjorie Whitlock always found time to prepare a home-cooked meal for her family. It was the only time they all sat down and just talked and they talked a lot. Sometimes Jessica would just sit and listen. Today, she placed her hand on her growing baby bump and thought to herself. *Hey little one, I hope you'll get to enjoy family dinners with your new family. I hope you get the chance to talk to your new mommy and your new daddy about your days and I hope you'll have brothers and sisters to love you and support you like your birth family supports us now.* Jessica discretely raised her napkin to her upper cheek where a tear sat waiting to fall.

Sarah sat at her bedroom desk staring at her calendar. She would be around 7 months pregnant by now if she had chosen life for her baby. She would never know if her baby was a boy or a girl. She would never know what her baby would look like. She would never know who her baby would grow up to be and because of her selfishness and ignorance, Cole would never know those things either. Sarah remembered little about leaving the abortion clinic on that dark day back in the spring, but she could remember Cole's face. She would never forget for as long as she lived how he had looked at her with such anger and grief. She had killed their baby and she didn't think Cole would ever forgive her.

Sarah had continued meeting with her post-abortion support group at Your Choice. Her mother had started coming with her. Both Sarah and Rachel knew that God had forgiven them both, but there were still days when the guilt was almost too heavy a burden to bear. Their counselor reminded them often of Satan's false accusations. "You must remember that Satan is the father of lies and guilt is a form of a lie. Guilt tells you that you can never be forgiven for what you have done. Guilt tells you that your past makes you unworthy of God's love and forgiveness. But the Bible tells us in the book of Romans *Therefore, there is now no condemnation for those who are in Christ Jesus, because through Christ Jesus the law of the Spirit who gives life has set you free from the law of sin and death. Romans 8:1-2"*

Lilly had been the friend to Sarah that she had always been. She had called Sarah regularly. She had come to Sarah's house often. Lilly's parents had been in touch with Sarah's parents. Since Rachel had become a Christian, Lilly's mother had met with Rachel weekly, discipling her into a deeper relationship with Jesus. Sarah's father had not yet received Jesus as his Lord, but Lilly's father had been meeting with Charles almost every weekend. They would go golfing, fishing, and hunting together. Sarah felt like he was getting closer to making a profession of faith.

Sarah had called Cole several times. She had left him numerous messages at first, but he had not responded to any of them. After a while, Sarah stopped trying to reach him, but she would occasionally ask Lilly about him. "I know you and Cole hang out together. How is he, Lilly?"

Lilly assured Sarah, "First of all, I want you to know that Cole and I are just friends. I would never betray you like that. Secondly, he's hanging in there. His parents convinced him to see a Christian counselor recommended by their pastor. He's getting the help he needs."

"That's good. I think it's safe to say that my relationship with Cole ended back in March. I don't blame him, Lilly. I want you to know that I'm glad you are there for Cole. You've been a good friend to both of us. Thank you for that."

"Of course. Things will get better, Sarah. Now that you know the Lord, you just need to trust Him with your future and with Cole's. Soon, all three of us will be at Pleasant Grove University. We'll meet new people. We'll get involved in new things. Your relationship with Cole might never be the same but God will bring you through this."

Lilly could always make Sarah feel better. "You're right as always. Speaking of meeting new people and getting involved in new things, I hear the Baptist Collegiate Ministry on campus is on fire. I look forward to getting involved in that. You plan to get involved in that ministry too, right?"

"I can't wait! It will be awesome!" The mood between the two girls lightened as they made their way downstairs and into the kitchen where the Scotts and the Campbells enjoyed dinner together.

Cole's counselor had scheduled a Saturday session. It wasn't the way Cole wanted to spend his afternoon, but he had agreed to go to every session unless an emergency prevented it. He pulled into his driveway, parked his car, and went inside into the kitchen. The timer on the Crock Pot indicated 15 minutes until his mother's homemade vegetable soup was ready. His parents were in the living room enjoying an Andy Griffith rerun. Cole grabbed a cold bottle of water from the frig and joined his parents in the living room. "Andy Griffith again?"

"Your dad has the entire series memorized but still, he watches it almost every evening. How did your counseling session go?"

"Ok, I guess." Cole drank a gulp of water.

"You guess? Do you want to talk about it, son?" Cole's dad turned off the TV.

Cole sighed. "I don't know. I mean, the counselor is great. I understand that Sarah's decision to have an abortion was not my fault. I know I did everything I could to stop her. Guilt is not my problem. My problem is forgiveness. I know I'm supposed to forgive Sarah. I know I'm supposed to forgive others like God has forgiven me, but that's a lot easier said than done. Mom, Dad, she killed my baby. How am I supposed to forgive that? I've been trying for months now. I just can't."

Cole's father tried to help. "Cole, remember that forgiveness is not just a feeling. It's a decision."

"I get that too but it's just not that simple, at least not for me. I can decide right now to forgive her, but I know I haven't because all I feel is anger toward her. Because of her, I have this burning anger in my heart, and I don't know how to put it out."

Cole's mother spoke softly. "We can understand your pain to some degree, Cole. That baby was our grandbaby. I've cried myself to sleep many nights just thinking about it. Your dad and I hurt but at the same time, we can't imagine how much harder this is for you. We have to keep trying."

"Your mother is right. We must keep trying. We must keep praying and trusting God to get us through this. The summer months have been long and hard because you've been in a waiting period, sort of a rut. You've had too much time to dwell on what happened. In just a couple of weeks, you'll be attending classes at Pleasant Grove University. It's a large campus. You might not see

Sarah at all, at least not much. You'll be able to concentrate on other things. You'll get involved in campus life with new people. You'll make new friends. You'll be able to get on with your life."

"True. You're right. I can't stop thinking about what Sarah did. It consumes me." Cole thought for a minute. His parents sat quietly, giving Cole a chance to regroup. "Yeah, you're right. In a couple of weeks, nothing will be the same. I'll be in a different school in different classes with different people. I found out about something else that might help."

"What's that?" Cole's parents asked in unison.

"They have this group on campus called Baptist Collegiate Ministries. I plan to get involved in that. They do a lot of things on and around campus to help share the gospel locally. They also go on mission trips to share the gospel around the world. I want to be part of that."

Cole's mother smiled as she checked her watch. "I think that's a wonderful idea, Cole. Now, the soup should be finished. Let's eat!"

The Quinn family sat down to dinner. Cole's father led the family in a prayer of thankfulness not only for the food God had provided for them but also for a son who had shown more strength in the past few months than any man he had known for a lifetime.

Luke and Emily had spent the day rearranging furniture. When their parents were in town for their graduation and wedding, they had moved Luke's things out of his dorm and into her apartment, but they hadn't had enough time to figure out where to put everything.

"How did you have all this stuff in that little dorm of yours?" Emily was still trying to squeeze Luke's favorite side table in between the sofa and a wall.

"Because I didn't have all of your stuff in there." Luke watched Emily push and squeeze his table into the spot where she wanted it.

He had decided it wasn't going to fit, but when Emily was determined to make something happen, there was no giving up.

"There! I got it in there. Perfect!" Emily stood back to examine from a distance. I think that looks fine. Don't you?"

"Yes. It looks great." It did, but he wouldn't have said otherwise even if it didn't. He had no idea what it might take to get that table back out of that spot. They might have to saw it apart.

"Whew! I think we're finally done. I can't believe it took us all summer to figure this out. Now everything is in its place. Welcome home, Mr. Westmoreland!"

"Welcome home, Mrs. Westmoreland!"

Emily was still getting used to her new last name, but she loved hearing Luke call her Mrs. Westmoreland. "I didn't realize how late it's getting. I'll find something in the kitchen for dinner."

"I saw a frozen pizza in the freezer. Let's just stick that in the oven. We can have pepperoni pizza and end the day with a relaxing movie."

Emily pulled the pizza from the freezer, removed the wrapping, grabbed a large cookie sheet, and placed the pizza in the oven. She set the time for 25 minutes. "Sounds good! What movie do you have in mind?"

"I don't know. Let's surf Netflix for a few minutes. Are you in the mood for a comedy or a drama?"

"Hmmm, how about a drama . . . no comedy . . . no drama . . . I don't know." Emily scanned the selection of movies as Luke moved the curser from one option to another.

"How about Fireproof? A perfect movie for a newly married couple." Luke knew they had both seen it before, but it was one of their favorite movies – a movie about a fireman and his wife whose marriage is in trouble, but they learn to overcome their challenges – a movie about promising to never leave your partner, especially in a fire.

"Sounds good to me." The timer on the oven sounded. "Did it really take us 25 minutes to decide on a movie?" Emily went into the kitchen to get the pizza from the oven.

"Another confirmation that we are now married," Luke teased.

Emily sliced the pizza and took two plates from the cupboard. She put a large slice of pizza on each plate and grabbed a bag of chips from the counter. Luke walked over to help Emily carry their dinner to the living room. They placed the food on the coffee table and then went back to the kitchen for drinks. Emily chose a Diet Coke can from the refrigerator and Luke chose to pour himself a glass of tea.

"When you say the blessing, remember our meeting tomorrow at Your Choice." Luke and Emily sat on the sofa.

"Remind me of the purpose for this meeting?" Luke had almost forgotten about it.

"Well, remember when I told you that Kathy wanted to pair me with Sarah as part of their Titus 2 Ministry?"

Luke was beginning to remember. "Yeah, you looked all through the paperwork, but you couldn't find anything about it."

"Well, it turns out that there was no Titus 2 Ministry." Emily raised her eyebrows.

"Then why did Kathy tell you that there was? It's not like her to lie."

"She wasn't exactly lying. I mean, she did, but she didn't mean it that way. It's just that she made it up in that moment. She sort of developed a Titus 2 Ministry right then and there."

"So what's tomorrow's meeting about, exactly?" Luke was still trying to figure it all out.

"It's about starting a Titus 2 Ministry. Luke, try to keep up."

"Wait, so there wasn't a Titus 2 Ministry, but Kathy said there was, but she wasn't lying about it because she made it up in that moment which means she started it back then. I still don't know what tomorrow's meeting is about." Luke wondered if all married women talked in circles like that.

"Well, Kathy called it Titus 2 because she had to think quickly. Her church has a Titus 2 Ministry but it's about pairing older woman with younger woman. At Your Choice, women might be paired with someone who is the same age or in the same season of life. We now have several clients paired with several volunteers, so we are meeting to discuss the ministry, the direction we want it to go, and come up with a new name for it."

"Now, I understand." Luke let out an exaggerated sigh of relief.

"You're so dramatic, Luke. Now pray. The pizza is getting cold."

Luke took Emily's hands in his and prayed a prayer of gratitude for all that God had given him. He thanked God for the campus jobs they both secured while they work on their graduate degrees in medicine and constitutional law. He thanked God for the roof over their heads and for the ministries God had led them into, Emily to Your Choice for Unplanned Pregnancies and Luke to a local medical missions group started by their church over the summer. He thanked God for the Godly wife He had given him, and for His blessing over their marriage. Then, he thanked God for pizza and said "Amen."

"I love you, Luke Westmoreland." Emily picked up her pizza and took a bite.

"I love you too Emily Westmoreland." Luke pushed the play button and as he did, he vowed that he would never leave his partner, especially in a fire.

Chapter Twenty-Four

Emily, Veronica, Kathy, and April arrived at Your Choice thirty minutes early. They placed refreshments on a table in the back of the room. They pulled a few tables together and brought in extra chairs so that they could seat more people. Veronica surveyed the room. "I think this will work just fine. Now we can all see each other as we discuss this new ministry that Kathy created off the top of her head." Veronica smiled and adjusted her glasses.

Kathy returned a surprised look. "I had no idea it would actually develop into something bigger."

April looked at a paper attached to a clipboard. "It has certainly developed into something. I have a long list of clients and a list of volunteers who would like to pair with someone." She looked at the second sheet. "I also have a long list of people who have signed up to volunteer to pair with a client, but they need to go through the training first."

Emily thanked them for including her as a leader in this new leg of ministry. She was excited about the growing list of people needing to go through the training. "It's a nice problem to have."

April heard a car pull into the parking lot. "Ok, we have people arriving. Emily, when everyone is here, Veronica will lead us in prayer to open the meeting. We'll give everyone a chance to grab refreshments and bring them back to the table. We'll start the meeting with you explaining exactly what you and Sarah do as part of this ministry."

"Sure. I'm happy to do that."

Sarah and her mother were the first to arrive. "Hello Emily, it's nice to see you again. Sarah talks about you all the time. I'm so glad God brought you both together."

"Sarah is such a blessing to me. I've learned a lot from her over the past several months. That's what makes this ministry special. We learn from each other." Emily gave both Sarah and her mother a warm, inviting look as she directed them to a table to sign in.

Jessica arrived next. Everyone was a little surprised that Jessica's mother, Marjorie, came too. Kathy welcomed Marjorie and shared a few encouraging words with them before directing them to the sign-in table.

Angela came in next. An older woman was with her. "Hello everyone. This is my grandmother. I call her Grandma Ruby. She lives in North Carolina where she volunteers for a pregnancy care center. She is very interested in what we are doing here. She said she might start this at her center so I invited her along so she can see what we do."

Veronica started to welcome Angela's grandmother. "We are more than happy to have her. Thank you for coming Mrs. . . ."

"You can call me Grandma Ruby. It's my favorite name of all." Grandma Ruby smiled with pride.

"Great. Then welcome Grandma Ruby. We are happy to have you join us today." Veronica loved the woman already.

April called the meeting to order. "I think we are all here. I'm going to ask Veronica to start us off with a word of prayer. Then, if you all would go grab a few refreshments from the back table and come back to your seats here, we'll get started."

Veronica opened in prayer. Then, everyone made their way to the back table for refreshments. There was lots of excited chatter as they were getting snacks. Veronica was waiting for them as they made their way back to their seats.

"I think we are all settled now. First, I would like to ask Emily McMaster, I'm sorry, that's Emily Westmoreland to tell us a little bit about what she and Sarah do together."

"It's OK." Emily beamed. "I'm still getting used to the Westmoreland name too." When the chuckling in the room quieted, Emily began. "First, let me say what a blessing this ministry has been to me. Until I visited here back in the Spring, I had no idea about all the things this little center with only a few employees does for our community. It's truly amazing and I am so happy to be part of it. As you know, Kathy paired Sarah and me together a few months ago. I'll save Sarah's personal story for her to tell if she chooses, but as part of what we have been calling our Titus 2 Ministry, Sarah and I meet at least once per week. We pray together. That's the most important part. This ministry must be built on a foundation of prayer. Sometimes we talk about deep emotional things and sometimes we talk only about light-hearted things. As the volunteer, I let Sarah choose the topics we discuss. I'm here for her. Once she brings up a topic, I'm free to lead her in the direction of healing. If a new volunteer is nervous about the counseling part, Your Choice offers training. When Kathy first paired me with Sarah, I didn't have that, but we have it now for new volunteers. I have loved every moment I have spent with Sarah, and I look forward to a life-long friendship with her."

"Thank you, Emily. Since you mentioned Sarah, I'll ask Sarah to speak next if she chooses."

"I would love to go next. Thank you, April. First, let me confirm for you, as a client and the first one to participate in this, that this ministry is needed. My sessions with Emily over the summer have helped me more than I could ever express. Some of you know, but perhaps not all of you know, that I came here after having an abortion back in March. I have been participating in the post-abortion support group and spending time with Emily. I'm still struggling with frequent attacks of guilt, but my time here has meant the world to me, and I don't know where I would be emotionally or spiritually if it wasn't for this ministry. Thank you all so much."

"If you don't mind, may I say something?" Sarah's mother asked nervously.

"Sure, Dr. Scott. We would love to hear from you." April was making notes as the meeting progressed.

Dr. Scott spoke in a quiet tone very different from her usual authoritative voice. Today she spoke from a heart of conviction. "I think most of you know that I'm Sarah's mother. I'm the one who pretty much forced Sarah into having an abortion. I'm an attorney who knows a lot of things about laws. I can make a good argument for any case brought to my desk, but I was ignorant concerning the development of babies in the womb. Like many women, I had been lied to and I blindly believed the lies. Thanks to Emily, Sarah, and this center, I now know the truth. Sarah and I can't get her baby back. Her baby is in the arms of Jesus now, but what we can do is help other young girls who are in situations like Sarah's. Thank you for allowing me to come here today and be part of this ministry moving forward."

Eyes were becoming misty. April tried to swallow the lump in her throat as she asked Angela to speak next.

"Hi, I'm Angela Cromwell. I first came to Your Choice back in the spring as well. I didn't want an abortion, but the father of my baby wanted me to have one. My Grandma Ruby who came here with me today volunteers at a pregnancy care center where she lives in North Carolina. She sent me a packet of materials that I shared with Brad, the father of my baby. The materials she sent helped us learn about the early development of babies in the womb. Like you, Dr. Scott, we had no idea how well-developed babies are even at the earliest stages of pregnancy. After reading the materials Grandma Ruby sent us and after seeing our baby's heartbeat on that big screen during our first ultrasound, we both knew that we wanted to choose life and parent our baby. Now, here I am with my growing tummy. My baby is due in October. My baby's father and I are not married yet, but we have lived separately since my first meeting here. Since then, we have entered into a relationship with Jesus and we are committed to live lives that honor God. I don't know what the future holds but I know Who holds our future. I would like to announce that I have accepted a position here at Your Choice as a full-time on-site counselor. I just received my degree in general psychology, and I look forward to serving here in that capacity and also as a volunteer in whatever we decide to call this Titus 2 Ministry after today. Thank you."

Sarah raised her hand. "I would like to add something if that's OK."

April motioned to Sarah. "Sure Sarah. Go ahead."

Sarah took a deep breath. "Angela mentioned the ultrasound. I want to tell you how important an ultrasound is for the life of an unborn baby. If I had seen one before my abortion, I know that I would have chosen life for my baby. I came here in the beginning, thinking that I might get an abortion here, but when I realized what Your Choice actually was, I left. I know how ridiculous that sounds now, but I was young, scared, and like my mother, misled. I was uneducated about fetal development, and I believed the lies. When I was in the room at the abortion clinic, they wouldn't let me see the ultrasound. The nurse told me it would just make things so much harder for me. Now, I know why she told me that. If I had seen an ultrasound. . . if I had seen my baby's heartbeat, my baby would be alive today. I just wanted to emphasize that. Thank you."

"That is important information. Thank you for sharing that with us, Sarah." Choking back another lump in her throat, April motioned to Jessica. "Jessica, would you like to go next?"

"Certainly. I'm Jessica. Like Sarah, I wanted an abortion as well. What I want others to know is that it isn't only non-Christians who seek abortions. I was raised in a Christian home. I am a born-again believer who considered abortion. In my heart, I knew abortion was wrong, but sadly, I cared more about what my parents, my church, and our friends would think of me than my baby's life. I tried to ignore the truth that I knew in order to justify what would have been a tragic decision for my baby. Like so many other ladies in this community, this center has been a lifesaver for me, especially for this little one still growing in my tummy. Veronica told me about two adoption agencies affiliated with Your Choice. I have chosen to make an adoption plan for my baby. My family has prayed with me, and we've discussed it many times. We believe an open adoption is the best choice for my baby. My baby's heart is still beating because you all gave me a choice I had not considered. Thank you."

Through her tears, Jessica's mother spoke up. "May I say a word or two, Miss April?"

"You certainly may, Mrs. Whitlock."

"I just want to thank you all for helping my Jessica choose life for her baby. I think all of you know our family situation and our financial circumstances. You reached beyond your boundaries to minister to our entire family." Marjorie began to feel the lump in her throat. "Choosing an adoption plan for Jessica's baby, my grandchild, wasn't an easy decision. We love this baby and he or she will always be our first grandbaby. You gave us many opportunities over the past several months to come here and speak with your counselors and adoption agency representatives. You lovingly guided us through this process. As hard as it is, we appreciate all you have done here to help Jessica and our entire family make this plan. We are so very grateful to you all."

"Yes," Jessica added. "You have all been so very helpful. We've been in touch with the adoptive family. They have been helping us financially as my doctor's appointments are more frequent. They are a good Christian family and so nice. We are thankful to God for bringing them into our lives. I know my baby will be loved well and I'll get regular updates from the adoptive family. Thank you all for making this very difficult process easier for us."

By now, there wasn't a dry eye in the room. Sarah, Angela, and Jessica had told their stories. Sarah's mother and Jessica's mother had shared how the ministry had reached beyond the walls of this center and ministered to their entire families. Angela will now work there full time after her baby is born and Emily will head up the new arm of the ministry that they had been referring to as Titus 2. Emily looked around the room at all the faces of testimony. Every face in that room had been personally touched by God's plan for life and not death, by God's generous mercy and grace, by the forgiveness Jesus offers. Their lives have been changed through a relationship with the Lord and babies hearts are still beating. Only Sarah would suffer the lifelong pain of a past abortion, but there was no doubt that her story would help save the lives of countless numbers of babies in the future. Only God would know how many babies would grow up and become influential people, maybe even pastors and missionaries, because Sarah was willing to share her story.

There were a few moments of silence as tears and sniffles were given a chance to subside. Veronica was the first to regain her composure. In true Veronica fashion, she wiped her eyes dry with a tissue, placed her fake diamond lined eyeglasses back on her tear-stained face and pulled everyone back into focus. "Wow, what a day we've had. We have rejoiced in God's goodness through a time of prayer and testimony. Now it's time to come up with a name for the ministry. Just to refresh your memory, we want to come up with a new name to more accurately reflect what we are doing by pairing two women together for support and encouragement. We will be pairing clients who need counseling and encouragement with a trained volunteer who may be the same age as the client and in some cases, even younger. This ministry isn't about having an older woman mentor a younger one but more about two women closer in age, a client and a trained volunteer acting as more of a counselor. Any ideas?"

Angela was the first to start offering her thoughts. "I keep thinking about how important that ultrasound was for us. I can't really think of a name but I'm thinking out loud to get our creative juices flowing."

"Yes," Jessica agreed. "The ultrasounds are key. Like Angela, I'm not sure how that will help us come up with a name, but maybe something related to it somehow."

Sarah spoke next. "If I had only seen an ultrasound first, my baby's heart would still be beating. If I had seen my baby's heartbeat . . . that's it!"

Angela caught on immediately, "Yes, how about Heartbeat?"

Jessica offered her thoughts. "I think you two are onto something. When abortion prone women see ultrasounds, most of them choose life for their babies, especially if they see the baby's heartbeat."

Angela added another layer of thought to the mix. "And even if the woman isn't abortion prone like Sarah or Jessica was, they are still coming here due to conditions of the heart. When someone like Emily is paired with someone who needs a different type of counseling, their hearts are still involved."

Sarah added another point. "Yes, it's like two women whose hearts beat as one, one heartbeat."

Emily agreed with Sarah. "Heartbeat. I like it and it will work for any counseling situation."

Veronica, April, and Kathy all agreed that Heartbeat sounded like a good name for this very important ministry.

Grandma Ruby added a final thought before the actual vote. "Thank you all for allowing me to come with Angela to sit in on this meeting. I have learned so much from listening to each of you share your stories. You have given me something to take back to my pregnancy care center in North Carolina. Will it be OK if I suggest the same name? I like Heartbeat too."

Veronica, April, and Kathy offered their approval. Then, Veronica called for the official vote. "OK everyone. All in favor of naming our mentoring ministry Heartbeat, raise your right hand."

Everyone in the room except for Grandma Ruby raised her hand and if Grandma Ruby had been part of this local Your Choice family, she would have raised her right hand too.

"There we have it, ladies. Heartbeat it is." Veronica gave instructions for placing the tables and chairs back in their original places. She asked for a few volunteers to clean up the refreshments table. She gave permission for anyone who wanted them to take home the leftovers. When everything was cleaned up and back in place, the group of ladies who had become like family stood in a circle for the closing prayer. Veronica asked for a volunteer.

"I would like to close us in prayer." Emily's own heart was overflowing.

Heavenly Father,

You are a good, good Father. Thank You for Your faithfulness in all situations. Thank You for Your sovereignty over all things. We come to You with grateful hearts for bringing us through very difficult times. Some who come to our center are preparing for a lifetime commitment of parenting that they had not planned for this season of their lives. Some come here preparing to separate from the babies they carry knowing that the decision they have made is in the best interest of their babies. Some come here who have already suffered loss of life and they need healing that only You can give them. And some, Lord, come here with the intention to have an abortion. For them, Lord, we pray for You to give us wisdom, knowledge, and understanding so that we will hear them and meet them where they are. Help us to reach them, Lord. Help us to educate them so that they will see that the babies they carry are knitted together in their wombs by You and that they are fearfully and wonderfully made. Help us point them to You, Lord Jesus, so that they may know You fully and serve You well. Guide us all as we go back to the homes where You have planted us to fulfill your purpose in our lives for this time and this season. We love You, Lord, and it is in Your name that we pray. Amen."

The group offered up an "Amen" in unison. There was hugging and a few lingering tears as each woman filed out of the room and headed for home on that Sunday afternoon but most of all, there was joy in their hearts, a joy that beat in unison, one heartbeat for one purpose under heaven.

For you created my inmost being;
You knit me together in my mother's womb.
I praise you because I am fearfully and wonderfully made;
Your works are wonderful,
I know that full well.
My frame was not hidden from you
When I was made in the secret place,
When I was woven together in the depths of the earth.
Your eyes saw my unformed body;
All the days ordained for me were written in your book
Before one of them came to be.
How precious to me are your thoughts, God!
How vast is the sum of them! Psalm 139:13-17 (NIV)

Letter from the Author

Dear Reader,

Thank you for reading Heartbeat. I hope you were able to identify with one of the four main characters. Perhaps you are an Emily who loves the Lord and works hard to live in obedience to God while serving others so that they may know Him and make Him known. Perhaps you are an Angela who does not want an abortion, but your baby's father does. You might be someone who first wanted an abortion, but you chose life for your baby and decided to parent that baby. Maybe you are a Jessica who sought an abortion but chose life and made an adoption plan for your baby. You might be a Sarah who followed through with an abortion and now you suffer from the scars that abortion left you. If you can identify more with Sarah, I hope you have found a place where you experienced forgiveness and healing. Angela, Jessica, and Sarah found themselves in an unplanned pregnancy situation. Each of them handled their situations differently. The one thing they all had in common was that abortion was not their only choice. They had other choices. Angela and Jessica chose life for their babies. Sarah chose abortion for hers, but she went to the right place to find Jesus and the forgiveness He offered her. Through Jesus, she is resolved to turn her tragedy into a testimony.

Oh Reader, if you are in Sarah's place, facing and unplanned pregnancy, there are beautiful options for your child that do not include abortion. I encourage you to reach out to your local pregnancy care center. If you don't have one in your area, I want to point you in the direction of LoveLine where you will find the help you need. Go to **www.LoveLine.com**. You can contact them 24 hours a day, 7 days per week, 365 days per year.

You might recognize LoveLine as one of Abby Johnson's ministries. The movie, Unplanned, is Abby's story. I recommend that you watch the movie if you get a chance.

No matter which character you feel represents you more, it's important for you to know that you are valuable. God loves you. If you have never entered into a relationship with Jesus, then I encourage you to go to my website at **https://www.tinatruelove. com/how-to-have-a-relationship-with-jesus** for more information about how you can know Jesus today.

Always remember that you are fearfully and wonderfully made.

Tina

More Resources:

Save the Storks: https://savethestorks.com
ProLove Ministries: https://proloveministries.org
Abby Johnson's Website: https://abbyj.com

Author's Website: https://www.tinatruelove.com
Author's Social Media Pages:
Facebook: TinaTrueloveAuthor
Instagram: TinaTruelove_Author
X (Formerly Twitter): TinaTruelove2
Pinterest: tinatrueloveauthor
Contact the author at: TinaTruelove.author@gmail.com.

Printed in the United States
by Baker & Taylor Publisher Services

Printed in the United States
by Baker & Taylor Publisher Services